You might also enjoy

The Rain Must Fall
By Evangeline Maynard

Epona's Gift
By Cat Spydell

THE LONG DANCE HOME

For Barb
With all best
wishes —
hope you enjoy
my story!
♡ *Julie Brown*

Julie Mayerson Brown

MISCHIEVOUS MUSE PRESS   WORLD NOUVEAU COMPANY

The Long Dance Home
Mischievous Muse Press
A Division of World Nouveau Inc.
Los Angeles County, California

Cover design by Gineve Rudolph

Library of Congress
Cataloging-in-Publication Data
The Long Dance Home
Mayerson Brown, Julie
Womens Fiction

Mischievous Muse Press/World Nouveau Inc.
ISBN 978-1-938208-07-2

Printed in the United States of America

10 9 8 7 6 5 4 3 2 1
BVG

Dedication

For my parents, Ruth and Sam
With endless patience, guidance, and love,
You taught me to do my best

For Mark
You have given me a life and a home
That allow me to pursue my dreams

For Mickey and Sammy
You are my ultimate "dreams come true"

Acknowledgements

The process of writing a book is at once thrilling and terrifying. It takes more commitment, time, and perseverance than one can imagine. Having the support from countless people who have enjoyed my writing over the years made me want to stick with it, even when it was hard.

Thank you to so many wonderful friends who have followed my musings on everything from toddlers to travel adventures. Knowing that I made you laugh makes me happy.

Thank you to my ha-ha-havurah girls who are my birthday group, my book club, and my dearest friends. To the early readers of this manuscript—Linda, Marcie, Shelly, Vickie, and my mom, Ruth—thanks for pushing me to keep at it through endless edits, rewrites, and miniscule corrections.

The members of the Millie Aames Writers' Group—you give great feedback, advice and criticism every time—Jean Shriver, thank you for welcoming me into writers group the first time, and the second.

I must acknowledge my BRUIN WOODS WEEK 9 literary circle, known as the Thursday Afternoon Poetry and Music Jam—you all listened to some of my earliest work. The hours we spent enjoying everyone's creative endeavors are some of my best memories from so many years of BW vacations. I miss you all a lot!

Also, thanks to my editor Cat Spydell. You made me slash characters, create new ones, and search for every tiny change that would improve my manuscript. You know better than anyone how hard an author works.

Finally, to my publishers at World Nouveau—Cat and Gineve—you are pioneers! Thank you for pushing me to take this step!

The Long Dance Home

CHAPTER 1

Cece Camden studied the painting clipped to an old, wooden easel in front of her. She titled her head and squinted. Sighing, she dipped her brush into a cup of water, touched it to the red paint, and dragged a watery streak of color through her subject's cascading, dark hair. Then, with her finest brush, she added a few jet-black lashes to the edges of the eyes.

"You know what they say—the enemy of good is better."

Cece looked over her shoulder at Patty. "I know, I know. I just can't seem to let it be finished." She stood and walked behind the back counter of The Art Stop, the trendy Venice Beach gallery where she and Patty worked, and washed her hands at the sink. "I feel like I need to keep trying to make it better, but if I mess with it too much, I'll ruin it."

Patty handed Cece a paper towel then boosted herself onto a stool. "Ah yes, the perfectionist predicament. Why do you think all artists are depressed?"

"First of all, I am not depressed. And second of all . . . I'm not an artist." Cece wound her long, light brown curls into a bun on the top of her head and stuck a pencil through the middle.

"Don't say that. You're a fabulous painter."

"I'm a good painter, but . . . ."

Patty cut her off. "The problem is that you don't believe in yourself. Too many years of ballet lessons and that mean lady telling you you're not good enough. It damaged your self-esteem."

"My self-esteem is perfectly intact. And besides, Miss Liana never told me that I wasn't good enough," Cece said. "She just told me I could be better."

Patty laughed. "Sounds like the same thing to me."

Cece scowled at her roommate. The two had met in an art history class at UCLA when Cece was a junior and Patty a freshman. They moved in together soon afterward. Their friends dubbed them "The Odd Couple," Cece, tall, graceful, and proper in her pearl earrings, a uniform of grungy, denim overalls, army green tank tops, and hiking boots, Patty stood barely five feet tall. She had short, red, spiked hair and little-girl hands, usually covered in wood stain and holding dangerous tools like saws and nail guns. She reminded Cece of a lovable, albeit annoying, comic book character.

"Don't you have artwork to frame?" Cece asked.

"I do." Patty headed to the workbench then turned back to Cece. "Hey don't forget, I'm taking you to lunch later for your birthday."

"How could I forget that? You buying lunch is a big event."

Cece walked over to a shelf on the wall and began rearranging a display of art deco figurines. "Where are we going?"

"Probably the taco stand on the beach," Patty said. "That's about all I can afford."

"It's fine. I love those tacos. And besides, I don't want to eat too much. Doug's taking me somewhere special tonight." Cece smiled at the thought of her boyfriend. "He's got it all planned out. Even said he has a big surprise for me."

"Oh crap, I bet you get engaged tonight. Then I'm going to have wear some hideous bridesmaid's dress, aren't I?"

"Yes you are!" Cece smiled. "And you will look adorable in the frilly, pink gown I'm going to pick just for you. But you'll have to cut your hair and soak your hands in turpentine before the wedding. Now, give me ten minutes to finish some paperwork, and then we'll go to lunch."

As Patty clomped into the back room, Cece sat down. She pushed the thought of Doug out of her mind so that she could focus on a stack of crinkled purchase orders, invoices, and receipts. An annoyed frown darkened her face. "What a mess."

Barbara, the owner of The Art Stop, was often away. She had an incredible eye for art, but no head for details, so she relied on Cece's meticulous micro-management skills. However, on this particular day, Cece couldn't concentrate.

She got up and went back to her painting. It was a watercolor of a face that Cece had seen only once in her life. Her subject was a young woman with long black hair, dark eyes, and flawless, ivory skin. She had a straight narrow nose, full, pink lips, and a thin, sculpted neck. Her eyes crinkled around the edges, revealing the smile that her lips did not.

For her ninth birthday, Cece's dance instructor, Ilana Lurensky, had taken her to San Francisco to see *The Nutcracker*. They were invited backstage after the performance. Cece froze when she saw the ballerina, still in costume, who had danced the part of the Sugar Plum Fairy. She looked down and placed a graceful hand on Cece's shoulder.

"Are you a ballerina?" she asked, her voice soft and musical.

Cece blinked and nodded, unable to speak.

"Will you show me?"

Cece nodded. She removed her shoes. In her stocking feet, she did her best *pas de chat*, leaping high into the air.

The ballerina's eyes sparkled. She took Cece's hands in both of hers. "You are a magnificent dancer," she whispered. "Work hard, and one day you will dance the Sugar Plum Fairy." The corners of her mouth turned up almost imperceptibly, her cheeks were flushed pink, and her eyes were fringed with thick lashes. It was the most beautiful face Cece had ever seen. And the most thrilling words she'd ever heard . . .

"Cece, you ready?" Patty said, interrupting her daydream. "I'm starving."

Cece stretched and pulled the pencil out of her hair. "Yeah, I'm ready. Let's go."

They slipped into their jackets and walked outside. A crisp, clear November day greeted them. They walked past a vintage clothing shop, a used bookstore, and a homeopathic pharmacist.

"Jesus, what is that smell?" Cece pinched her nose.

"It's frankincense," Patty said. "Great aromatherapy—calms anxiety, increases concentration, cures almost everything. Let's stop so you can inhale it for a while."

"The only thing I want to smell right now is a fresh, homemade tortilla sizzling on a hotplate. Keep walking."

On the boardwalk, they jumped out of the way of skateboarders, cyclists, and a rollerblading club. Beachgoers dotted the sand, vendors sold everything from toys to churros, and mimes twisted skinny balloons into silly hats and animals.

Patty froze. "Oh my God, look at those guys playing volleyball with no shirts. Aren't they beautiful?"

"I thought you were into girls this month."

"That was last month. See the one with the blond mohawk? Wait here, I'm gonna go meet him."

Cece grabbed Patty's wrist. "No you're not. We're having lunch and going right back to work."

"Fine." Patty frowned. "You're no fun."

"And you," Cece said as they got into a long line in front of the taco stand, "are freakin' crazy."

It was mid-afternoon when Cece finished the paperwork. She looked up at the sound of bells jingling as Barbara's best friend whirled in. Mae Adamu, a jewelry designer and boardwalk icon, was half Nigerian and half Italian. The ageless hippy with smooth, brown skin and beaded cornrows in her hair wore Birkenstock sandals, a jean jacket, and a bright yellow, flowing, skirt.

"Hi girls!" Mae closed the door. She had her tabby cat, Goldie, on a leash and held a brown grocery bag. "I brought some new designs for you to look at. And, hold onto your hats, an entire pan of my famous tofu lasagna!"

"Oh yum," said Patty, who was sitting on the floor sanding a long strip of molding. "But you know what? I'm allergic to tofu."

Cece choked. Who could be allergic to tofu? She stood and gave Mae a tight, affectionate hug. "I'd love some," she said.

"Wonderful! It's so delicious." Mae unhooked the cat's leash. "There you go Goldie, be good."

The golden orange cat went straight for Cece, slinking around her ankles. Cece nudged Goldie with the back of her hand. "Go on, scoot."

"Goldie knows you don't like her," Mae said. "She can sense it. That's why she pesters you."

"It's not just Goldie. I don't like any cats."

"I don't know why," Mae said, unwrapping her casserole. "You love dogs and monkeys."

"Dogs listen, and monkeys are adorable and intelligent. Cats are ornery, and they make me nervous." Cece stepped aside, but Goldie followed her. "And why does she wind herself around my legs like this?"

"She's releasing her pheromones on you, marking her territory."

"See? That's just not right." Cece grabbed some plastic plates and forks from behind the counter.

Goldie jumped into a chair as Mae scooped lasagna onto paper plates. Cece sat, avoiding Goldie's suspicious glare, and took a bite. The tofu squished in her mouth.

"Good, huh?" Mae said, finger-feeding Goldie bits off her plate.

"Mmmm." Cece forced herself to swallow. She didn't know which was worse—eating tofu lasagna or watching the cat eat it.

"Patty dear," Mae said, "don't you want to at least try it?"

4

"Seriously Mae, tofu gives me like that closed up throat thing. And besides I had a huge beef burrito for lunch."

Mae frowned. "You really ought to cut down on your consumption of meat. Being vegetarian is so much healthier."

Patty turned over the piece of molding and continued sanding. "I'm a farm girl from Texas, Mae. Sayin' you're vegetarian is worse than sayin' you don't believe in God."

Mae tsk-tsked and turned her attention back to Cece. "Let me show you my new pieces." She took a wooden box out of her bag and opened it. Each piece of Mae's jewelry was one-of-kind, made of sterling silver, crystals, beads, and semi-precious stones.

Cece picked up a necklace—a small butterfly of sapphire blue crystals hanging on a sterling chain. "This is stunning."

"Let me see it on you," Mae said.

Cece fastened it around her neck. The butterfly landed just below the soft spot between her collarbones.

"Ahhh, fabulous."

Cece reached for a hand mirror and looked at her reflection. With her wide-set blue eyes, fair skin and long, brown hair, it was truly stunning on her.

"It's such a pretty piece, Mae. And I love the blue crystals." She reached back to unclasp it.

"No you don't." Mae grinned at her. "Happy birthday, dear."

"Oh Mae, I couldn't."

"You most certainly can. What's the point in my creating beautiful things if somebody is not enjoying them?"

Cece kissed her friend's cheek. "Thank you, Mae. I love it."

"Cece's gonna get another piece of jewelry tonight," Patty offered from her seat on the floor. "A diamond."

Mae gasped. "From Doug? An engagement ring?"

Cece's heart quickened at the thought of Doug and the night ahead. "I don't know, maybe. He hasn't said anything about getting engaged, but he's been acting kinda weird, like he's planning something special."

"Well," Mae said. "That is exciting news!"

Cece toyed with the butterfly. "I'm not expecting too much, am I? I mean, we've been together for three years, I'm twenty-nine, and we're completely in love. It's time, don't you think?"

Mae patted Cece's hand. "Absolutely. And husbands are wonderful. I've had four of them myself."

Patty pulled Goldie onto her lap. "And now you have a cat."

"Exactly," said Mae.

Cece rubbed her forehead. "We have to stop talking about Doug now. I don't want to jinx it."

"You're right about that," Mae said. "So let's get down to business. What pieces do you want me to leave with you?"

Cece picked up a pair of earrings made from wooden beads and peacock feathers. "I hate to tell you this Mae, but the jewelry's not selling. It's discounted already, and we'll probably cut prices again after Thanksgiving."

Mae shrugged. "The money's not that important, Cece. You know that as well as I do. An artist just wants her work to matter. Especially to the person who is lucky enough to possess it." Mae looked over her shoulder at Cece's watercolor.

Cece felt her throat constrict. Mae was right. She didn't paint for money, although a sale would be nice. She painted because she loved painting. In the end, she just wanted her art to belong to someone who would cherish it as much as she cherished the memory that inspired it.

Mae closed the box on her creations. "Tell you what. I'll take these down to the boardwalk this weekend. I always make a few good sales there." She stood, packed up her things, and clipped Goldie to her leash.

Cece pushed away from the table. "See you next week."

"Definitely," said Mae. "And good luck tonight, honey. I hope you get your wish."

"Thanks. Me too."

Mae gave Cece a quick hug then stepped back and looked at her neck. "My goodness, those sapphire crystals practically match your eyes. I'd swear that necklace could have been made just for you." Mae winked, giving her a mischievous smile, and left.

CHAPTER 2

The restaurant hung out over the Pacific in Malibu, and the moon cut a silvery streak of light through the water. Cece and Doug sat at a table by the window, candles casting soft shadows across their faces. They had just finished eating dinner, and the waiter cleared away their plates. Doug picked up Cece's hand and clasped his fingers through hers.

"You look great tonight, Ceece," Doug said.

"Thanks." Cece's right leg bounced nervously, and she felt like she was about to overheat. She had on a sheer, white silk blouse with long sleeves and draped neckline. Her hair fell in loose curls over her shoulders.

"Pretty necklace." Doug's eyes drifted down. "Matches your eyes." He lifted the jeweled butterfly, his hand brushing against her skin.

"A birthday gift from Mae," Cece said. "I love her jewelry." *Why did I just mention jewelry?* Cece thought.

"That was nice of her." Doug reached under the table, squeezed Cece's leg and smiled. At almost thirty, he could have passed for a college kid. But in his crisp blue dress shirt, brown leather jacket, and khaki slacks, he looked handsome and sophisticated. His hair, brown that tended toward dark blond in the summer, curled around his shirt collar.

"Dinner was delicious," Cece said. "And this spot is beautiful. What a view! I didn't even know this restaurant existed." Cece rambled, waiting for the moment she had been anticipating ever since she was a starry eyed little girl. There was no doubt in her mind that Doug Whitman was her dream come true.

They had met three years ago. Barbara had just expanded her gift shop into a coffee bar and gallery to showcase local artists and jewelry designers. They needed a photographer for a new brochure, so Cece asked for a referral at the camera store down the street. The manager handed her a tattered business card.

"Used to develop his film here before everyone went digital," he said. "Real good photographer, too. Haven't seen him in while though. Don't even know if he's still in business. Good luck."

Back at work, Cece called the number on the card.

"Hello?" It was a woman's voice.

"Hi, I'm calling for Doug Whitman. Is this his number?"

"Doug doesn't live here anymore. This is his mother—I could take a message for you."

Cece couldn't help smiling. His mother, how cute. "Thank you. I'm looking for a photographer. Is he still in that line of work?"

"He is. Is it for a wedding or bar mitzvah or something?"

"Oh, no, I just need photographs taken of an art gallery in Venice Beach."

"Oh, you're in L.A.," Mrs. Whitman said, "I know Doug would love the job, but he lives in San Diego now."

"Okay, well, thanks anyway." Cece started to hang up.

"Wait," Mrs. Whitman said. "Why don't you give me your number, and I'll tell him to call you. If he's not busy, maybe he'd drive up."

An hour later he called the shop, and Cece hired Doug Whitman over the phone.

Two days later, on a warm Saturday morning in September, Cece looked up when the gallery door opened.

"Hi." He was tall with broad shoulders accentuated by a tight, blue T-shirt. He had on faded Levi's and white, slip-on tennis shoes. His hair was a mass of light brown curls. "Are you Cece?"

"I am." Cece wished she had put on make-up and a cuter outfit.

They worked together for several hours, Cece arranging art pieces, adjusting the lighting, and asking casual questions. They took a break and walked down to the boardwalk for lunch. By the time they finished hotdogs and lemonade, Cece was beyond infatuated with her photographer.

Late in the afternoon, as Doug packed up his equipment, Cece watched him, trying to work up the nerve to invite him to dinner.

"I'll go through the photos tonight," Doug said, "and have a file to you by tomorrow."

"Great. Tomorrow's great. Or the next day will . . ."

"Do you want to get some dinner?" Doug asked.

Doug refilled their champagne glasses. "Oops, I almost forgot—one more little present."

Cece's stomach flip-flopped as Doug handed her the second gift. It was the size of a box of spaghetti and covered in little kid birthday wrap.

"Very cute paper, love the balloons." She tore it off, unveiling a plain white gift box. "Hmm," she said. "It's heavy."

"Open it." Doug leaned forward on his elbows.

She lifted the top. Inside the white box she found a wooden case. Cece unlatched the delicate brass hook. Her mouth dropped open. A paintbrush—the Da Vinci Kolinsky fine point sable—the brush she had coveted for years, but could not justify buying. After all, no starving artist spends over $200 on a paintbrush. "How did you know I wanted this?"

"I was looking at your catalog," he said. "You'd circled this in red and written 'someday' beside it. So babe, today is someday."

"Doug, wow, thank you. I love it. And it'll last forever." Cece recalled the commercial slogan "a diamond is forever," but she banished the thought from her mind and any of sign of disappointment from her face. "Thank you for such a great birthday."

"You're welcome." Doug touched her hand. "What do you say we get out of here?"

Cece nodded, and Doug motioned to their waiter to bring him the check.

At the door, Doug stood behind Cece and helped her put on her jacket. As he lifted it over her shoulders, he nuzzled her neck and nibbled on her ear.

They hurried across the parking lot to Doug's truck. Cece hopped in, her teeth chattering. "I'm freezing."

Doug started the motor and turned on the heater. "Come here," he said. "I'll warm you up."

Cece leaned against his strong chest.

"I'm crazy about you," he said. He kissed her, lightly at first, then his lips parted, his smooth tongue slipped around hers, and his fingers caressed the back of her neck. Cece responded the way she always did, melting into him as if she were still a teenager.

"Can't wait to get home," Doug whispered.

Doug turned out of the parking lot onto Pacific Coast Highway. As he drove, he rested his right hand on Cece's leg. Trying to put all thoughts of a ring out of her mind, Cece avoided looking at the blue Tiffany box in her lap. It was an uncomfortable reminder of her childish disappointment.

They cut over to Ocean Avenue and into downtown Santa Monica.

"Want to get a quick drink before we end the night? Your birthday's not over for another half hour."

"Actually, I'm kinda tired. Let's go home."

"All right. Your place?"

Doug had an apartment in Culver City, but they both preferred Cece's house. Patty didn't mind when Doug stayed over. She adored him. And tonight she had gone out clubbing in West Hollywood, a scene that didn't get started until midnight.

"Yeah. Patty won't be home 'til late . . . if at all."

"Great." Doug picked up her hand. "I'll build a fire in the fireplace."

"Sounds good."

Doug stopped at a red light. He brought Cece's hand up to his lips and kissed it gently. "You okay?"

"Of course, why?"

"You seem a little quiet."

Cece looked out the car the window. Crowds of people were milling about the street, going in and out of restaurants and bars. She turned back to him.

"I'm fine, a little stressed about work. Sales are slow. Barbara comes back tomorrow, and . . ."

"You're upset. I can tell."

"I'm not."

The light changed, and Doug let go of her hand. They drove the few remaining blocks without talking. Doug turned into the narrow driveway and parked his truck. "Cece, tell me what's wrong. I know you way too well for you to hide anything from me."

Cece leaned down to get her purse and the white bag containing her presents. "It's just, I . . . I was . . . you know what? Forget it. It was a wonderful night. Perfect in fact." She reached for the door handle.

Doug stopped her. "You don't like your gift, do you? Did I get the wrong paintbrush? I can exchange it."

Cece felt awful. "No, no—it's the exact one I've been wanting."

"Then the picture? You don't like that?"

"Of course I like it. I love it—the picture and the frame. You put so much thought into everything." She looked at him, his eyes wide and adoring like a puppy's.

"Okay," he said. "If you're sure . . ."

Cece squeezed his hand. "I'm absolutely sure. Now let's just go inside. We have the whole night ahead of us."

CHAPTER 3

Cece slipped out of her coat and hung it on a hook by the front door. The house, a Spanish-style, pink stucco bungalow, with arched windows and red tile roof, was on the border between Santa Monica and Venice. It was a tiny, two-bedroom house, with one bathroom, living room, dining area, and kitchen.

Cece turned on a lamp. In the dim light, she could see Doug's preoccupied expression, but she ignored it. "Aren't you going to take off your jacket?"

"Oh yeah. Sure." Doug slipped it off and threw it over the back of the couch. The white slipcovered sofa stood in the center of the small living room across from the brick fireplace. The coffee table in front of it was an old leather trunk Patty had picked up at a flea market. An antique armoire that held their television was angled into the corner of the room.

"Want tea?" Cece asked. "Or something stronger?" She walked from the living room through the narrow, arched doorway that opened into a breakfast nook and cozy kitchen.

"Tea's good," he said. "Where are the matches?"

"On the mantle where they always are."

"Don't see them."

Cece went back toward the fireplace. "They're right here," she said, her tone impatient. "Oh, wait, sorry. I left them in the kitchen yesterday."

She went into the kitchen, reprimanding herself for being irritable. After all, Doug had no idea what was going on in her mind.

Cece put the matches on the coffee table. "Here you go."

"Cece, is there something . . ."

"I'm fine, Doug. Please stop asking."

Doug rubbed the stubble on his face. "Maybe I should go."

Cece turned around. "No, don't leave. I didn't mean to snap at you." She went to him, reached up, wrapped her arms over his shoulders, and wound her fingers into his curls.

Doug leaned into her, nuzzling and kissing her neck and shoulders. "I love you, baby." His lips brushed over her ear. "And all I want is to make you happy, but you seem upset."

Cece stepped back. "I thought you were going to propose!" Cece clamped a hand over her mouth as if to trap her words.

"What?" Doug looked like he'd been slapped.

"Oh my God, I'm sorry! I didn't mean to blurt it out like that, but you're right, I am upset."

Doug stood immobile, while Cece wrung her hands. "I feel like such a fool now, but I did expect, or at least I was hoping . . . I don't know. I'm such an idiot! I even thought you might have hidden a ring in the chocolate soufflé, but . . . " Without warning, Cece burst into tears.

Doug sat on the back of the couch, his face pale. "I'm, ah, I don't know what to say."

Cece wished that she were dreaming. She felt exposed and humiliated, having bared her soul. She wanted to open her mouth and suck the words back inside, like tapping a delete key on the entire conversation.

"We've never even talked about it," Doug said, still looking at her in disbelief. "I had no idea that, that . . ."

Cece straightened her shoulders, wiped her nose with the back of her hand, and frowned. "No idea that what?"

Doug looked like he was under interrogation. "That you wanted, uh, wanted me to . . ."

"Doug, I'm twenty-nine today, and you're almost thirty," Cece said, suddenly feeling less foolish and more practical. "We've been together for three years. Did you plan to just date me forever?"

Doug's jaw dropped. "Oh God, are you pregnant?"

"No I'm not pregnant! But I'd like to be someday, before my grade A eggs are grade C."

Doug swallowed. "Oh. I get it, the biological clock thing."

"It's not the biological clock thing, Doug! It's that I thought you, that we . . ." Cece paused as the wooden clock on the mantel chimed. It seemed to have an opinion as well. "Wait. I can't believe we're not on the same page about this. You said I was the one."

"I know. And you are." Doug pushed his hair back with both hands. "Could I have that drink now? A shot of tequila would be good."

Cece's eyes opened wide. "Seriously? I tell you I want to marry you and you ask for tequila?"

Doug picked up his jacket. "You know what? Forget the tequila. I'm gonna go now. We'll talk tomorrow, okay?"

Cece nodded, her eyes brimming with tears. He looked at her as if she were a complete stranger before walking out and closing the door behind him.

CHAPTER 4

Patty's jaw hung open. "And then he just left?" She poured coffee into two large mugs.

Cece nodded. She looked at her watch. Almost noon and Doug still hadn't called. Her eyes were red and swollen.

"On the one hand I feel awful, and on the other I feel like, you know, is he a complete idiot? I mean, how could he not think that I'd want to get married? I don't know of any woman who'd date a guy for three years and not expect to marry him."

Patty stood. "Maybe it's ultimatum time."

Cece groaned. "Jesus, I never thought I'd be the kind of girl to say 'marry me or else I'm leaving.' What a cliché I've become!"

Cece's cell vibrated. Her eyes met Patty's.

"Doug?" Patty whispered.

Cece nodded and picked up the phone. "Hi." She kept her voice soft and calm. "Okay. Uh-huh. Sure, yeah. Bye." She touched 'end call' and looked at Patty. "He's coming over in an hour."

They sat on the couch. Doug's back was stiff, his feet planted flat on the floor, as he tried to explain himself. "You just caught me off guard, Ceece. It's not that I don't want to, um, you know, get, well, get . . ."

"Married, that's the word you're struggling with," Cece said, trying to sound patient.

Doug laughed and cracked his knuckles. "Right. Married. I can say it." He rubbed his hands on his legs. "I just need some, some time, I guess, to think, and you know, well, to um . . ."

"It's okay, I get it."

Cece had decided to stay calm. There would be no more emotional outbursts. Nor would there be the ultimatum that Patty had suggested. At least not yet.

"You do?" Doug looked relieved.

"I do." Cece forced herself to give him a reassuring smile. "Let's just forget the whole thing ever happened."

"Are you sure?"

"I'm sure."

Doug hugged her. "I wish you weren't going up north. We should spend Thanksgiving together. My mom would love it if I brought you home with me."

"Sorry, but I already promised my dad I'd come home. Besides, I'm bringing Patty with me. I'll only be gone a couple of days though."

"Good, because I'm really gonna miss you." Doug put his hands on either side of her face. He kissed her, his lips soft. "I'm crazy about you, you know that."

Cece knew. He said it all the time. She smoothed a hand over his cheek, noticing that the light brown stubble on his face had grown softer overnight. "Yes, I know. Now, I have to get ready for work." She tried to stand, but Doug pulled her back.

"You have time. Where's Patty?"

"Not here."

Doug slipped his hand around her and tickled her lower back. "Lucky me."

Cece giggled. "Damn right, lucky you." She crawled onto his lap and wrapped her legs around his hips. "But I only have a few minutes."

"A few minutes is all we need."

Barbara leaned against the counter beside the espresso machine, twisting her short, dirty blond ponytail around her fingers. "I hate to cut hours right before the holidays, but I promise it's only temporary. Sales will pick up after Thanksgiving, I'm sure, and then we'll be back in the black."

Cece looked at her boss with a skeptical eye. "I worked on bills yesterday, Barbara. The account was low, but it wasn't that bad."

"Oh, I know that dear," Barbara said, pulling at a loose thread on her oversized red sweater. "But my sister manages the payroll account, and, um, well, evidently that one is running short. But don't worry, she's going to be here for the entire holiday weekend and will help me sort everything out." Barbara smiled. "You both will be back at work Monday after Thanksgiving."

Patty put a hand on Barbara's shoulder. "No problem, Barb, we'll be fine."

Cece pinched Patty on the arm.

"Ouch!"

"Be quiet." Cece mouthed the words. She turned her attention to Barbara. "Let me make sure I understand. Patty and I take off all next week, without pay, including Black Friday, and come back to work on Monday, right?"

Barbara nodded. "Exactly."

"That's great," Patty said. "More time with your family!"

Cece smacked her.

"And," said Barbara, "once my sister gets me organized, I'll definitely be able to pay you for the week—vacation time and holidays." She gave them a hopeful smile. "Sound good?"

"Does to me," Patty said.

"I guess," Cece said.

"Now, you girls just have a wonderful time up north with the family. Everything will be straightened out in no time."

"Phil's going to be so excited," Patty said, referring to Cece's father. "He adores me."

Cece rolled her eyes and tried to ignite a flicker of enthusiasm. The original plan was to spend only two nights, but now they might as well make it a longer stay. And Cece knew that her father would be thrilled to have them a few extra days. Ever since she had moved away at eighteen, her father constantly asked, "Aren't you ready to move back home?" A firm "No" was always the answer. But it wasn't her home she wanted to avoid—it was her hometown, where everybody knew everybody's business, the word 'privacy' had been erased from the city charter, and too many people remembered an extraordinary young ballerina named Cecilia Rose . . .

Doug sat on Cece's bed eating pizza and drinking a Corona from the bottle. He watched her pack. "My mom said to tell you to have a good trip, and that she's *very* disappointed you won't be at our Thanksgiving dinner."

"Very?"

"That's what she said. *Very.*"

"Sweet. Tell her I promise to come over when I get back."

Doug drank some beer. "Maybe my parents can take us to the club next weekend. We haven't done that in a while."

Cece went to her dresser and rifled through a drawer. "That would be fun." She pulled out an old, comfy UCLA sweatshirt and stuffed it in. "I just wish I was more excited about going up north," Cece said.

Doug took another slice of pizza from the box. "You'll have a good time. Your dad's a great guy, and you love Julia."

"I know," Cece said, tucking socks into the side pockets. She adored both her father and her stepmother. They'd been married only two years, but Julia had been a family friend forever. When Cece's mother left and ran off with a younger man, Julia stepped in to help Phil deal with his mortified daughter and his traumatized son. "I just hate going into town. And now that we'll be there for the week, I don't know how I'll avoid it."

"When are you coming home?"

Cece groaned. "Probably Saturday. I'll call you when I get close, maybe we can catch a movie or something."

"I'm working that night. In fact, I'm working all weekend."

"You are?" Cece asked.

"Yeah, I told you the other day. Some spoiled girl's sweet sixteen in Beverly Hills on Saturday night and a wedding Sunday afternoon."

Doug had never said a word about either, but she didn't want to make it an issue. And just hearing him say the word "wedding" set her on edge. "If you did tell me, I . . . never mind, it doesn't matter."

Doug put a hand on the back of her thigh. "Why are you so grumpy?"

"I'm not."

"Yes you are."

Cece rubbed her eyes. She had to shake off this bad mood. "I'm just worried, you know? About work, going up north . . . "

"Come here." Doug pulled her onto the bed next to him. "You worry too much."

Cece tried to smile. She looked into Doug's eyes, fringed with long lashes that most girls would envy. Even in November he was tanned from surfing whenever the waves were good. She lifted her lips toward his and initiated a deep, delicious kiss. Cece felt his hands slide under her shirt and up her back.

"How much time do I have?" Doug asked with a boyish smirk.

"Enough." Cece stood and shimmied out of her pants, stripping down to a black thong.

Doug put his hands on her buns and squeezed them. "I love your ass," he said, gazing up at her.

"It's too big."

"No way—it's perfect. Probably my favorite part."

"Oh please, it couldn't be," Cece said.

19

"Well, maybe your boobs, I can't really choose—both are perfect."

The front door slammed, interrupting Doug's assessment of Cece's body.

"Stop whatever you're doing in there," Patty called from the living room. "I'm home!"

"Lock the door," Doug said.

But it was too late. Patty waltzed in as if she had been invited. "Hi Dougie!" She plopped herself onto the bed. "Well, aren't you little miss sexy? Shame your girlfriend is so unattractive, Doug. Aren't I more your type?"

Doug laughed and adjusted his crotch. He ruffled Patty's spiky hair. "You're cute, but a sexually confused punk-rocker is more than I can handle."

Patty gave his shoulder a shove. "I'm not confused, Doug, I'm flexible."

"That's right," Cece said, pulling her pants up. "Patty's just open-minded."

"Yeah," Patty said. "Hey, why are you putting your clothes on? Thought we could finally have that three-way."

"Oh Christ!" Cece said. "Get out of here and go pack. We're leaving early. I promised Dad we'd be there by dinner time."

Patty jumped on the bed like a little girl. "I can't wait to see Phil! Why did he have to get himself married? I thought he had a thing for me."

Cece looked at Doug. "Get rid of her, would you?"

"With pleasure." Doug lifted Patty and threw her over his shoulder. "Whoa. You've put on a few, little one."

"Shut up, I have not!"

As Doug carried her out, Patty lifted her head, grinned, and blew a kiss in Cece's direction.

CHAPTER 5

The mountains shimmered in the morning sun as Cece rounded the curve from the 405 onto the 101 North. Early on a Sunday one could get from Santa Monica to the San Fernando Valley in twenty minutes, a drive that would take an hour during the week. Cece glanced at Patty, who had been dozing since Sunset Boulevard, and yawned. She hadn't slept well, worrying about how she had left things with Doug. He seemed to have forgotten about her embarrassing outburst the night of her birthday, which was a both a relief and an annoyance. For the millionth time at least, Cece wished she had kept her mouth shut. But now that the subject of marriage had been brought up, there was no undoing it.

"Wow!" Patty bolted up straight. "We're almost through the valley. How long was I asleep?"

"Only about a half-hour."

"Want me to drive?" Patty asked.

Cece sipped her coffee from a travel mug and looked at the fuel gage. Her old but reliable BMW, a car passed down from her father when she graduated from UCLA, did not get very good mileage. "Soon. We'll stop in Ventura to fill up the tank and take a potty break."

"For a tall girl, you sure pee a lot."

"For a tiny girl, you hardly pee at all."

Patty leaned her head back then turned toward Cece. "You do know that he's in love with you, don't you?"

"How do you know?"

"I just know. Give him some time, he'll come around."

Cece looked in her side view mirror and changed lanes to pass the car in front of them. "That's just it, Patty, I have this horrible feeling that I'm running out of time."

"It's only because of your birthday."

"Maybe. But if I feel that way, and if I'm ready to, you know, get married, and if Doug's not, which seems to be the case, then, well, I . . ." Cece felt tears threaten and squeezed her eyes to keep from crying.

"Stop right there. I know what you're thinking—right love, wrong time and all that crap. Don't even go there, Cece. You two are gonna be fine. Now let's have some fun."

Patty picked up her iPod and scrolled, stopping on Lady Gaga's "Bad Romance." The song blasted through the speakers, and they sang along.

"Charlie King, third grade." Patty looked over her shoulder and changed lanes to go around a truck.

"Third grade? You got your first kiss at, what, eight years old?"

"Yup, on the lips but no tongue. Your turn."

They were heading toward Santa Barbara along the ocean. The waves were tall and clean, and Cece could see two surfers in wetsuits carrying their boards into the water. *Doug's probably surfing right now,* she thought.

"Come on," Patty said. "Let me hear it."

"Okay, okay, my first kiss." Cece gazed up and smiled. "Good story. 1993, sixth grade, I'm at my first boy-girl party."

"Go on," Patty said, squirming in her seat.

"So we're playing seven minutes in heaven, and Ross Tucker, who was a year older, picks me to go in the closet with him."

"Oh my God!"

"Yeah, so, I can barely contain myself, 'cause I'd had a crush on him for like two years!"

Patty gripped the steering wheel and bounced in her seat. "You naughty girl, give me details!"

Cece laughed at the long forgotten memory. "He closed the door, and there was just enough light coming in for me to see his face. He was so cute, and I was so nervous. Oh, wait, and someone puts on Bon Jovi 'Bed of Roses'!"

"I loved that song!" Patty squealed.

"Then he asks me if I'd ever kissed a boy before, and when I say no, he says to me: 'Your first kiss should be special, so if you don't want to, it's okay. I won't tell.'"

"Oh my God! That's the sweetest thing I've ever heard!"

"So I say, and get this, I say to him, 'Kissing you would be special.'"

"You said that? I don't believe it!"

"That's what I said. So he bent down, and he put his lips on mine—cool and soft—and he kissed me." Cece shivered at the memory.

"That is the best first kiss story ever! What happened after that?"

"That was it. He got with some older girl the following week, you know, the stuck-up cheerleader type, but he always said hi to me at school. Then his family moved away, and I never saw him again."

"Geez, no wonder you're such a hopeless romantic."

"Yep. I blame everything on Ross Tucker." Cece looked dreamily out the window for a minute. Then she turned her head to face Patty. "Don't you have to pee yet?"

"Again?"

"Sorry."

They stopped in Pismo Beach, a small, seaside town halfway between LA and San Francisco, to eat lunch. Patty parked the car on the side of the road beside a small park nestled in between jagged cliffs. They sat on a bench that looked out over the water and unpacked the lunch Cece had made that morning.

"Peanut butter and jelly," Patty said. "Oh boy."

"You like peanut butter."

"I would rather have grabbed a burger somewhere."

"We're unemployed, remember?"

"We're not unemployed, Cece, we're on a temporary hiatus from work. You need to chill out a little."

Cece licked some peanut butter off her thumb. "I know, you're right. Sometimes I wish I could just relax and be more like you."

"Believe me, so do I!" Patty nudged Cece with her shoulder. "But then we'd probably kill each other."

Storm clouds began to form over the ocean and the air turned colder.

"Let's get going," Cece said. "I'll drive."

They finished eating and got back into the car as a light rain began to fall. Cece turned on the windshield wipers, smearing muddy streaks across the window. Patty reclined her seat and dozed off again.

"Nice nap, sleepy head."

Patty yawned. "How long was I out this time?"

"About an hour." Cece smiled at Patty. "You're so cute when you're sleeping."

Patty put her seat up and stretched. "Ceece?"

"Yeah?"

"If we both were gay, would you be into me?" Patty asked.

Cece groaned. "Where the hell do you come up with these questions?"

"I don't know, they just pop into my head. I'd totally be into you."

"Really?"

"Sure, why not? You're amazing, and you're already my best friend in the whole world."

Cece smiled. She reached over and squeezed Patty's knee. "In that case, yes, if I were gay, I'd be into you."

"Thanks."

"You're welcome."

Shafts of light from the setting sun cut through gaps in the gray clouds. Cece slowed down to let an RV change lanes in front of her and noticed a sign for the exit to Gilroy.

"Hey, have you ever had garlic ice cream?" Cece asked.

"Yuck no. Is it good?"

"It's weird, kind of sweet and savory at the same time.

"Sounds terrible."

"Definitely an acquired taste," Cece said. "But they do make it right here in Gilroy, garlic capitol of the world. Want me to stop?"

"Not really, but believe it or not, I have to pee."

The traffic was heavy as they drove across the Golden Gate Bridge from San Francisco into Marin County. A blanket of fog was rolling in, but the sparkling lights from the city still glimmered in the distance.

Cece glanced over at Patty. "Feeling any better?"

"No. Maybe I should make myself throw up," Patty moaned.

"I told you not to eat so much ice cream."

"But it was so good. I can't believe how good it was."

Cece shook her head. "Dad's making enchiladas for dinner, so you need to get your appetite back, missy."

"Enchiladas? Oh Jesus, I wish I hadn't eaten that second scoop."

"I knew you'd regret it," Cece said.

Patty inhaled deeply. "Just one more thing to add to the list."

"What list?" Cece asked.

"My list of regrets," Patty said. "Don't you have one?"

"No." Cece thought for a moment. "Well, not a list anyway. I don't think I have enough regrets to even bother making a list."

"Well I have a list, and it's long."

"What's on it?"

"That second scoop of garlic ice cream for starters."

Cece laughed. "That's a fleeting regret. A real regret is something you wish you had done differently because of how it impacted your life. I want to hear about one of those."

Patty rubbed her belly. "I have to think. You go first."

They reached the end of the bridge, and Cece opened her window to pay the toll. An icy blast of wind blew into the car. She rolled the window up quickly. "That's easy. I regret telling Doug that I thought he was going to propose."

Patty pulled a sweatshirt on over her head. "Oh yeah, I get that. What else?"

Cece brushed some hair off her face. "Well . . . I think that now, in hindsight, I regret quitting ballet."

Patty snorted. "Every girl quits ballet. I quit after two lessons, even though I looked like an adorable little strawberry in my pink leotard and tutu. When did you quit?"

"When I was sixteen."

"Sixteen? I didn't know you danced that long."

Cece stretched her neck. "Over thirteen years without a break, and I had just auditioned for the San Francisco Ballet. I was good."

"Then why'd you quit?"

Cece said nothing for several seconds. She lowered her eyes. "To get back at my mother."

"Oh," Patty said. "For leaving your dad, huh?"

Cece nodded. "And because she had an affair that sent the whole town into a tizzy. Do you know how embarrassing that was for me to hear people talking about my mother's sex life?" Cece rubbed her forehead. "So first she humiliated us, and then she left us. My brother was only twelve."

"That must've sucked."

"Oh it did. God, I hated her."

Patty adjusted her seatbelt over her tummy. "Why did she care so much that you quit ballet?"

"Well," said Cece. "Partly because she was the quintessential stage mother. My success reflected on her. But more than that, I think she dreamed that I would achieve what she never could." Cece tapped a nail on the steering wheel.

"She was a ballerina, too?"

Cece saw brake lights in front of her and slowed down. "She was, and she was good. But not as good as I was. Anyway, I was so mad at her that I took away the one thing I had control of, and there was nothing she could do about it."

25

"Did it work? Was she mad?"

Cece remembered the day she told her mother that she had quit dance. She still could see the hurt and anger in her eyes.

"She was furious. Livid. Kept saying: 'how could you do this to me?' and 'do you know the sacrifices I've made for you?' Which was true. My parents spent a bundle on my dance lessons. But I didn't care. All I wanted was to get back at her."

"Jeez." Patty swung her head side to side. "That's some story."

"Yeah, revenge feels good, but the satisfaction is short lived. And there's usually a downside. It might have been my mother's dream that I become a prima ballerina, but it was my dream, too."

Patty sniffled.

"Are you crying?"

"It's so . . . so sad."

"You think that's sad? Now my mother is on her third husband and living in Seattle raising his teenagers." Cece stopped at a red light and looked at Patty. "Probably making them crazy, now."

"Is she miserable?"

"No idea, we haven't spoken in almost five years." Cece took a few deep breaths and put her mother out of her mind "Okay, now it's your turn. Tell me a regret." She poked Patty's stomach. "And a bigger one than eating too much ice cream."

"One time I drank too much vodka," Patty said with a grin.

CHAPTER 6

Cece rounded the corner of the street she had lived on for eighteen years. Her house was in Clearwater, a small town in Sonoma County. Named after a lake on the outskirts, Clearwater consisted of a long main street with a village square in the middle and family owned businesses on both sides. The quaint town was surrounded by farms, wineries, and houses situated on oddly shaped plots of land. Most of the homes had been built in the forties and fifties for families in search of a rural area not far from Oakland and San Francisco.

"Here we are," Cece said as she pulled into the driveway.

She parked right in front of the house, a traditional craftsman bungalow that sat at the end of a long gravel driveway on an acre of land. It had a low-pitched roof, broad eaves with exposed rafters, dormer windows on the second floor, and a wide, wooden porch that stretched around the entire perimeter.

Patty and Cece got out and stretched just as Phil Camden threw open the front door and walked toward them.

"You made it!" He hugged them both at the same time.

Over six feet tall, with broad shoulders, excellent posture, and thick, mostly gray hair, Phil looked like a rugged, older Marlboro man. All he needed was a horse and a cowboy hat. Cece pushed her nose into his chest and breathed in the familiar scent, a mixture of sawdust, autumn leaves, and musky cologne.

"Hi Daddy." Cece kissed his cheek.

"Hi Phil." Patty kissed his other cheek.

"My girls are home. I'm a happy man. Come on in, dinner's almost ready."

The warm kitchen smelled of hot, spicy chili and melted cheddar cheese.

"Where's Julia?" Cece asked.

"Just ran to the store. Should be back any minute."

"Hey," Patty said. "I'm gonna run up and take a quick shower." Patty mimed to Cece that her stomach still hurt.

"Go right ahead," Phil said. "Julia put towels out already."

As Patty headed upstairs, Cece turned to her dad and gave him another hug. She relished a few minutes alone with him.

"How's my girl?"

"Good. Just a little tired. Where's the dog?"

As if in answer to her question, Boomer, her father's sweet, old boxer, flew in through the doggie door.

"There you are," Cece said to the dog. She sat on the floor and let Boomer lick her chin. He wagged his stubby tail while she petted his square head and massive neck.

Phil peered out the window above the sink. "Looks like Julia's back."

Cece heard the car door slam and Julia's familiar quick steps crunching the gravel on the driveway. She got up and opened the door. "Julia!"

"Cece!" Julia dropped her grocery bags on the table and gave Cece a huge hug. "I'm so glad you made it in time for dinner. I was terribly worried about you girls driving in the rain. I've been checking the weather for days to be sure . . ."

"Slow down there, sweetheart," Phil said. "Where's my kiss?"

Julia looked at Phil with an adoring smile. She lifted her face to his, and Cece watched as they kissed, their lips puckering in matching fashion. It made her happy to see her father with a woman like Julia. When Cece's mother left, she thought her happy-go-lucky dad would never be himself again. But now, with Julia, he was happier and more content than Cece ever could have hoped.

"Let's unpack these groceries," Julia said. "Where's Patty?"

"In the shower." Cece pulled a brick of cheddar cheese out of a reusable, cloth bag. "And I'm starving. Is Tommy coming?"

Phil looked out the window again. "Just drove up."

Boomer barked and jumped on the door, pushing his nose against the glass. Tom, Cece's younger brother, blew in, knocking the dog down to all fours.

"Tommy!" Cece said.

"Hey sis." He wrapped his sister into tight hug. Tom was built just like his father only bigger. A football star in high school, he was strong and handsome, if a bit disheveled, with the same blue eyes and curly brown hair as Cece. "Been a long time since you were here."

"I know." Cece ruffled her brother's hair. Ever since their mother had left them, the two had watched out for each other. "I've missed you. You should visit me more."

"Oh no," Tom said. "I can only take so much city life, especially in LA."

He let go of Cece and turned his attention to Boomer, petting the dog's face excitedly with both hands. "Who's a good boy? Who's the best boy?" After roughing up Boomer he kissed Julia on the cheek. Then he went to his father. The two men embraced in a tight man-hug. "Hey Pop."

"Hello son." Phil put his hands on Tom's shoulders and squeezed them, as if Tom still were a teenage boy. Cece smiled at the obvious affection between her father and brother. After his wife moved out, Phil had dedicated every possible moment to his children, and especially to Tom, who never could comprehend why his mother had left him.

Patty appeared, her hair wet from the shower, dressed in gray sweat pants, a large blue sweater that draped off of one shoulder, and fuzzy white slippers. "Hi Tommy!"

Cece watched her brother's expression. She suspected that Tom, three years younger than Cece, had been nursing a crush on Patty ever since they'd met when Tom was still a teenager.

"Hey you!" He scooped Patty up as if she weighed nothing.

"Put me down! You're squeezing me to death." Patty giggled like a little girl.

"Enchiladas are ready." Julia clipped back her long auburn hair and put an apron on over her flowered peasant top and black leggings. "Let's eat!" she said, waving her hands, a thick stack of bangle bracelets jingling on her arm.

Cece loved Julia's style—half Audrey Hepburn and half hippie-chic.

They sat down at the long farm table that separated the kitchen from the family room. Tom filled everyone's wine glasses, and loud conversation, interrupted by spurts of laughter and raucous teasing, filled the room.

"Where's Ryan tonight?" Cece asked, referring to Julia's sixteen-year-old son.

"Dinner with his father," Julia said. "Although he really wanted to stay home to greet you. He'll be back in an hour or so."

"I can't wait to see him." Although they never had lived in the house together, Cece considered Ryan her little brother. She buttered a square of cornbread and licked her fingers. "This is delicious."

Phil poured hot sauce on his food. "So how was your birthday?"

Cece pushed her fork through an enchilada topped with chili. "Good. Doug took me out for a fabulous dinner. We had a great time."

"Are you kidding? It was awful!" Patty said.

"Patty . . ."

"What? Why?" asked Phil.

"Cece thought Doug was going to propose, and he didn't." Patty took a large bite of food and looked at Cece. "Right . . . ooooh dat hot."

"You have the biggest mouth I've ever seen," Cece said.

Tom reached for a second serving. "So what happened?" He glanced at Patty and winked.

"Now hold on," Julia said. "If Cece would like to keep it private, that's up to her." She patted the back of Cece's hand.

"If that young man disappointed my little girl, I'd like to know."

"Daddy, it's fine. I just, you know, got a little ahead of myself. And then, well, I kind of caught Doug off guard."

Tom's jaw dropped. "You mean you told him? Why'd you do that?"

"What do you mean why'd I do that? I didn't do anything wrong. I just, well, I guess I mentioned that I thought he might've gotten a . . . a certain gift that . . . " Cece drank down half a glass of wine. It all sounded so awful now.

Tom leaned his elbows on the table. "Ceece, had you guys even talked about it? Has he ever said he wanted to marry you?"

Cece frowned at her brother. "He says that I'm the one all the time. And he always tells me he's crazy about me."

"What are you? Seventeen? All guys say that shit. It's how we get . . ."

"Stop right there, son," Phil interrupted. "Now Cece, you know I like Doug very much. But if he doesn't think my little girl is good enough for . . ."

"Phil!" Julia almost jumped from her chair. "Nobody has suggested that. Cece, honey, don't you worry. You may have surprised him with your, um, suggestion . . ." Julia wiped her mouth with a napkin. "But give him a little time to digest the idea. He'll come around."

"I hope so." Patty picked up her wine glass. "Cece is almost thirty."

"Jesus! I just turned twenty-nine last week!"

"So thirty's right around the corner," Tom said. "Now I get it, it's the whole biological clock thing, isn't it?"

Cece pushed her plate away. "Why is it that all men think that? Why can't it be that he's the man I love and want to spend the rest of my life with? But, truthfully, yes. I'm twenty-nine now and will be thirty in one year, thank you Patty, and I want to know. A woman likes to have a plan. We don't like to be left hanging."

"And we men don't like to be blind-sided," said Tom.

The room fell silent.

Phil cleared his throat. "Well, now that that's settled, what's for dessert?"

CHAPTER 7

Cece pushed and squeezed the pillow underneath her head, trying to get comfortable.

Patty groaned from the trundle alongside Cece's bed. "Can we switch beds tomorrow night? This cot is too small."

Cece turned the pillow over. "If it's small for you, it'll be way too small for me. Besides, I'm mad at you."

"I know. You'll get over it though."

"And by the way," Cece said, "Ryan's room is right next door, so no running around in your underwear."

"He's sixteen and a total hottie. You think he's never seen a naked girl before?"

Cece kicked Patty's leg. "I have no idea, but he's my little brother, and I don't want him traumatized."

Patty sat upright. "Oh my God, me naked would traumatize him? He'd probably love it!"

"Patty, could we just go to sleep?"

"Fine." Patty flipped herself over. "G'night."

"G'night."

Cece turned onto her back. A sliver of moonlight illuminated her childhood bedroom, and she could see the comforter her mother had picked out for her fifteenth birthday, all flowers in pale, pastel colors. Cece had wanted to her room to be turquoise and purple, but her mother insisted that would be impractical. Neutral, soothing colors would stand the test of time. Maybe her mother had been right. After all, the bedding was still there, but her mother wasn't.

Cece drifted in and out of sleep. Tom's suggestion that she had blindsided Doug renewed her worries, and she wondered how, or if, she ever could make everything go back to the way it was.

The house was quiet when Cece awoke, and Patty's bed was empty. She stretched her long legs, crawled over the trundle, and went to the closet for her old bathrobe. It was hanging on a hook on the back of the door—purple chenille—the one her father bought her the year her mother left. "To hell with practical," Phil had said, "you pick any crazy color you want." She slipped into the robe and tied the sash tightly. It smelled fresh, like spring rain laundry detergent.

"Patty," Cece said as she padded down the stairs. "Are you here?"

"In the kitchen," Patty called out.

Cece found Patty standing in front of the stove. She sniffed. "Do I smell bacon? And coffee?"

"You do. I got up early and had breakfast with Phil before he left for work. Hey, I didn't know that Tom was working for him."

"Yes you did. That's why the truck says: Camden *and son*, Electricians. You saw it last time you were here."

"Oh wow, you're right." Patty handed Cece her coffee. "Never really thought about it before. How do you want your eggs?"

"Are you doing this so that I won't be mad at you anymore?"

"Yes," Patty said, a piece of crispy bacon hanging out of her mouth.

"Well, it's working. Scrambled with cheese, please, missy."

"Comin' right up. How'd you sleep?"

Cece nibbled on a piece of toast. "Awful. You?"

"Like a baby."

For the next few days, they cleaned and prepped, shopped and baked. To Phil Camden, Thanksgiving weekend was the kick-off of a two-month celebration that lasted all the way until Super Bowl Sunday. The serious cooking began Wednesday afternoon.

"Oh no!" Julia said. "I forgot celery. How could I forget that? Patty, look in the fridge and see if there's any in the crisper."

Patty pulled open the drawer. "Nope. Want us to run to the market and get some?"

"Would you? That would save the day."

Cece looked up from chopping onions, her eyes red and watery with black mascara smeared underneath. The last thing she wanted to do was venture into town. She ran a paper towel under cold water and wiped her eyes. "I'll go get my keys," she groused.

33

Cece pulled the car into a parking space and turned off the motor. She looked in the rear-view mirror, licked a finger and wiped the residual black smudges from her eyes. "I look like crap."

"You probably won't run into anyone you know."

Cece looked at her roommate. "You don't understand small towns, Patty. Let's just get in and out. You have the list?"

Patty shook the piece of paper as they got out of the car. "Right here. That one little bunch of celery turned into fifteen things."

They scurried through the grocery store aisles with Julia's list, filling the cart. "Okay," Cece said. "Did we forget anything?"

Patty ran her finger down the list. "Ummm, we just need a box of cornstarch."

Cece pushed the shopping cart around to the next aisle. "Oh my God," she said.

"What?"

"Someone I know." Cece stepped to the other side of their cart. "I have to say hello."

"Where? Who?"

"Natalie," Cece said. "Hi."

A tall, slim woman with dark, straight hair blunt-cut to her shoulders and golden-green eyes approached. "Cece?" She extended her long arms and hugged Cece. "My God, I haven't seen you in ages. You look great."

"And you!" Cece said, "gorgeous as ever. How have you been?"

"Good," Natalie said, glancing down at Patty.

"This is Patty, my roommate." Cece put a hand on Patty's shoulder. "Natalie's an old friend of mine from ballet."

"Old friend?" Natalie said. "How about old best friend? Cece and I were practically sisters, weren't we? I don't think a weekend went by when we didn't have a sleepover at one of our houses."

Patty dropped a box of cornstarch into the cart. "Now I'm her best friend, and we have sleepovers every night."

Natalie laughed. "Well, you're the lucky one then. Cece was the most wonderful friend I ever had." She reached out and took both of Cece's hands in hers. "You really were. I've missed you."

Cece noticed Natalie's eyes grow misty, and she felt a lump form in her own throat.

"I can hardly believe you're standing right here in front of me," Natalie said. "It really is good to see you."

Cece relaxed. She and Natalie had been friends since their first ballet class together at the age of three, but when Cece quit dance, their friendship withered. "How's your mom? Still running the studio with an iron fist, I'll bet." Cece looked at Patty. "Natalie's mother owns the ballet school where we took lessons."

Natalie scratched the side of her neck. "She's, well, she's not too good."

"Is she sick?" Cece's former teacher and mentor had been a formidable Russian woman—strict and exacting—whether the girls were perfecting their arabesques or making their beds.

Natalie nodded.

"I'm so sorry. I hadn't heard anything about it."

"We're trying to keep it private." Natalie chuckled. "Which is not easy around here, small town and all that, you know?"

"I sure do," Cece said. She wanted to know more, but she didn't want to pry.

"Anyway," Natalie continued. "She still teaches some of the time, but it's . . . it's been hard."

Cece felt an unexpected rush of emotion. She had loved Natalie's mother, Miss Ilana, more than her own. "I'm really sorry, Natalie. Will you tell her hello for me?"

"How long will you be here? If she's feeling okay on Friday, she'll be at the studio. You could stop by. I know she'd love to see you."

Cece took a deep breath. "I . . . I don't know. We're leaving first thing in the morning."

Patty interjected. "I thought we were . . ."

"I have to get home and back to work." Cece fibbed. "I manage an art gallery, and, well . . . "

"No, I understand. Listen, you're a busy city girl now. I'm happy for you." Natalie extended a slender hand to Patty. "So nice to meet you. And Cece, wow, I can't believe here we are, running into each other at the grocery store of all places. Give your family my best, won't you?" She hugged Cece again.

"You know, we could extend our stay, I guess," Cece blurted. "What if I came by about ten?

Natalie's head sprung up. "Oh my gosh, yes, that'd be wonderful." She pulled her cell out of the black satchel sitting in her cart. "Let's exchange numbers."

As Cece recited her cell phone number, Natalie punched it in. "I'll text you with my number," she said. "I'm so excited! We'll meet in front, okay? Just like when we were little. My mother will be so happy to see you."

Cece moved to the front of her cart. "Okay. Great. I'll see you Friday, then."

Natalie flicked a tear from the corner of her eye. "I'm so glad we ran into each other, Cece. You have no idea how much this means to me."

CHAPTER 8

The sound of clattering dishes woke Cece Thanksgiving morning. She leaned over the side of her bed and pulled her cell phone from the charger. It was too early to call Doug, so she texted: *Hi call me when you're up xoxo.*

They'd missed each other's calls yesterday, but Cece was not concerned. Maybe a few days apart would end up being a good thing, a break from the tension she had created with her outburst. When she got home, she told herself, she would put marriage out of her mind, and make sure that everything with Doug returned to normal.

She climbed over a sleeping Patty and went downstairs. The kitchen already smelled delicious.

"Hey," Cece said.

"Good morning. You're up early."

"There's work to be done." Cece filled a mug with coffee and watched Julia smear butter over the turkey's pale skin. "I'm so happy you married my dad." She kissed Julia's cheek.

Julia looked over her shoulder at Cece and smiled. "So am I, honey."

Cece took a sip of coffee. "That is an enormous turkey."

"We'll have lots of leftovers for the weekend. You're staying, aren't you? You know how your dad likes to start putting up Christmas decorations right away."

"Oh, I know. He rolls right from one holiday into the next." Cece poured cream in her coffee and stirred it with her finger. "We'll probably leave early Sunday. Doug's working all weekend, and I don't have to be at the gallery until Monday, so there's no rush for me to get back."

Julia turned on the oven. "Good. Your dad will be thrilled. He misses you a lot, you know."

"I know he does."

Julia washed a bunch of herbs and patted them with a paper towel. "By the way, I heard that you're going to the studio to see Ilana."

"Yep. Tomorrow morning at ten."

" I think it's very sweet of you to visit her."

"I didn't know she was sick, did you?"

"No." Julia looked concerned. "I did hear that she wasn't working as much lately, but that was all. It can't be serious or the whole town would be talking about it."

"I guess," Cece said. "But she's one tough lady. Nobody can suffer in silence better than she can. Anyway, put me to work."

The house phone rang.

"Why don't you grab that for starters," Julia said.

Cece put her coffee down and picked up the receiver on the yellow wall phone with the long, curly cord. "Hello?"

"Hey there!" Doug's voice greeted her.

"Doug! Hi, you got my text."

"Sure did. You didn't answer your cell."

"Oops, I left it upstairs. How are you?"

"Lonely."

Cece glanced at Julia who was busy chopping celery. "Me too." She walked around the wall into the hallway, stretching the telephone cord, and sat on the floor, her knees bent. "I wish you were here with me."

"So do I. But you got Patty there."

"Not the same."

"I hope not," said Doug. "I miss you, Ceece."

"I miss you, too. A lot."

"Hey, I was thinking you should come with me to that birthday party I'm working. It'll be fun, well, maybe not fun, but entertaining."

Cece took a deep breath and exhaled. "I'm not driving back until Sunday."

"I thought you said you were coming home sooner."

Cece wrapped the cord around her foot. "I . . . I was, but there's so much going on here, and my dad likes me to be around to start the Christmas decorating."

"Okay."

Cece could hear disappointment in his voice.

"I'm really sorry."

"No big deal."

"You're not mad, are you?"

Doug cleared his throat. "No."

"I would've come home earlier, but you said you were working all weekend."

"Yeah, but I was thinking we could have hung out together at the party."

Cece played with the phone cord. They had just gotten through a rough couple of days, and she wanted to avoid any more tension. "I'll tell you what, let me talk to my dad. He'll understand if . . ."

"No, don't do that," Doug said, his voice apologetic. "You probably won't be back up there for a while, so you should stay."

"Are you sure?" Cece asked, feeling a surge of love for him.

"Yeah. I just really miss you, babe."

"Me too. I can't wait to get home and have everything, you know, just go back to normal."

"Same here."

Cece sighed. "By the time you see me on Sunday, you'll want me even more."

"I don't think that's possible. And don't get me thinking about it either. I'm at my parent's house!"

Cece laughed. "Say hi to your family for me, okay?"

"All right, babe. Have a good time."

"I will. And I'll call you after dinner. Love you."

"Love you, too. Bye."

•

The farm table looked like a Norman Rockwell painting with the huge turkey browned to perfection, white tablecloth, gold napkins, antique china, and a centerpiece of orange daisies, yellow mums, and red lilies surrounded by ivory candles in crystal hurricane lamps.

"Okay family," Phil called. "Time for dinner! Tom, bring the wine, would you?"

"Got it right here, Pop."

They took their seats—Julia and Phil at the heads of the table, Ryan next to Tom on one side, Patty and Cece across from them.

Cece squeezed Patty's hand. "Thanks for being here," she said.

"What? Are you kidding? I love your family, probably more than my own." Patty laughed.

Ryan, a shy boy with a slight build and straight blond hair that covered one eye, looked at Patty. "Where is your family?"

"All over the place. My parents practically live in their RV traveling around and visiting my siblings who are scattered all across America."

"So she belongs to us this Thanksgiving," Julia said. "And we are delighted to have her."

"Thanks, Julia," Patty said. "I love it here."

Phil went and stood beside his wife. He put an arm around her and placed a soft kiss on her head. "This is the most magnificent turkey I've ever seen." He picked off a strip a crispy skin.

Julia slapped his hand playfully. "Wait! We need to take a picture. Who has a camera?"

"I do." Ryan pulled out his cell phone and snapped pictures of the food and all the family, while Tom poured wine.

"Make a toast, Pop." Tom handed him a glass.

"Okay, but I'm not very good at this."

"Yes you are Daddy, you're the best."

"Thank you darlin'. Well," Phil said lifting his glass, "to this wonderful family. All of you, everyone at my table is my family, and I am so happy you all are here." He winked at Patty and ruffled Ryan's hair. "And to the start of the holidays, my favorite time of year—gift giving and non-stop football—doesn't get better than that. Cheers everyone, now let's eat!"

Cece took her cell into the living room and sat on the couch. It was after midnight, and she had meant to call Doug earlier. Dinner had been wild and full of laughter, and it was not until they finished cleaning up that Cece realized how late it was. But she knew Doug would still be awake.

She listened to the rings, surprised that he didn't pick up right away.

"You've reached Doug Whitman Photography. Please leave your name and number and we'll get back to you. Thanks and have a great day."

"Hi sweetie. Thought you'd still be up, maybe you are . . . um, just wanted to say g'night and, well, sorry about this weekend. Call you tomorrow. Love you."

She pressed 'end call' and tossed her phone onto the coffee table. Uneasiness stirred in her stomach. *I need to get home*, she thought. *I need to get back to Doug.*

CHAPTER 9

For the second morning in a row, Cece was awakened by noise. It sounded like Santa was clomping around on the roof.

Patty bolted upright. "What the hell was that?"

"My father started putting up Christmas decorations."

"Oh. Okay." Patty put the pillow over her head and went back to sleep.

Cece lay on her back and stared at the ceiling. Today she would see Ilana Lurensky for the first time in more than ten years. "It's going to be an interesting day," she said to herself. She got out of bed and went downstairs to the kitchen.

The sight of Tom, bent over with his head in the refrigerator, welcomed her.

"Don't you have your own apartment?"

Tom turned. "Good morning to you, too."

"Sorry, but what are you doing here so early?"

"I told Dad I'd come help him with the lights. And besides, I have no food at my place, so for breakfast I'm making a Thanksgiving leftovers omelet, want one?"

"Yuck, no. Any coffee left?"

"Sorry, just took the last of it. Hey, did you see those light up reindeer things Dad bought? I think he's getting a little whacked."

"He is not. He just loves Christmas. Where's Julia?"

"Driving Ryan to soccer or something."

Cece reached out. "Gimme your coffee, Tommy."

Tom handed his mug to her. "You won't like . . ."

"Bleeeeech! Did you dump in the entire sugar bowl?" Cece handed the mug back to Tom.

"You can make a fresh pot, you know."

"I'll get some at the bakery on my way to the studio." Cece picked up a sponge and wiped around the coffee maker.

"Weird that you ran into Natalie Lurensky the other day. She still so hot?"

"Hotter than ever. Exceptional actually, in that exotic Russian model sort of way." Cece leaned on kitchen sink. "But there's something different about her, not as confident as she used to be."

Tom scooped yams, stuffing, and a few slices of turkey into a frying pan. "Maybe it has to do with her mother."

"Maybe." Cece watched Tom pour eggs over his concoction. "That looks disgusting."

"That's okay because I'm not giving you any."

Cece punched his arm. "That's okay, 'cause I don't want any."

Tom smiled at Cece. "It's good to have you home, sis, it really is."

A chilly breeze blew against Cece's face as she stepped outside. She buttoned her black peacoat and wrapped a red muffler around her neck. The cashmere scarf had been a gift from Doug their first Christmas together. Putting it on reminded Cece that they hadn't spoken since Thursday morning. She would call him as soon as she finished visiting with Natalie and Ilana, unless he called her first.

As she walked down the steps, she looked up to see her father at the top of a ladder leaning against the roof. A long string of white lights trailed across the front lawn. Boomer was barking and jumping around in circles underneath his master.

Cece patted the dog. "Don't worry, he'll be fine." She looked up. "Daddy!"

Phil turned. "Hey there baby girl, where're you going?"

"In to town, to see Natalie and her mom. I won't be gone long."

Phil waved. "All right, have a good visit. When you get back I'll let you help me set up my new reindeer. Patty, too."

"Okay, that sounds fun," Cece said with a smile. "See you in a bit."

Cece got into her car and rubbed her hands together. She considered going back inside for the red matching gloves, but at the moment getting a coffee was more important than having warm hands.

She backed her car down the driveway and into the street that had been a dirt road until Cece started high school. She drove underneath a canopy of bare branches created by the California Oaks that grew on either side of the road.

In less than five minutes, Cece turned onto Main Street. She drove past the shoe repair, beauty salon, and candy shop—businesses that had been in Clearwater for as long as Cece could remember. She pulled her car into a space right in front of Nutmeg's Bakery and hopped out. She realized that she had reached into the ashtray for change for a parking meter that didn't exist. "Gotta love a town with free parking," she said to herself, smiling.

In front of Nutmeg's windows were some tables and chairs for the customers who preferred outdoor seating. A number of people were already there clustered under the heaters. Cece pushed open the glass door and stepped inside, inhaling the sweet, familiar smell. She waited in line at the counter behind an older woman ordering an entire box of pastries.

The bakery had been the favorite hangout where Cece and her friends went every day after school for freshly-baked cookies and treats. Shortly before Cece left for Los Angeles, the owner's daughter, fresh out of Stanford with a business degree, decided they needed to do something to keep Starbucks out of Clearwater. She transformed the little bakery into a trendy and picturesque coffee bar, with state of the art espresso machines, round wooden tables, and intimate seating areas in the corners. Historical photos lined the walls. Of the few things Cece missed about her hometown, Nutmeg's was one of them.

"Help you?" a teenage boy asked. He had short, bleached hair, a gold hoop earring in one ear, and a thin goatee. Over his T-shirt he wore the requisite brown apron with "NUTMEG'S" embroidered on the front in orange lettering.

"Large black coffee, please."

"For here or to go?" the boy asked.

"Um, to go I guess. And do you have any pecan sticky buns left?" Those were her favorite.

"Lemme take a look."

He disappeared for a moment and came back with a giant square pastry covered in chopped nuts and buttery, brown sugar icing.

"You're in luck, last one."

Cece clapped her hands together. "Oh, I haven't had one in ages." While she waited for her order, Cece checked her cell. Nothing from Doug—no text, no missed calls. Disappointed, she dropped the phone back into her purse.

"That'll be $7.40."

Cece looked at the teenager. "Really? How much is the sticky bun?"

"Six bucks."

"Wow. Guess prices aren't what they were in the '90s." She handed him a ten-dollar bill.

"Wouldn't know. I was a baby." The boy looked at Cece as if she were from another century and handed back the change.

Cece spotted an open chair on the patio under a heater and headed outside. She had a few minutes to enjoy her breakfast before going to meet Natalie. As she was about to sit, the person in the chair behind her scooted backwards and collided with her, knocking into her arm.

"Oh no!" Cece gasped as she watched her coffee spill and her pastry tumble out of the bag onto the ground.

"I'm so sorry! I didn't even see you."

Cece turned. A tall man stood beside her chair. He looked down where Cece's coffee was flowing like a tiny stream toward the sidewalk. "Don't move. I'll be right back." He disappeared into the bakery.

Cece sighed. As she picked up her cup and plastic lid, a dog came by and sat down beside the sticky bun. He looked up at Cece. "Go ahead, you might as well take it," Cece said. The dog wagged his tail, grabbed it, and ran off. Cece sighed and dropped the cup into a trashcan and went back to her table.

She wiped up the mess with a handful of napkins and thought about Doug. Maybe she should drive back today. Phil would be disappointed, of course, but Cece felt a yearning to get home. She looked at her watch and calculated. After a quick visit at the studio, she could run back to the house, pack up with Patty, and be on the road by mid-afternoon. *It'll be good to get home tonight*, she thought, *then Doug will come over and everything can go back to the way it was . . .*

"Here you are." The man placed a white mug in front of her. "Bad news," he said. "No more of those cinnamon roll things."

Cece touched the coffee mug and looked up at the man who had ruined her breakfast. He appeared to be in his thirties, with broad shoulders, neatly trimmed, dark hair, and a beard that was several days old. It made him look rugged and masculine, and Cece was unable to overlook the fact that he was gorgeous.

She cleared her throat. "Yeah, I know. I got the last one." She picked up the mug and was about to mention that she had wanted a to-go cup. Instead she took a sip. The coffee was hot and smooth, and a real mug made it taste even better. She smiled at the man. "So what are you going to do about my sticky bun?"

The corners of his mouth turned up, and his eyes narrowed. He pointed one finger in her direction. "Stay here." He took two steps toward the doorway then turned back. "Please," he added with a polite nod of his head.

Cece sensed a stirring in her chest. Had she just flirted? She peered through the window to see the man talking to the teenage boy. He shook his head, leaned to the side, and pointed to something behind the glass. Cece sat up straight. "I'm being ridiculous," she whispered to herself. A minute later the man appeared carrying a large plate with what looked like a giant square of pecan pie.

"You've got to be kidding," Cece said.

"What? I saw that huge sweet roll you were about to eat."

"I was only going to have a few bites. The rest I was taking home."

"I'll bet you were." The man held out a white cloth napkin with a fork resting on top. She took it from him.

"Thank you." Cece pressed the side of the fork through the pecans, gooey filling, and dense crust. She tasted it. "Oh, really, really good," she said, her mouth full.

The man looked like a schoolboy showing a good grade to his mother.

Cece licked a crumb off her lip. "There is no way I can eat all this."

"Then you can take it home."

Cece motioned to the chair across from her. "Please, sit down and eat some."

"Well, if you insist." He sat and pulled a fork and knife out of his pocket.

Cece laughed. "Are those weapons, or do you always walk around with silverware?"

"I didn't want to seem presumptuous." He sliced off a thin piece.

"No, no, you have to do better than that." Cece picked up the knife. She cut the pecan bar directly through the middle then squinted at it. "Does that look even?"

The man took a bite. "Like you measured it with a ruler," he said chewing slowly. "Mmm, that is good."

The teenage boy appeared with a carafe of hot coffee. "Refill?"

"Oh," Cece wiped her mouth with a napkin. "Yes, please."

"Would you like a cup of coffee, sir?"

The man glanced at Cece. "Um . . ." he looked at the teenager. "Sure. That'd be great."

The boy filled another mug and placed it on the table.

The man picked it up, and steam rose in front of his face as he sipped. "Best coffee in town. Have you had it before?"

"Only about a thousand times," Cece said. "High school hangout."

"Really? You live here?"

"Not anymore. Just home for Thanksgiving. I live in LA."

"Ahhh, city of angels. I love that town."

Cece took another bite, feeling awkward.

"I used to live in Manhattan Beach," the man said.

Cece looked up. "I live in Santa Monica."

"Very nice. And what do you do in Santa Monica?"

"Actually, I work in Venice Beach. I manage a small art gallery." Cece said, taking another bite. "What do you do?"

"Lawyer."

That was all he said. Cece eyed him over the edge of her coffee cup. "Small town lawyer, huh? Come to think of it, you do look a little like Atticus Finch."

The man threw his head back and laughed. "Oh wow, if only! I do have an office here, but I'm in the city most of the time."

A truck pulled up, and two men with fresh pine wreathes got out. They each picked up a half dozen or so and started hanging them on every lamppost.

"Can't believe the holidays are already here," the man said.

"I know. Clearwater sure loves Christmas. Main Street will be twinkling and sparkling in no time."

"It will." The man watched as one of the workers attached a wreath to a lamppost. "Maybe I'll decorate my house this year."

They continued their small talk and finished off the pecan square. Cece licked her finger and picked the remaining crumbs up from the plate. "So good." She put her finger in her mouth. Suddenly chagrined by her lack of manners, she looked up. The man seemed amused. "Oh, wow, that was completely uncouth of me. I'm sorry."

"Not at all. I thought it was . . . adorable."

A layer of clouds moved across the sky and blocked the sun, darkening the patio where they sat. Cece looked at her watch. "I'm afraid I have to go. I'm meeting somebody in a few minutes."

The man nodded. "All right, well, again, sorry I knocked over your coffee and ruined your sticky bun." He rubbed the stubble on his cheeks. "Do you think I could make it up to you with, say, dinner tonight?"

Cece nearly choked. This handsome, slightly older man was asking her out. "Oh, I . . . I'm sorry but . . . no, I can't tonight." She felt her face grow warm.

"When are you heading back to LA? Maybe another night would work."

Cece shifted in her chair. She felt clumsy and inept. "You're so nice, but I'm, you know, I'm in a . . . it's just that . . . "

"Ah, you're in a relationship," the man said. He smiled and ran a hand through his hair. "I should have guessed. I hope I didn't

45

embarrass you. It's just that, well, you're very cute . . . and funny. I thought that, maybe, bumping into you was somehow meant to be."

Cece blinked and cast her eyes downward. She couldn't speak, and for a few seconds she let herself imagine what a date with this man might be like. He stood and extended his hand. She reached up and felt his strong grip.

"It was a pleasure having breakfast with you," he said.

She let go of his hand, surprised by her reluctance to do so. "I enjoyed it, too." Cece rose and scooted her chair back, tipping it to the side. She caught it and pushed it into place. "Well thank you for the coffee and the, uh, delicious pecan thing."

The man smiled, and a dimple appeared near the corner of his mouth. "You're welcome. Have a safe drive home."

Cece buttoned her coat and willed herself to stop behaving like a silly teenager. "Good-bye," she said, wrapped her scarf around her neck. As she walked to her car, she glanced back. The man was still looking at her. Embarrassed, Cece turned away and quickened her steps.

CHAPTER 10

From two blocks away Cece could see the old Mayfair Hotel on the corner at the end of Main Street. The two story, southern style inn with white wood siding, pitched roof, and wrap-around porch no longer accommodated guests, but from the outside it looked the same as it had when it was built in 1925. It was sold in the sixties and converted into office space on the upper floor. When Ilana Lurensky leased the expansive lobby, she transformed it into her dance studio, maintaining much of the original décor.

Cece parked her car. She took a deep breath and got out. Natalie was standing on the porch in front of the entrance to the Lurensky Dance Academy. She raised her hand and smiled. Cece did the same and walked toward her childhood friend. Nervous about seeing Ilana, her lightheartedness from the handsome-man-encounter faded as she approached.

"Good morning." Natalie hugged her. "I'm so glad you're here."

"Me too," Cece said, keeping her tone light.

There were three sets of French doors across the front of the building, and the middle one was ajar. Natalie put her hand on the doorknob then stopped. "I told my mother last night that you were in town, and that you'd be coming to see her. But she's a little off this morning. She didn't remember."

"Okay." Cece nodded. She still did not know what was wrong with her former instructor.

"She's getting a little ditzy. Might not recognize you right away."

"That's understandable. She hasn't seen me since I was a teenager."

Natalie pursed her lips. "Well, it's a little more than that."

Cece hesitated. "I don't want to upset her."

"I don't think that'll happen. If anything gets weird, I'll take care of it," Natalie said with a small laugh.

They stepped inside. Nothing had changed. The high, dark wood ceiling, crystal chandeliers, and carved moldings that Cece had loved as a little girl were still polished and gleaming. Shiny mirror-covered the walls, and ballet bars of differing heights cut horizontal lines across each. Cece closed her eyes and inhaled the familiar, musty smell she remembered from thirteen years of dancing in the same room where they stood.

"She's in the office," Natalie said.

They walked to a door in the far corner that opened into a long hallway.

"This is amazing," Cece said. "Same bathrooms, same cubbies, same everything. And still immaculate."

"Remember how my mom would make us polish the wood around the cubbies if she didn't think we had practiced enough?"

"Does she still do that?"

"She doesn't, but I do, with my pupils." Natalie smiled. "Let me tell you, it works."

At the end of the hall was an open door, and Cece could hear classical music playing on the old record player.

"We're rehearsing for *The Nutcracker*," Natalie said. "Every Christmas, same show. You'd think this town would get tired of it, but they don't."

"Hey, it's tradition." Cece's felt warm, and nervous. She slipped off her coat and folded it over her arm.

Ilana Lurensky sat behind an antique French desk in front of a large window. On either side of the window were panels of beige drapery that fell in sumptuous gathers on the floor. A crystal chandelier, similar to those in the studio, hung from the middle of the ceiling, and large, framed prints of famous ballerinas lined the walls. Natalie went ahead of Cece.

"Look Mamma, Cece has come to see you."

Miss Ilana looked up. Cece noticed that her face hadn't changed. A few wrinkles around her eyes, smile lines deeper, but that was all. Her dark, almost black, hair, now streaked with gray, was pulled into a tight bun at the nape of her neck. She wore the same uniform Cece remembered—long, black ballet skirt over a black leotard, tights and ballet slippers. Cece felt intimidated just being near her again.

Ilana looked at her daughter and then at Cece. She seemed confused, her lips pursed. Then she glanced at the wall clock and frowned.

"You are late."

Cece smiled and raised her eyebrows. "It's just a little after ten," she said.

"I tell you a thousand time, lesson begins on the hour." Ilana clapped her hands twice. "Go Cecilia, dress. Quickly. And you, Natalia, we rehearse all day today."

Cece blinked and swallowed. Ilana thought that she and Natalie were children.

"Mamma." Natalie took her mother by the shoulders. "Look at me. Cece is here for a visit. She's all grown up now, just like me. You know that."

Ilana's harsh expression softened. She focused on her daughter's face. As reality dawned, her eyes cleared. "Of course I know zat," she said, looking up at her daughter. "Who has come to visit?"

"It's Cece. You remember Cecilia Rose, don't you?"

Cece took a few steps forward and touched Ilana's hand. "It's wonderful to see you, Miss Ilana."

Ilana smiled at her, but still without recognition.

"Come on, Mamma," Natalie said, her voice impatient. "It's Cece, my best friend my whole life." She walked across the room and opened the doors of a large armoire. The shelves were lined with black, leather albums. She ran a shaky finger over the spines of the books until she found what she was looking for.

Natalie placed the album on the desk in front of her mother and opened it. Cece caught her breath as she glimpsed a picture of herself. She was twelve or thirteen, dressed in a crimson and gold costume, and standing on pointe with her left leg extended behind her. Her brown curls were wound into a tight bun on top of her head.

Natalie tapped on the photo with one finger. "Remember this, Mamma? We were doing Don Quixote, and Cece was Dulcinea. Look at how well she did her arabesque."

Ilana's eyes grew watery. "Ah, Cecilia Rose, to see her dance . . ."

"Mamma, she's right here in front of you!"

Ilana looked at Cece. She stood and put her hands on Cece's cheeks as recognition dawned. "Cecilia? I tink I never see you again. Vat a beautiful girl you become."

Cece felt her eyes fill with tears as she hugged Ilana. The woman was smaller than Cece remembered.

"Come. Vee sit down." Ilana pulled Cece's arm.

They sat at the desk and continued looking through the album.

"I have book for my best dancers. In turty years, I make maybe eight book." Ilana smiled at Cece and patted the open album. "This dancer here, my best ever."

Cece trembled as she turned the pages slowly, and long forgotten memories of her days as a ballerina unfolded. She smiled at a snapshot—a line of girls, only four or five years old, in pink tights and tutus. It was Cece and Natalie's very first recital. The two little girls stood side-by-side holding hands.

She turned the page. "Look at this one," Cece said, pointing at another picture. "That's me with Jenna. I idolized her. Didn't she go to London?"

Natalie nodded. "She did. She danced there for a long time then married some wealthy British guy and started having babies. Sends a card every Christmas."

Suddenly Cece wished she had kept in touch, not only with Ilana and Natalie, but with some of the wonderful friends she had had.

"I'm sorry I never came back to see you in all these years, Ilana."

"Ah," Ilana waved her hand, dismissing the apology. "I understand. It vas difficult time for you."

The scrapbook captivated Cece. Photos, newspaper articles, recital programs—all recognizing Cecilia Rose Camden as the ballerina to watch.

"I can't believe these pictures," Cece said, turning through the last few pages. A piece of stationery fell out of the back of the album and fluttered to the floor. Cece leaned over to get it, but Natalie got it first and tried to slip back into the book.

"What's that?" Cece asked.

"Just an old letter, it's nothing."

But Cece had caught a glimpse of the header on the stationery. It was from the San Francisco Ballet. "Please," she said, extending her hand with palm up.

Natalie hesitated. She handed the letter to Cece.

March 3, 1998
Dear Ilana,
So disappointed to learn that Cecilia has stopped dancing. The committee had just accepted her when I got your message. At this point we have filled our openings, but if she changes her mind in the next week or so, I will see if I can pull some strings. I haven't come across a ballerina like her in ages. She is the kind of dancer we dream of, and I truly believe that she has what it takes. Do what you can to get her to rethink it and if . . .

Cece gasped. "I made the company?" It had been a lifetime ago, but the news made her hands shake. "I had no idea."

She closed her eyes and recalled a vague memory of Ilana leaving countless messages for her after she had quit coming to her classes, but Cece would not return her calls. Her life was in chaos, her dancing days over. She was not about to let Ilana try to lure her back.

Cece put the letter on the desk and went to the window. A light rain was falling, and moisture dripped from the leaves on the trees behind Ilana's office. Cece stared outside.

"You okay?" Natalie asked.

Cece nodded. "I need to use the restroom." She hurried down the hall, her heels clicking on the wood floor. Inside the bathroom, she leaned on the sink and pressed her palms on the cold tile. She took deep, even breaths. Following the audition, she had waited and waited, checking the mailbox every afternoon in the hope that she would hear from the ballet, but before she got that answer, her mother left the family. Her world unraveled and ballet no longer mattered. If there had been a letter, she never received it.

Cece looked in the mirror and wiped her eyes. "You had every reason in the world to quit dancing," she said to herself.

She returned to Ilana's office. All she wanted to do was say goodbye.

"Cece," Natalie said. "I'm sorry. I didn't even know the letter was in there."

"It's fine. Ancient history now." Cece glanced at Ilana. She was going through the album again. The clock on the wall chimed. "I need to go."

"Okay." Natalie touched her mother's shoulder. "Mamma, Cece's leaving."

Ilana continued looking at the book as if she hadn't heard her daughter speak.

"Wait just a sec, I'll walk you out." Natalie stood behind her mother and coaxed her out of the chair. "I think you should have a little nap, Mamma, before rehearsal starts."

Ilana stood. "Did I have tea?"

"Not yet, Mamma, I'll get it for you after your nap. Say goodbye to Cece."

Cece hugged her teacher. "It was good to see you, Miss Ilana."

"And you, my dear." Ilana put her hands on Cece's shoulders and studied her face. "Like second daughter to me, Cecilia Rose." She kissed her on both cheeks.

Natalie walked her mother to the couch against the wall. "I'll be back in a little bit, Mamma."

"Thank you, Natalia." Ilana curled her legs up and put her head on a cushion. Natalie covered her with a thin, pink blanket.

Cece followed Natalie through the studio and out the French door. The rain had stopped, but water dripped from the balcony above the porch. Natalie put a hand on Cece's arm.

"I am so, so sorry Cece."

Cece exhaled. "Don't worry about it. It all happened so long ago. Probably one of those 'all for the best' things."

"Still . . ."

Cece crossed her arms against the cold breeze. The rain had cleared and the air smelled of fresh pine from all the Christmas wreaths on the lampposts.

"Listen, what you're dealing with is way more important," Cece said, changing the subject. "I had no idea what you meant when you said your mom wasn't well. I was thinking, I don't know, arthritis or something."

"It is tough, but her problem kind of comes and goes. She can be completely normal for weeks, and then she has a bout of total lunacy."

Cece put her hands in her pockets. "She was so tough when we were young."

"She's still tough, but only on her good days."

"What does her doctor say?"

"He put her on an anti-depressant. Then all she did was sleep, so he took her off it." Natalie crossed her arms. "We're going back right after the holidays."

"You really have your hands full, don't you?"

Natalie took a breath. "What are you going to do? Life gets messy."

They stepped off the porch, and Cece saw a girl in a gray jacket, ripped jeans and clunky boots coming toward them.

"Hey Dawn," Natalie said putting on a cheerful face. "How was your Thanksgiving?"

"Fine."

"This is Cece, an old friend of mine."

"Nice to meet you," Cece said. The teenager had wisps of blond hair sticking out a black knit cap. "Do you dance here?"

Dawn nodded.

"Dawn is fabulous. She's our Sugar Plum Fairy this year."

"Congratulations," Cece said. "That's a tough part."

"I guess," said Dawn.

"Go on in," Natalie said. "I'll be there in a few minutes."

"Nice to meet you, Dawn," Cece said. "Good luck."

"Thanks." Dawn's sour expression didn't change as she went into the studio.

"Geez, were we like that?" Cece said.

"Who can remember? Teenagers are so cranky these days. I suppose they always were, just seems worse now that we're the old ones."

A minivan pulled up and five little girls in pink tutus poured out. "Miss Natalie!" they shouted.

"Hi you guys!" Natalie said. The girls swarmed Natalie. They wrapped their arms around her waist and hips, giggling and pushing on each other like puppies trying to get attention. "Run inside and start stretching, lots to do today. Hurry, hurry."

The little pink girls scurried inside.

"Oh my gosh," Cece said. "How cute was that?"

The woman driving the van honked and waved Natalie over.

"Oh no," Natalie said under her breath as she approached the car. "Hi Wendy, what's up?"

Cece hung back, but she could hear everything. The woman leaned toward the open passenger window. "Where on earth is your mother? I've been trying to reach her."

"Just busy time of year, Wendy. Can I do something for you?"

"Well, yes, the new instructor you hired. I don't like her."

"Kendall? Why's that?"

"She seems to favor certain girls over the others. I watched the lesson the other day, and she practically ignored Brittany. Now you know I'm not one of those mothers who thinks her daughter is better than everyone else, but let's face it, Brittany is better."

Cece squirmed. The woman sounded like her mother.

"I'll check on that, Wendy, and I'll talk to Kendall. Don't worry, Brittany will get all the attention she needs."

Wendy's frown went away. "Okay, thanks. I'll be back shortly, just running a few errands. Then I'll come in and watch the snowflakes. And by the way, I got a great referral for the costumes—tell you about it later." She waved as she took off down Main Street.

Natalie stepped back from the curb.

"Between the mothers and the teenagers, I don't know how you do it," Cece said, shaking her head.

"It's hard sometimes, but the little ones always cheer me up."

"They are adorable. And still wearing pink tutus, just like we did."

They started walking toward Cece's car.

"That mom," Natalie said. "Wendy. She drives me crazy, but she's right. The new instructor is, well, just too young and inexperienced. I wish you lived here, I'd offer you the job."

"Yeah, right, like I could teach ballet."

"Are you kidding me? You'd be amazing." Natalie bumped her with her shoulder. "The pay's pretty good—can I tempt you?"

Cece laughed. "Me leave LA? Not a chance." Cece crossed her arms and shivered. "It's 75 degrees and sunny where I live."

Natalie stretched her shoulders. "I don't blame you. What I wouldn't do for a few days of sunshine right now."

Cece brightened as she thought about the weather and the smell of the ocean and Doug waiting for her in Los Angeles.

They stopped beside Cece's car.

"It was great seeing you Natalie. And I'm really glad I saw your mom."

"Thank you so much for coming. And again, sorry about that letter."

"Listen, I changed my life a long time ago. I might have a few regrets, but who doesn't?"

"Very philosophical." Natalie hugged her with strong arms. "Please stay in touch. Let's not let another decade go by before we see each other again."

"It's a deal," Cece said as she got into her car. "Bye, Natalie, take care."

"You too." Natalie gave her a nostalgic smile. She turned and walked back into the studio.

CHAPTER 11

"Patty! Where are you?" Cece said, slamming the front door.

"Jesus, I'm right here in the kitchen. Making lunch with Phil. Want a turkey and cranberry sauce sandwich?"

After the overly sweet breakfast, real food sounded good. "Sure. Make a couple and wrap them in foil. We're going home this afternoon."

Phil stopped slicing meat. "What do you mean? I thought you were staying through the weekend! I was going to get the tree tomorrow, so we could all decorate it together."

"I'm sorry, Daddy, but I just have to get home. We've been here five days already."

"I know baby, but what's another day or two? And you haven't even said if you'll be back for Christmas."

"I'll try to come up for a few days," Cece said. "Maybe, if Doug can come." There was no way she would leave him behind again.

Patty pulled off a long piece of foil. "I can't believe we have to leave. I love it here."

Cece's father hugged Patty. "You can come back any time you want, with or without Cece."

Boomer jumped up, his paws on the counter, and stole a slice of turkey from the platter.

"Hey!" Phil hollered at the dog. "Bad boy! Get outside!" Boomer flew through the dog door into the backyard, turkey hanging out of his mouth. "You'll wait for Julia to get back, won't you? To say goodbye?"

"Of course we will. Come on Patty, let's pack up."

Ryan carried their suitcases to the car and put them in the trunk.

"You know the Grapevine can be very foggy this time of year," Phil said. "Which route are you taking?"

"We'll stay by the coast, Dad." Cece squeezed her father's hand. "Don't worry."

"And be sure to call me when you get home. I don't care how late it is."

"I will." She hugged her father and then Julia. "Take good care of him, okay?"

"Oh, you know I will, honey." Julia kissed Cece's cheek. "See you soon I hope."

Tom came down from his ladder, and gave Cece a big hug. "Bye, sis," he said.

Cece wrapped her arms around her little brother. She looked up at him. "Don't be such a Northern California snob, Tommy, come visit us."

"Maybe." He released Cece and hugged Patty, lifting her off her feet.

"Bye Tommy," Patty said in a playful tone. She planted a big kiss on his cheek. Then she went to Phil and hugged him.

Cece kissed Ryan, making him squirm, and pulled Patty off of Phil. "Let's go, missy."

Cece rolled her window down. "Be careful stringing the lights, Dad. I don't want to hear about you breaking any bones."

"He'll be fine, he's got me," Tom said, putting his arm over Phil's shoulder.

The four of them stood together.

Patty leaned forward. "God, they look like the perfect family don't they?" She picked up Cece's cell phone a snapped a picture.

Cece felt her heart swell as she backed down the driveway. "They really do," she said with a little catch in her voice. "They really are." She brushed a single tear off her cheek.

"Are you okay?" Patty asked.

"It's been a very strange day." Cece pushed the button to turn on the heater."

"What happened?"

"Well," Cece said. "I'm not really sure where to start . . ."

They were passing Palo Alto by the time Cece finished telling Patty about Ilana, the letter that fell from the album, and her encounter with the man at the bakery.

"You must be exhausted after all that," Patty said.

"I'm definitely running on adrenaline."

"Tell me again what that magnificent man looked like."

"No. I've told you twice already."

"I love it that he replaced your sticky bun with a real dessert. That was really nice."

"I know," Cece said. "Now let's stop talking about him." The only thing Cece wanted to think about was getting home to Doug.

"Wait, one more question. What was his name?"

Cece titled her head and thought for a moment. "You know what? I don't think we ever introduced ourselves."

"Seriously?"

"Doesn't matter. It's not like I'm going to cyber stalk him."

"Well I could. You already have a boyfriend. Maybe a cute, tiny girl with red hair is just Mr. Sticky-bun's type."

They had been on the road over two hours when the rain let up, and the sun started peeking through the clouds.

"I can't believe I haven't heard from Doug," Cece said. "Check to see if I have any missed calls."

Patty picked up Cece's cell. "Does he know we're on our way home?"

"No, I just left a message for him to call me back."

Patty held up the phone. "There's a voicemail."

"There is?" Cece reached for her cell, but Patty slapped her hand away.

"Keep driving, I'll put it on speaker."

Cece smiled at the sound of Doug's voice.

"Hey babe—got your message. What's up? Call me back. And, um, I really miss you. Can't wait to see you on Sunday."

Cece was standing in line waiting for the bathroom in a McDonalds when her purse started vibrating. She reached in and grabbed her phone.

"Hi!" she said to Doug.

"Hey, babe, I got your messages. You've been hard to reach."

"I know. My service has been spotty."

"How's everything going up there? Your dad put up the Christmas tree yet?"

Cece grinned. "Guess what . . . I'm on my way home." She squeezed the phone anticipating an enthusiastic response.

"You're kidding, right?" He didn't sound happy.

Cece's heart dropped. "No. We're on our way. I decided to leave this afternoon, like you wanted me to, remember?"

"But I'm not home."

"What do you mean? Where are you?"

"I'm down in Coronado, staying at my brother's place. The waves are phenomenal, so we decided to go surfing."

"But I thought you were working this weekend?"

"I gave the jobs to Mike. He really needs the money, you know?"

Cece's feet felt like they'd been glued to the floor. She didn't want to be mad, but she was. It seemed that Doug never made work a priority.

"I'm sorry, Ceece, if I'd known you were coming home, I never would've gone. But I didn't think you'd be back until Sunday."

"Well," she said, trying to keep her voice in check. "I assumed you'd be home because you had to work, so I . . . never mind."

"I'm really, really sorry. Tell you what. I'll only stay one night. I can surf with the guys tomorrow morning and leave in the afternoon. I'll be home in time to go to dinner. Sound good?"

"I guess."

"I'll call you when I'm on my way."

"All right," Cece said. The restroom door opened and a woman walked out. "Bathroom's free, I've got to go."

"See you tomorrow," said Doug. " Love you."

"Love you too. Bye."

CHAPTER 12

Cece stood in her bedroom wrapped in a towel, water dripping on the carpet. It was Saturday afternoon, and she still hadn't heard anything from Doug. She dried off and put on a pair of sweat pants and a white long sleeve shirt. She looked at her cell phone, willing it to ring. Then it did.

"Doug?"

"Hi, I'm at a gas sta . . ." static interrupted him.

"You're where?"

"Encinitas. Truck broke down."

"Can't you fix it?"

"No I can't fix it. I need a new radiator hose. I'm getting towed to the nearest garage, and I'll call you from there."

"Okay," Cece said. "When do you think you'll be back on the road?"

"Depends on the garage. If they have the hose, probably in a few hours. I'm really sorry."

"Don't worry, just let me know."

"We'll go to a late dinner or something."

Water dripped from Cece's hair into the phone. She flicked it away. "Okay. See you tonight."

Cece pushed 'end call' and threw the phone onto her bed. It bounced off and fell to the floor, knocking the battery out, which slid under her dresser. "Aaaaaaaargh!"

Three hours later, Doug called again.

"The mechanic didn't have the right hose, so he tried to patch the old one, but it kept leaking coolant, so that means . . . "

"I don't know anything about hoses and coolant, Doug. Did they fix it or not?"

"Not."

"Now what?" Cece could feel her blood pressure rising.

"My brother's gonna come pick me up. I won't get home until tomorrow."

"But I rushed home just to be with you, Doug!" Cece wanted to scream.

"Don't be mad Ceece, these things happen. You know that."

"If you'd stayed in LA and worked the parties, the ones that prevented you from going with me to my Dad's by the way, then you wouldn't be in this predicament."

Doug didn't respond.

"Guess I'll see you tomorrow. If you make back by then."

"I'm sorry, Cece."

"See you later."

"See you later. I'm really . . ."

Cece hung up before he could apologize again.

It was late Sunday night when Cece heard a knock on the front door. She and Patty were sitting on the couch in their pajamas watching *It's A Wonderful Life.*

"That's probably Doug," Cece said.

"Want me to get it?" Patty asked.

"Sure."

Patty paused the movie on Jimmy Stewart's face, got up, and opened the front door. "Hey Doug."

"Hi Patty."

Cece didn't turn around. She heard Doug walking toward the couch where she sat. "Hi Ceece."

Cece looked at him through the corner of her eye. He looked tired and guilty and as adorable as ever. "Hi."

"What're you doing?"

Cece didn't answer.

"Looks like you're watching TV and eating Christmas cookies."

Cece put a whole butter cookie into her mouth. "That's right." Crumbs blew off her lips.

Doug started to laugh. "Can I have one?"

Cece tried not to smile, but she couldn't help it. She wanted to stay furious with him, but she was so happy to see him that she couldn't. "I guess."

Patty came around the front of couch and picked up the plate. Here," she said, offering the last cookie to Doug. "I'll get more while you two make up. But be quick about it. I want to get back to my movie."

"Do you have any with the red and green sprinkles?" Doug asked. "Those are my favorite." He sat down on the couch.

"Yes we do. And would you kiddies like hot chocolate with that?"

"Hell yeah," Doug said, popping the cookie into mouth.

"Thanks Patty," Cece said. "You're the best."

Patty disappeared into the kitchen, and Doug picked up Cece's hand. He kissed it. "Look at that, you have red frosting on your knuckles."

Cece twisted her hand to see, but Doug pulled it back toward his mouth. He licked the frosting with his soft tongue. Cece raised a shoulder. "If you think kissing my hand's going to make everything fine, you are mistaken."

"Then how about this?" Doug leaned in and kissed her mouth gently, his lips soft and parted. Cece could taste the sugar cookie he'd just eaten.

"Better," she said.

Doug wrapped Cece into a tight hug. "I'm sorry babe, you were right. I should've stayed here. The waves weren't even that great."

Cece sighed. "And I'm sorry I was so hard on you. It wasn't your fault that your radiation thing broke."

"Radiator."

"That, too," Cece laughed and leaned her head on Doug's shoulder. "I missed you."

"I missed you more." Doug put his nose against Cece's damp hair. "God, you smell good."

"It's my shampoo."

"I don't think so. You always smell like, I don't know, like a rain forest."

Cece laughed. "How do you know? You've never been."

"I just know." Doug took the clip out of her hair, and it fell in soft waves over her shoulders. "Someday I'll get there though, and I'll bring you back a monkey."

"Promise?"

"Promise." He nuzzled Cece's neck, and she felt his lips and tongue against her skin. Then he took a little nip.

"Hey," Cece giggled. "None of that!"

"Sorry, I lost my head. Your intoxicating scent overwhelmed me."

Cece gave him shove. "You know I still have to punish you for messing up the weekend, don't you?"

"Of course. What's it gonna be, boss?"

"You have to sit right here on the couch between Patty and me and watch the rest of our sappy movie with us."

"I haven't seen you for a week, and you're making me sit through a movie before I can get you into bed?"

"Yes, and that's not all. At the end, when we are crying, you have to hand us tissues, as many as we need. And after that, you will explain to us why it's a happy ending."

"Geez, you're killin' me!"

"And if you get it right," Cece kissed his ear with wet lips. "Then you can take me to bed."

"You two are disgusting." Patty said, coming back into the living room. She put a tray on the coffee table. "Here, Christmas cookies and hot chocolate, grown-up hot chocolate."

Cece picked up a mug and took a sip. "Mmmm, hot cocoa with Kahlua. I love it."

"So yummy," Patty agreed. She snuggled in next to Doug, picked up the remote, and un-paused Jimmy Stewart's face.

"Tissues," Cece said through her tears, "Doug, we need the tissues."

Doug leaned forward, pulled a bunch of tissues out of the box and held them to either side.

Cece and Patty sniffled and sang 'Auld Lang Syne' with the movie, their faces as red as the poinsettia plant sitting by the fireplace.

"You two look really, uh . . . sad. " Doug pushed the blanket to the side and stood up. "Please just tell me you understand the happy ending."

Cece straightened her back and curled her legs. "Nope. You have to explain it." She looked at Patty. "That's the last part of his punishment."

Patty scooted next to Cece, pulled her knees into her chest, and spread the blanket out again. "We're ready."

"Okay, it's a happy ending because George's friends bring him the money, and that solves all his problems."

Cece looked at Patty, her head shaking. "Close, but that's not the answer we're looking for."

"Is this a test?" Doug asked.

"Sort of," Patty said. "Come on, try again."

"Um, it's a happy ending because George didn't really jump off the bridge, and his wife didn't become a librarian."

"No!" Cece and Patty said together.

"Jesus, gimme a hint then."

"Okay," Cece said, "ting-a-ling-a-ling-a-ling." She moved her hand back and forth as if she were ringing a bell.

"Oh! It's a happy ending because Clarence got his wings!"

Patty and Cece cheered.

"Finally," Patty said.

"You figured it out," Cece said. She put her hand in the air. Doug grasped it and pulled her up off the couch. "Now I'll let you take me to bed."

"About time." Doug tossed the blanket over Patty's head. "G'night little one."

"Just keep it down in there you guys," Patty said, her voice muffled by the blanket. "I need my beauty rest."

CHAPTER 13

"Good morning," Cece said. She kissed Doug's cheek. He stirred and stretched.

"G'morning," Doug said without opening his eyes. He rolled over and pinned Cece with his arm. "Let's stay in bed all day."

Cece wiggled out from under him. "Wish I could sweetie, but I have to get ready for work." She stood and put on her white, terrycloth robe. "God only knows what I'll be walking into."

Doug reached for Cece's hand and pulled. "Sit down a sec, I want to ask you something."

Cece sat. "What?"

"I was thinking, you know, about, uh, that thing after your birthday last week . . ."

"I told you, just forget it."

Doug sat up in bed. "No really, listen Cece, what if, what would you think if . . . if I moved in here with you and Patty?"

Cece wasn't sure she heard him correctly. "Did you just suggest that you move in with me and Patty?"

Doug raised his eyebrows. "Uh . . . yeah."

"In this house? The three of us?"

Doug gave her a hopeful smile. "I think it'd be great. I stay here half the time anyway, and well, I can leave some stuff at my parents' house, so I wouldn't need much room in the closet. There's plenty of parking out front, just need to move my truck on street cleaning day . . ."

"You've really thought this out, haven't you?"

"It's a good idea, Ceece. I mean . . . we'd be moving in the right direction, you and me. And Patty's great. She'd love the idea."

Cece stood up. "I don't think she would."

Doug pushed the blankets off his legs. "Well I do, and besides, think of the money we'd save, all of us."

Cece tightened the sash on her robe. "Don't even mention money, Doug. If that was your concern, you wouldn't have given up work to go surfing."

Doug got out of the bed. "I thought we were past that."

"So did I, but you're the one who mentioned money."

"Just forget it then," Doug said. He ran his hands through his hair. "It's obviously not what you want."

"I don't know, but I don't think it's what you want, either. I think you're just trying to appease me so that . . ." Cece stopped herself.

"So that what, Cece? Tell me."

"It's just . . . no, never mind—I have a roommate, Doug, and I don't need another one."

Cece left the room, slamming the door. She went into the kitchen and made a pot of coffee. A few minutes later, she heard her bedroom door open and Doug's heavy footsteps coming toward her. He leaned against the door jam. "I'll call you later."

Cece didn't even want to talk to him, but she decided that would be childish. "Okay," she said, rinsing the dishes that were in the sink.

"I hate fighting with you, Cece. I thought you'd like the idea of my moving in."

"That isn't what I want, Doug! I'm sorry."

"Yeah, I got that. Do you want me to call you later or not?"

Cece raised a shoulder and glanced up. Doug looked more sad than mad. "Okay," she said.

"All right. Bye."

He turned and walked away.

Cece went back to washing dishes. She dried two mugs and put them on the counter.

"Good morning." Patty came into the kitchen looking like a sleepy little girl. Her hair stuck out in all directions, and she had on a red nightshirt with a picture of Santa Claus on the front. "Coffee ready?"

"Yeah." Cece told her about Doug's suggestion that he move in with them.

"It'd be fine with me," Patty said. "We could use some testosterone around here."

"It's not going to happen. I don't want to live together. It's not part of my plan."

"Your plan, huh? You're pretty rigid with that plan of yours." Patty held out a mug, and Cece poured coffee into it.

"Statistically speaking," Cece said, "couples that live together before marriage have a higher divorce rate. That's just a fact."

"Really?" Patty raised her eyes at Cece as she sipped her coffee.

"Yes, really."

"Okay, fine. So why do you look upset? Did Doug get mad?"

"He didn't. I did."

"Again, huh?"

Cece nodded and took a deep breath, realizing that she probably had overreacted and wishing that she hadn't started the argument with Doug.

"Listen, Ceece, I know I'm not an expert when it comes to relationships, but I think you need to loosen up a little. Doug's great, and you're kinda being a pain in the ass."

Cece looked at her friend. She was right.

The alleyway was wet from the late night rain as Cece and Patty got out of the car. They walked around the building to the front. Cece unlocked the glass door and pushed it open, tinkling the bell.

"Angel got his wings," Patty said.

"Yep." Cece closed the door behind her and locked the deadbolt. They wouldn't open for an hour or so. She walked over to the thermostat. "Jesus, it's freezing in here!" She flicked the switch to turn on the heat.

"Cece! Cece come here!" Patty stood at the long table where she did the framing and repairs on artwork.

"What is it?"

"Look what Barbara left here." Patty held up a poster that said:

"GOING OUT OF BUSINESS SALE;" A second one said: "EVERYTHING MUST GO" and another: "CLEARANCE—75% OFF."

"I knew we shouldn't have left town!" Cece said.

Patty leaned down and pulled out a piece of foam core board.

"What are you doing?" Cece frowned.

"I'm mounting the signs, why? You think I should use a frame?"

"No! I think you should throw them out!" Cece was so angry she wanted to tear the signs up. "Shit! Can things get any worse?"

The bell tinkled again, and Barbara walked in. She had dark circles under eyes, disheveled hair, and no make-up. "Oh, girls! So happy to see you, so sorry you had to come home to such bad news."

Cece pounced on her. "Barbara, what is this? Going out of business? 75% off, what on earth happened?"

"So, you saw the signs." Barbara sighed. "I know. I can't believe it either. I never should have opened this business."

"What are you talking about?" Cece asked.

"It's a failure," said Barbara.

"It's not," Cece argued. "You had a vision and look at it. It's delightful—the gallery, the coffee bar, all the handmade jewelry and artwork we sell."

Barbara took a few steps toward the girls. "Yes, I'm brilliantly creative. But I'm not very good with finances."

"Cece is crazy smart when it comes to math, she can help you straighten it out, right Ceece?"

Cece nodded. She felt dizzy, like she might get sick.

Barbara picked up Cece's hand. "It's too late. I quit paying the bills months ago."

Cece pulled her hand away. "You what?"

Barbara started to cry. "I just buried my head in the sand. At first I only put off the minor ones. I thought if I got organized and the holiday shoppers boosted sales, well, then I'd get everything sorted. But it just got worse."

"Wait a minute," Cece said. She walked over to the thermostat—it was not working. She pushed the button for the overhead lights. "They shut off the electricity?"

Barbara swallowed. "And the gas. We still have water though. Landlord pays that one."

Cece tried to stifle a cynical laugh. "This is great. Just great. Barbara, what were you thinking?"

"That's just it, I wasn't thinking."

"I thought your sister was coming to help you figure out the finances," Cece said. "What happened with her?"

"She's the one who told me to liquidate. I've borrowed a lot of money from her the past couple of years. I think she wants to kill me."

"Can you blame her?" Patty said out of the side of her mouth.

Barbara toyed with a Kleenex. "I'm so sorry, I really am."

A knock on the door startled them. Mae Adamu, cupping her hands around her eyes, was peering through the glass.

Cece opened the door, and Mae blew inside with Goldie tucked underneath her yellow slicker. She pushed the hood back, and her beaded cornrows fell around her shoulders. "Brrrrrrrr, it is cold out there!"

"Don't take off your coat," Cece warned her. "It's cold in here, too."

"Any coffee?" Mae asked, placing Goldie on the floor. The cat immediately went for Cece.

Patty picked up some mugs. "I'll go to the book store—they always make a big pot."

"Oh, Mae," Barbara said, giving her friend a hug. "I've made such a mess of things."

Cece stepped away from Goldie. "Goldie, stop it," she whispered. She pulled a hand knit blanket out of a basket. At a hundred dollars a pop, not many had sold. She wrapped it around her shoulders.

Mae took off the slicker and put on a blanket, too. "Let's sit down and see if we can straighten out this mess."

The three of them sat at one of the tables in the coffee bar. Mae clasped her hands and put them in front of her. "So, Barbara, if I understood you correctly, your sister ordered you to close up shop?"

Barbara nodded.

Mae raised her eyebrows. "Is that what you want to do then? Throw in the towel?"

"Of course not. "

"Are you still paying rent on this space?"

Barbara raised a shoulder. "Well, sort of. Allen gives me a nice break on it since we're . . . you know, friendly."

Mae looked at her. "Still sleeping with him, huh?"

Cece's mouth fell open. Barbara looked at her and turned bright red.

Cece put her palms up. "Hey, whatever works. I'm not going to judge."

Mae pulled a laptop out of her satchel. "Before I became an artist, I was an accountant."

Cece's head snapped up. "Seriously?"

"Yes I was, and a damn good one. Barbara, let's get your financials out, and we'll do some forensics to figure out why this business is hacking and coughing its way toward death."

Cece wound her hair through her fingers, trying to remain calm. If Mae was right and The Art Stop was dying, she and Patty could end up in the unemployment line.

"All right," Barbara said. "Come with me, would you Mae? There are a couple of boxes in the back."

The two women vanished just as Patty returned with four mugs of hot coffee. "Where's Mae and Barbara?"

"In the back working on the financials."

"It's bad, isn't it?" Patty sat down. Goldie jumped onto her lap and rubbed her orange head against Patty's arm.

"Not if you think it's a good idea to pay your rent with sex."

"No!" Patty said, her eyes popping, "Barbara's doing the nasty with Allen?"

"Oh, and by the way, Mae used to be an accountant."

Patty shook her head back and forth. "Too many revelations for one morning. I'm exhausted. Hey, hand me one of those blankets, would you?"

Cece leaned her chair back and pulled one out. Patty shook it open and put it over her shoulders. The price tag dangled by her chin. "Huh, a hundred bucks less 75% and our employee discount? We should buy a few of these."

The four women went through checking account statements, sales receipts, and inventory lists. Cece and Patty figured out which items needed to go back to the artists and which ones could be kept for the fire sale.

A few customers wandered in and purchased from the clearance table. The prices made Cece cringe.

They took a break for lunch and ate cheese and tomato sandwiches that Mae had brought with her.

"Thanks for lunch, Mae," Cece said. She got up from the table. "I'm going to go take a little walk."

Outside the air was cool. The sun went behind a cloud, and Cece's shadow disappeared. She walked around the corner and sat on a bench near a coffee shop to call Doug. As soon as he answered, she started to cry.

"I'm sorry," she said. "I was such a bitch to you this morning."

"It's okay, babe. I'm sorry, too."

"No," her voice quivered, "you didn't do anything wrong."

"I kinda did. I should've known that my moving in was a stupid idea."

"Let's just forget it, okay?"

"Good idea," said Doug. "What's going on at work?"

Cece shook her head side to side. "Complete disaster. You won't believe it." She told him the whole story.

"Don't worry Ceece. I'm sure it'll all work out."

Cece wished she felt so confident. "What are you doing tonight?"

"Basketball with the guys. Want me to come over after?"

"Yes," she said. "I really do."

"I love you, babe."

"Even though I was so mean to you?"

"Yes, even though."

"Good. I love you, too."

A little after four, Cece looked up from her work. It was starting to get dark. She leaned back and stretched. Goldie had settled herself deep into a basket of wool yarns imported from Australia. Cece shook the edge of the basket to get Goldie out, but the cat just buried herself in deeper. *What the hell,* Cece thought, *nobody's going to buy the yarn anyway.*

Patty was inside the front window making a new display. She had spent hours moving everything for the sale up to the front, while Barbara called the artists and designers who needed to come pick up their pieces.

Cece leaned toward Mae. "Well? Any news?"

Mae, with skinny reading glasses resting on the tip of her nose, had just combed through three years of financial information. "It's not good, honey. Not good at all."

Cece dropped her head onto her folded arms and sighed. It was becoming clearer by the moment that she might not have a job anymore, a job that she loved at a place that she loved—one that she helped Barbara build.

At 6:30 Barbara locked the door. Candles were burning everywhere, which cast a haunting and romantic light through the gallery. Mae stood up. "Gather 'round ladies, I'll tell you what I think."

Goldie lifted her head and meowed, then tucked her face back into the yarn.

The four women wrapped up in their blankets and sat at the table. "Looks like we're about to have a séance," Patty said.

"If anything needs to be brought back from great beyond, it's this business," Mae announced.

They all looked at Barbara, who had been crying off and on all day. "Give it to me straight, Mae. I have to face the truth."

"Okay, Barbara, here it is. You're in debt, and your personal finances are all mixed in. If you liquidate everything and collect money owed to you, you might be able to avoid bankruptcy."

Barbara chewed her fingernails. "I see."

"A lot of artists owe you money, Barbara," Cece said. "I went through five years of receipts, and when you paid them after their pieces sold, you didn't keep your percent."

"I did that on purpose, Cece," Barbara said with a trembling voice. "They needed the money more than I did."

"Oh, wow, Barbara, that was so sweet of you," Patty said.

"No," Mae said, "that was incredibly stupid of you."

Cece glanced at Mae, appreciating her candor.

"I'm all for helping artists," Mae continued, "for goodness sake, I am one. But this is business, Barb, and you won't have a business where those artists can sell their work if you don't change the way you operate."

"Okay," Barbara said, straightening up in her chair. "Tell me what to do, and I'll do it."

Under the table, Patty reached for Cece's hand and squeezed it. Cece returned the squeeze with a clammy hand.

"Well, first thing we'll do," said Mae, "is get out of this freezing concrete building and go to my house where it's warm."

"That sounds good to me," Patty said.

"Hold on there, cutie pie, you girls aren't invited." Mae pointed in Cece and Patty's direction. "Barbara, I'm going to help you develop a new business plan. But in the meantime, I'm sorry to say, you have to close to The Art Stop, at least until you get your utilities back on. Then maybe, *maybe* you can reopen. But probably not until after the first of the year. I'm guessing your landlord won't evict you, right?"

"I'll make sure of that," Barbara said.

Cece clenched her teeth. "What about us?" she asked. "When can Patty and I come back to work?

Mae reached over and took their hands. "Right now she's got nothing to cover payroll, so unless you want to be paid in peanuts, you'd better find new jobs, at least for the next month or two."

"I'm so sorry, girls, so sorry," Barbara started crying again.

"For Christ's sake Barbara, nobody's dying here." Mae stood. "Now let's all have a big hug and say good night. But first, Barb, give these girls some stuff, because you don't have a nickel to pay them."

Patty sniffled. "Can I keep this blanket?"

Barbara nodded. "Here, take all of them. They were cheap." She gave Patty the entire basket.

"Cheap?" Cece said. "They sell for a hundred bucks."

"Huge mark-up on blankets, girls, remember that."

"Keep going," Mae instructed. "These two are the best, and you'll be lucky if they're even willing to come back and work for you again."

Cece felt uneasy accepting the gifts, but they weren't really gifts, she reasoned. Barbara probably owed her over a thousand dollars in back pay.

"You're absolutely right," Barbara said. "The least I can do is make sure you leave with all the Christmas gifts you need." She went to the back and came out with two exquisite, inlaid wood music boxes. "My sister just brought these last week. They're from Italy. I want you each to have one."

"They're so pretty," Patty said.

"And here." Barbara handed them a box of delicate, hand painted ornaments, a basket of colorful bangle bracelets made of silk threads, and an armload of knit scarves.

"Go on now, get out of here before I start crying again."

It was no use. The four of them sobbed together for another half hour before Cece and Patty could tear themselves away. They said their goodbyes, and Cece was about to open the door, when Mae stopped her.

"Cece, wait." Mae walked across the gallery and picked up Cece's painting of the ballerina's face.

"Oh my God," Cece said. "I forgot it was even there."

Mae handed it to her. "It's finished, my dear. And it is magnificent."

"Thank you," Cece whispered.

"And remember what I told you," Mae said, her voice soft. "We just want our work to matter."

Cece nodded, blinking back tears. "I know."

She gave Mae a kiss and went out into the cold night.

CHAPTER 14

Patty picked up a sharp knife and sliced herself a piece of cake. They were sitting at the table in the breakfast nook with their checkbooks, calculators, and a holiday fruitcake that Patty's aunt had sent her for Christmas. Cece yawned. She had gone through Barbara's finances all day and now she was going through Patty's and her own.

Patty got up. "I'm getting some milk."

"Okay," Cece said without looking up. Her cell vibrated and flashed Doug's cute face.

"Hey," she said, her voice flat.

"Hey. How's it going?"

"We're figuring things out, but it's looking grim."

"I'm sorry, babe. Listen, we just finished playing. I'm going to run home and take a quick shower before I come over."

"You know what," Cece said, "It's almost ten, and I don't think I can stay awake much longer." As much as she wanted to see Doug, she was exhausted.

"Are you sure? I'll bring cookies."

"I would love to see you, but I'm a mess." She picked a pecan off the top of the fruitcake before her and ate it.

"All right. I'll call you in the morning on my way to work. I've got a job downtown."

"Really? Where?" Cece asked, perking up for the first time in hours. At least Doug was working.

"Office building. A decorator just finished some huge project in a law firm and hired me to photograph the space."

"Oh, that's cool," Cece said. "Come over after you finish, okay?"

"Sure. You making dinner?"

"I can. Macaroni and cheese from a box most likely."

"One of my favorites. See you tomorrow, babe. I love you."

"Me too, 'night."

Patty came back. "Do you think if I slept with the landlord, we could have free rent?"

"Works for Barbara," Cece said.

"I don't know. He's kinda creepy."

"Yeah, but it works for her," Cece said. She dropped her head on the table. "I can't keep my eyes open, Patty."

"Me neither. Let's call it a night."

As they headed toward their bedrooms, Cece put an arm over Patty's shoulders. "Maybe we'll come up with something brilliant in our dreams."

Cece rolled onto her back and stared at the ceiling. The sun was just rising. She'd slept solidly for a few hours then woke with a start when she dreamed that she was back in Clearwater living in her father's house. And that was what gave her the idea. At first she hated it, but after contemplating for half the night, she started to think that maybe it wasn't so bad. She recalled her conversation with Natalie. *Did she really mean it when she said she'd hire me?* Cece asked herself. She got up to make coffee.

The fact that she was even thinking about calling Natalie made her sweat. But going up north for a few weeks was not a big deal. She could help Natalie get the show ready, make some money, and be back in time to spend New Year's Eve with Doug. She wrestled with the plan and waited for Patty to get up.

"I hate it. It's a terrible idea!" Patty said. She picked up the coffee pot and refilled her mug. "I knew that gorgeous Amazon woman wanted you back."

"You're being ridiculous, Patty, and a little immature, too. "

Patty pushed out her lower lip. "I don't care."

Cece put her arms around Patty. She loved her like a little sister. "Listen, you are my best friend in the whole world. Nothing's ever going to change that."

"No matter what?"

"No matter what." Cece ruffled Patty's messy hair. "The truth is, I can't even remember exactly what Natalie said the other day. And if she did say something about hiring me, she probably didn't even mean it. She knows I no longer call Clearwater home."

"But what if she did mean it?"

"Well," Cece said. "Then I go up north for a few weeks, make some money, and come home. Hopefully, Mae and Barbara will get things figured out, and in another month, everything will go back to normal."

Patty took a deep breath and exhaled loudly. She raised her shoulders. "Okay. It's not like we have a ton of options."

"Yeah? Really?" Cece was relieved.

"Yeah, really." Patty got up. "What about Doug?"

"I'm calling him first, don't worry."

"Okay then," Patty said. "Do what you gotta do. I'm going to shower."

Cece watched Patty trudge off to the bathroom. She sat at the table in the breakfast nook and called Doug. No answer. Cece almost left a message but changed her mind. Maybe he was just in the shower. She'd try again in five minutes.

Cece went into her room and made her bed. Then she picked up her dirty clothes, put them in her laundry basket, and dialed Doug again; still no answer.

I'm being ridiculous, she thought. *It probably won't even happen so there's no reason to even bring it up to Doug.*

Relieved that he hadn't answered, Cece searched her cell phone for Natalie's number. Her hands were clammy as she pressed 'call.' She readied herself to leave a message, mulling over what she'd say. Natalie picked up after the third ring.

"Cece, what a surprise," Natalie said.

"Natalie, hi. Um, how's your mom doing?"

"Oh, well, not too bad. Actually, she was good yesterday, but today's not going so well."

"You must really busy." Cece knew she was beating around the bush, but she couldn't help it.

"Like you can't imagine. Hold on a sec. Robby! I told you those don't go there—put them in the back, and make sure you cover them!" Natalie returned. "Sorry about that."

"If it's a bad time, I can call back later."

"No, I'm just working on *The Nutcracker* and screaming at everyone. What's up?"

"Well, um, here's the thing, I came home to LA, you know, and it's such a long story, but where I work, the business isn't . . . Oh shit Natalie, were you serious about hiring me to teach dance?"

"Really?"

"I just need to work for a few weeks. The gallery's going to reopen in January, so I . . ."

"Oh my God, Cece, you have no idea how much I need you. When can you get here?"

"Wow," Cece said, surprised by Natalie's eagerness. "When would you want me?"

"Is today too soon?" Natalie laughed.

"Yeah, well, I have to get a few things organized around here first, but . . ."

"Doesn't matter, just get here as soon as you can."

"Okay." Cece stood and started pacing around her room. "I guess I can pack today and drive up tomorrow."

"That's great, excellent. I can't wait. Listen, it'll be intense, Cece. *The Nutcracker* opens in just over two weeks, and we are far from ready. We'll be rehearsing late almost every night."

"That's okay. I remember how crazy it gets."

"Crazy is an understatement! See you when you get here."

"Okay. And thanks, Natalie."

"Don't thank me. You're my Christmas angel!"

They said goodbye and hung up. Cece went into the living room. She sat on the couch and put her hands on the top of her head. "Wow," she said aloud. "Wow."

Patty came out of the bathroom wrapped in a towel and sat down next to her.

Cece folded her lips together and gave her friend a thin, almost apologetic smile.

"You got the job?"

Cece nodded.

"Good," Patty said, her voice firm. "That's good. What did Doug say?"

Cece's heart skipped a beat. Suddenly she wasn't so sure that spending a few weeks up north really was no big deal.

"I . . . I couldn't reach him. He didn't answer."

"Oh. Well, he'll probably be okay with it," Patty said, her tone unconvincing.

Cece stood. "Yeah. He'll be fine with it. I'm . . . I'm sure he will."

CHAPTER 15

"Hey," Doug said as he walked in the door. He pushed over a stack of mail and put his camera bag on the table in the entry. He took Cece into his arms and gave her a big kiss. "How did your day go?"

Her stomach had been churning for hours, and she felt mildly nauseated. "Fine," Cece said. "How about yours?"

"Really good, busy. This space I photographed was amazing."

"What did it look like?" Cece asked. She wanted to put off telling Doug her news as long as she could.

"Well, let's see, hardly any walls, the coolest furniture you've ever seen, and huge windows—at least twelve feet high."

Cece put silverware and plates on the table in the breakfast nook. "Must have had a great view."

"Oh, God, you could see everything—Santa Monica, the harbor, the mountains. And Ceece, the snow level is so low. Maybe we could go skiing next weekend."

Cece felt one eye twitch. "Do you want a beer?"

"Sure. Where's Patty?"

"She's out." Cece reached into the refrigerator for two bottles of Corona. "Are you hungry?"

"Starving," Doug said. "Worked right through lunch."

"That's great."

"Great?"

Cece looked up. "I'm sorry, what?"

"I said I worked through lunch and you said 'that's great.'"

"Oh, I must not have heard you." Cece brushed it off and tried to suppress her growing anxiety.

She put the casserole on the table along with a bowl of green salad and handed Doug a spatula. "Take a big serving, sweetie, and just give me a little bit. I'm not very hungry."

"Looks good, babe. Thanks for cooking."

"You're welcome."

They sat. Cece took a small bite. The food felt like paste in her throat.

"I'm going to get water. Want some?"

Doug raised his eyebrows. "Are you okay?"

"Fine. Just thirsty." Cece went to the kitchen. She stood at the sink and filled a tall glass with ice and water from the tap. Through the window she could see the glow of a half-moon. Guilt was chewing her up. *What was I thinking? Why didn't I talk to Doug before I made my decision?*

Cece took a deep breath to steady herself. Two Netflix DVDs that she had found while packing caught her eye. They belonged to Doug. She grabbed them on her way back to the table.

"I have a couple movies that I think are yours." She placed them beside his arm.

Doug picked them up. "Where did these come from?"

"I was, um, cleaning out some stuff and found them in my nightstand. They're yours, aren't they?"

"Yeah. I was looking for them a few weeks ago. You said you didn't have 'em."

"I know, sorry. I guess I misplaced them."

Doug put them back on the table. "You might as well keep them, I already paid the fine."

"Then you keep them."

"I don't want 'em. They were in your queue." He swallowed the rest of his beer, got up, and went to the kitchen. "Shouldn't have told you my password."

"What was that?" she asked.

"Nothing," Doug said, coming back with another beer. "I was kidding."

But Cece heard a hint of annoyance in his voice. "We're talking Netflix, Doug, not your bank account. What is it with you and your passwords anyway?"

"Can't be too careful, babe," Doug said. "You have any idea how bad it is if something gets hacked and all your . . ."

"So now you don't trust me, is that it?" Cece pushed her half-eaten plate of food away.

Doug put his beer bottle down. He leaned in. "Ceece, what's going on with you?"

"Nothing."

Doug's eyebrows went up. He tilted his head. "This isn't really about passwords, is it?"

"No."

"Then what the hell are we arguing about?"

Cece tapped her fork on the table. "It's nothing. I'm just a little anxious."

"About what? Work?"

" Kind of."

"Cece, if this about money, don't worry. I'll help you."

His offer made her bristle. Doug had more money than she did, but it had never been an issue between the two of them. Cece remained fiercely independent, and Doug respected that. He was, however, generous beyond belief.

"And besides," he continued, "the gallery's going to reopen after Christmas. So until it does, you should just enjoy being on vacation. We can go . . ."

"I got a job. A temporary job."

"Oh. Well. That's good news. What's the job?"

"Not something I ever thought I would do."

"Okay . . ." Doug gave her one of his adorable, crooked smiles. "Pole dancer?"

"No." Cece didn't find his joke funny. "But it is dance, teaching ballet and stuff, you know, like I used to do when I was kid."

Doug took her hand in his. "Sounds perfect for you."

"Yeah, I know. It is."

"They why aren't you happier about it?"

Cece looked into Doug's eyes, full of love and concern. "It's in Clearwater."

Doug let go of her hand. "Oh."

"It's just for a few weeks, no more than three or four. I'll probably be home in time for Christmas."

Doug nodded and rocked his chair back. "How, um . . . when did this happen? You didn't mention it last night."

"It just happened today. I was talking to Natalie, and . . ."

"Who's Natalie?"

Cece realized she had never mentioned her old friend to Doug. "Natalie runs the studio where I took dance lessons when I was a kid."

Doug took a drink of beer. "Okay . . . and?"

"Well, we were just, um catching up, talking, and I started telling her about the gallery and how I was temporarily unemployed. And then she said that she was looking for someone to help her with the Christmas show that they do every year, and, well . . . she offered me a job, like, totally out of the blue." Cece closed her mouth. She had spun the story and felt horrible.

"All right." Doug rubbed his chin. "So is this something that you and I are going to discuss? Or have you already decided?"

Cece saw no purpose in prolonging the inevitable. "I've already decided. Since I need the money, I said yes."

Doug gripped the edge of the table with both hands. "I'm a little surprised we didn't, you know, talk about it first."

"I know, sweetie, and I'm sorry, but I am so worried about paying my bills and keeping this house, I just jumped on it." Cece felt perspiration pool under her arms. She could see that Doug was on the edge of getting upset. "Please don't be mad."

"I'm not mad. When do you think you'll leave?"

"I leave . . ." Cece winced. "Tomorrow."

"Tomorrow." Doug repeated what she'd said, as if he had to think about what the word meant. "Tomorrow?"

Cece nodded. "Tomorrow," she whispered.

Doug stood and bumped his chair. It fell over and crashed to the floor. He picked it up and shoved it back in place. "Now I'm mad."

"I know it happened fast, but I . . . I can jump in and do this work so easily. And you know I can't stand uncertainty. I hate not knowing what's next." Cece got up and walked over to Doug. She tried to put her arms around his neck, but he caught her wrists and stopped her. She swallowed hard. She had never seen him look so hurt.

Doug closed his eyes. "I don't know what to say to you."

Cece pursed her lips, trying not to cry.

"Wait." Doug held up one finger. "I do know what to say. You give me a hard time about being impulsive, and now you do this? Without even talking to me, you decide to take job out of town for a month? That's pretty goddamn impulsive, Cece."

Cece started to acknowledge that he was right, but her defensiveness got the better of her. "I have a problem with impulsive when it means giving up jobs to go surfing. This may come as a surprise to you, but I have to work. I don't have rich parents to fall back on whenever I run a little short on cash!" As soon as she said the words, she regretted it.

Doug turned his back on her. He clasped his hands over his head as if he was holding it down and walked into the living room. He stopped, and Cece felt panic rise in her throat.

"Doug, I'm sorry, I . . ."

He turned and faced her. "I don't know what's happening with us. Two weeks ago, we were the happiest couple I knew. And now, it's like, I feel like . . . I don't even know what I feel like."

Again Cece tried to get close to him, but he stepped back.

"I don't know what you want from me," Doug said.

"What do you mean?"

"I feel like I can't get it right. Whenever I see you lately, I do something wrong. I'm always disappointing you."

"That's not true." Cece brushed tears off her cheeks.

"Yes it is. Ever since your birthday, it seems that all we do is fight." Doug leaned on the back of the couch shaking his head.

Cece nodded. He was right. "It's because of what I did, what I said. It's my fault, I know it."

Doug pushed his hair back with one hand. "And your whole, I don't know, uptightness and freaking out over everything, it's just not good."

Tears spilled from Cece's eyes. It was true. She was uptight and controlling, and she wanted to fix it, but she didn't know how.

"Cece, we have a great relationship. Why are you messing it up?"

His words jolted her.

"Why am I messing it up?" she repeated.

"You've changed. In the past couple weeks, you . . ." his voice trailed away.

Cece started to shake. She had changed, and she knew it. Worry and disappointment and frustration had made her act like somebody she didn't want to be.

"I feel like you're not sure you want to be with me anymore, Ceece. Like you've given me the ultimatum."

"But I didn't."

"You didn't say the words, but you . . ." Doug looked lost and completely worn out. "You might as well have."

He was right. She had expected him to propose, and when he didn't, she reacted like petulant child.

"What should I do?" Cece could barely get the words out.

"I don't know," Doug said, pacing back and forth across the living room. "I just want everything to go back to the way it was."

"I do, too."

He turned and looked at her, his face frozen as if he were wearing a mask. "Do you? Do you really?"

Cece couldn't speak. His question was a slap in the face. "I . . . I don't know." Her legs felt like they could no longer support her weight. "But I know that I love you."

Doug got up. He put his hands on her shoulders and gave her the saddest smile she had ever seen. "I love you, too, more than anything in the world, but . . ." He looked down at her, tears in his eyes. "I thought I knew where we were headed, but I guess I don't." Doug wiped his eyes with his palms.

"Doug, please," Cece cried. "You know what? I won't go. I don't have to. I'll stay here, and we'll figure it out together."

"No. Then you'll just resent me."

"I won't. I'd never resent you."

Doug looked down at the floor. When he looked at Cece again, his anguish was palpable. "You already do."

Cece reached for him, but he put his hands up as if to shield himself from a blow. "I need some time."

Cece trembled. She felt as if somebody had swung a bat into her gut. She leaned over, her hands on her knees, and tried to breathe, but she couldn't catch her breath.

Doug went to the door and opened it. He stopped, but he didn't look at her. "I don't know how I'll live without you," he said. "I just don't know."

CHAPTER 16

Cece cried into her pillow until it was damp and smeared with mascara. She turned it over and cried herself to sleep. She awoke to soft knocks on her bedroom door and heard it open slowly.

"Ceece?" Patty whispered.

Cece sat up and turned on her bedside lamp.

"Oh my God, what happened?"

"We . . . we . . . broke up."

A whole new set of tears started.

"Oh sweetie," Patty said. "I'm so sorry."

Patty held Cece while she sobbed. Then she curled up behind her, wrapping a warm arm over Cece's body. They nestled together like two puppies and fell asleep.

"This all you're taking?" Patty said, pointing to Cece's small bag. "You'll be there a while."

Cece was sitting on her bed. She had dumped out her purse and was repacking it. "Don't need much. I'll be wearing ballet pants and sweatshirts most of the time." She got up and looked in the mirror that hung over her dresser. She pulled her messy hair into a ponytail and tried to wipe off the remnants of her makeup, but it was hopeless. "I look like hell."

Patty didn't contradict her. "I'll go get your coffee."

"Thanks." Cece took one last look in her room to make sure she had everything. On her desk, propped against the wall, was her ballerina painting. The dancer looked at Cece as if she were saying: *take me with you.*

A sob caught in her throat. Doug had watched her paint the picture. On many occasions they had gone to the beach where he set up her easel for her. Then, while she painted, he would take pictures of dolphins and whales. But most of the time, he took pictures of her.

Cece picked up the painting and started to pack it, but what was the point in that? The picture would be there, waiting for her when she got home. Even though Doug wouldn't.

She went into the kitchen. Patty handed her a travel mug. "Drink it slowly, or you'll have to pee at that yucky gas station by the freeway."

Cece tried to laugh, but it hurt her head. "You're going home for Christmas, right? See you parents?"

"I don't know, maybe."

Cece took a sip of coffee, burning her tongue. "Ouch."

Patty handed her a napkin. "You have to talk to me every single day, okay?"

"Yes, I promise."

Patty nodded. "You'd better go. It's a long drive."

"Right." Cece hugged her best friend.

"And no more crying," Patty said. "It's not safe to cry and drive."

"I'm pretty sure I'm all cried out."

Cece got stuck in traffic on the curve from the 405 onto the Ventura Freeway. She glanced at her cell phone lying on the passenger seat. She didn't expect Doug to call, but wondered if he would. This was her first real breakup. All her prior boyfriends had lasted a year at most, and when they broke up it always ended with "and we'll stay friends." Of course they didn't, but it cushioned the hurt at least to say it.

She was in uncharted territory and had no idea what the protocol was. The pain in her chest and in the pit of her stomach was unbearable. She turned on the radio. An old '70s song was playing. '*I would give everything I own, just to have you back again, just to hold you once again...*'

Cece reached into the tissue box and pulled out the entire stack. There weren't enough tissues in the world to absorb the tears that she shed.

She stopped at a gas station just outside of Santa Barbara.

"Forty dollars on seven," she said. "And two candy bars." She pushed two twenties and a five under the bulletproof glass.

The man at the register looked at her with what Cece construed as a sympathetic smile. *How pathetic. Even this guy feels sorry for me.*

He took the money and passed her a small amount of change.

"Thanks," Cece said. She picked up two Snickers and went to pump her gas. Then she used a bathroom that wasn't too disgusting and got back on the road.

In the mid-afternoon Cece decided to take a detour. She drove through Cambria, a small town on the Pacific Ocean, and turned onto a narrow street lined with art galleries, small hotels, and exclusive shops.

She parked a block from the cliffs. It was cold and windy, and the ocean air smelled fresh. She put on her jacket and walked along the pathway toward a beach where elephant seals had been mating and giving birth for over a hundred years.

Cece leaned on the railing. Below her, sprawled all over the sand, were dozens of seals. They were the size of compact cars. Several of the males were as big as minivans. A harem formed around the dominant male as he bellowed and thrashed to intimidate the competition.

A few yards away, Cece watched a fight break out between two other males. They appeared to be vying for a gentle looking female. She lifted her head and looked at them, as if she were wondering which suitor would win.

With a sigh, Cece tore open the wrapper of her second snickers bar. *I wish I could be an elephant seal. Fatten myself up all year long, then lie at the beach and watch the boys fight over me.* She shoved the rest of the chocolate bar into her mouth, went back to her car, and continued the drive up north.

Phil Camden walked across the lawn as Cece pulled into the driveway. She got out of the car and fell against her father.

"Hi Daddy."

"How you doin', sweetheart?"

"I'm okay."

They walked toward the house. Cece looked at the Christmas lights all around the roof and winding through the trees. The silly reindeer stood on the lawn next to a couple of snowmen. "House sure looks festive, Daddy. You and Tommy did a great job."

"We did, didn't we?" Phil wrapped his arm around her. "Let's get you inside, it's freezing out here. They're even talking snow, believe it or not." Cece smiled to herself. In awkward moments, her father always brought up the weather.

Tom was standing by the door as they walked up the steps. He had on ripped jeans and an old Cal Berkeley sweatshirt. "Hey sis."

"Hi Tommy."

"You look like shit."

Cece couldn't be mad at him. "I know."

They stepped inside. Julia walked toward Cece, her arms outstretched. Her hair was scrunched on top of her head, and she wore a white apron over her red maxi dress. "Hi sweetie," Julia said, pulling Cece into her arms. "How are you?"

"Terrible."

"I know."

Cece had called Julia before she'd left and given her the 'in a nutshell' account of what was happening.

"I hope you don't mind, honey. I told the guys about you and Doug."

"It's okay," Cece said. "Better than me having to tell them."

"Want me to get your stuff?" Tom asked.

"Thanks." Cece handed him her keys. "Be sure to lock it."

"You're back in Clearwater, Ceece, we don't lock up here."

Cece followed Julia into the kitchen. She inhaled the warm smell of something delicious. It made her hungry and sick at the same time. "What are you making?"

"Roast chicken," Julia said. "Should be ready in about ten minutes. Are you hungry?"

It was after seven, and she hadn't eaten all day except for the two candy bars. "Kind of. Not really. I'm going upstairs to wash my face."

"Okay honey, let me know if you . . ."

Cece left the kitchen without hearing the rest of Julia's sentence.

At the table, Cece picked at a baked potato. She had taken off her clothes and put on her purple robe. Julia, Phil, and Tom exchanged concerned looks.

"Where's Ryan?" Cece asked, staring at her plate.

"Wednesday night dinner with his dad," Julia said.

"That's right. It is Wednesday, isn't it?" Cece took a tiny bite of chicken. Only one week ago, she was happily preparing for Thanksgiving. Now, it seemed, her life was in shambles.

"So," Phil said. "Thought we'd do the tree this weekend. How does that sound, baby girl?"

"Fine."

"We were supposed to do it last weekend, but we got so busy stringing lights, we just ran out of time."

"Uh-huh," Cece said. She took a sip of water.

"You want to go with us, honey?" Julia asked. She ran a hand over the back of Cece's hair.

"Where?"

"To get the Christmas tree," said her father. "We can hunt for the perfect one together, just like we did when you were little."

Cece gave her dad a weak smile. "Maybe. I'm not sure. I might be at the dance studio. Natalie said rehearsals are non-stop."

More silence.

Tom cleared his throat. "So how's Patty?"

"Almost as heartbroken as me," Cece said. She looked at her brother. "Oh, that's not what you meant, is it?"

"What do you mean?" Tom asked.

Cece put her fork down. "You're such an idiot, Tommy. We all know you have a crush on her, so quit pretending you don't."

Phil and Julia eyed each other, but they didn't say a word.

"Whoa. Where did that come from?" Tom looked at his sister.

"You act like it's a big secret. And it just, I don't know, pisses me off."

"First of all, Cece, I'll let that go because of your, whatever, your broken heart. And secondly, if I did like Patty, which I don't, at least not that way, it really wouldn't be any of your business. Besides," Tom grinned at his father. "She's way too little for me. I'd probably crush her."

Cece's mind wandered back to Cambria and the gigantic male elephant seals mating with the much smaller females. She shook the image of her brother on top of Patty out of her mind. "Whatever."

Tom got up. "Anyone want a beer?"

"I'll take one," Cece said.

Tom returned from the kitchen. He flipped the caps off with a bottle opener and handed one of the beers to Cece. She took a drink, and the taste reminded her of dinner with Doug right before they broke up. She put the bottle down, dropped her head into her hands, and sobbed.

Julia rushed to her side.

"I don't know what's happened to me." Cece blew her nose into her napkin. "I never cry like this. I'm not a crier."

Phil nodded. "That's true. You were a very low-drama teenager."

Tom shifted in his chair. "Yeah, this really isn't like you."

"I know it. I'm sorry." Cece wiped her face with her bathrobe sleeve.

"You have nothing to apologize for, baby-girl. We're your family," Phil said. Tom nodded in agreement.

"And, well, maybe," said Julia, "when you get home after being away for a few weeks, you and Doug can sort this all out, and, you know, patch things up."

Cece looked up at Julia. Maybe she and Doug could recover. Couples broke up and got back together all the time. She closed her eyes and pictured his devastated face as he left her house less than twenty-four hours earlier. It was an image she knew she'd never forget. How could Doug get over the hurt she had caused?

"I know it's a cliché," Julia said, "but sometimes things really do happen for a reason."

"Then what's the reason for this? To ruin my life?"

"Well," said Julia, "I don't know. Reasons usually aren't revealed right away."

Cece got up. "I really need to go to bed. I'm sorry."

"That's fine honey," Phil said. He stood and hugged her. Cece leaned against her father's broad chest and pushed her nose into his soft flannel shirt. He stroked her hair. "A good night's sleep is what you need. You'll feel a whole lot better in the morning. I'm sure of it."

Phil released her. Cece turned and trudged up the stairs. *If sleep could solve my problems,* she thought, *then I need to sleep for a year.*

CHAPTER 17

Cece slept for thirteen hours. When she woke up, she raised her head. It felt like it had been hit by hammer on both sides. She put her head down, and went back to sleep.

It was after eleven when she dragged herself out of bed. She opened her bedroom door and bumped into Julia.

"Cece," Julia said. "How are you feeling, honey?"

"I have a little headache."

Julia reached into the linen closet and pulled out a fluffy blue bath towel. "Take some Advil, it's in the medicine chest, and a nice hot shower." She handed Cece the towel.

"Thanks." Cece took the towel and went into the bathroom. She got in the shower and stood under the hot water, letting it pound on her head and neck and back.

She got out, brushed her teeth, and examined her eyes in the mirror. They were still red, but the swelling had gone down.

Back in her bedroom, Cece lifted the window shade, and bright sunlight flooded her room. "Great." She yanked the shade down. "A cheerful, sunny day. Just what I'm in the mood for."

She put her suitcase onto the bed and opened it. She caught her breath. On top of her clothes was the wooden case holding the paintbrush Doug had given her. Lying next to it was the picture in the Tiffany frame. She hadn't packed them, so Patty must have slipped them in.

Cece looked at the picture. Seeing herself leaning against Doug as they sat on the beach made her heart feel like it was about to crack.

Her eyes burned and filled with tears. She wiped them away and stuck the picture in a dresser drawer.

Cece opened the latch on the wooden case. The paintbrush rested on a bed of black velvet. She picked it up and swept the fur over the inside of her wrist. It was a remarkable brush. She put it back into the case and placed it in a box that held all her old art supplies. Her desire to paint had vanished.

Inside her closet, Cece rifled through clothes on hangers searching for a pair of dance pants. "Ah-huh," she said, "I knew I left these here." She put on the stretchy black pants that were at least fifteen years old. They were a bit tight, but wearable. She layered two tank tops over her workout bra and threw a white, wide-neck sweatshirt on over the tanks. After one more glance in the mirror, she picked up her purse and went to start her new job.

The dance studio looked empty when Cece arrived. The doors were locked. She walked around to the back of the building and went in through the service entrance. It opened into an old, narrow hallway used by the staff when the Mayfair Hotel was still in operation.

"Hello? Natalie?"

"Whoa!" A young man jumped. "Who are you?" He had a mop of blond hair that hung over his eyes, wore black, skin-tight jeans, a checked flannel shirt, and clean, white Converse tennis shoes.

"Cece Camden, who are you?"

"Robby Olsen. I work here." He pulled a rolling garment rack jammed with costumes out of a closet. "I do the grunt work."

Cece sized him up. "I see. Do you know where Natalie is?"

"Running an errand. Should be back anytime."

"Okay, well, I'm meeting her here," Cece said. "I'll just wait in the office."

"I can't let you do that."

"What do you mean?"

"I'm also the head of security."

"Really? Security?" Cece almost laughed at him.

Robby jingled the set of keys hooked to his belt. "Until I receive confirmation as to who you are, I cannot unlock any doors nor allow access to restricted areas." He spoke as if the line was an announcement he had made many times before. Cece thought he might salute.

Natalie came down the hall from the other direction. "Cece, you're here!" She approached with outstretched arms.

"Guess she does know you," Robby said to Cece.

Cece gave Natalie a hug. "Your head of security here takes his job very seriously."

Natalie rolled her eyes. "Head of security? Robby, I told you to quit calling yourself that."

"Yeah, but it sounds better than *schlep*."

"Sorry, but that's what you do," Natalie said.

"Fine. Where do you want these costumes? The basement is damp, and I don't want them to get mildewed," Robby said.

Cece opened her mouth. She leaned toward Natalie and whispered, "Is he for real?"

Natalie held up one finger to Cece. "Put them in the girls' changing room. And after you do that, run to Nutmeg's and get two large black coffees. And you can get yourself one, *one*, cookie on my account."

"Thanks! Be right back," Robby said, pushing the costume rack down the hall.

Natalie led Cece into the office and closed the door behind them. "Please, don't ask. He's the son of some friend of somebody around here."

"What a character," Cece said. "Real cute, but a little strange."

"Ya think?" Natalie put her bag on the desk. "He's a pretty good worker though, and meticulous with the wardrobe."

Cece looked around Ilana Lurensky's office. If somebody had told her that she'd be back in less than a week, she would have said they were crazy. "Where's your mom?"

"At home. She's been up and down for few days." Natalie opened her bag and pulled out a variety of pain relievers.

"Do you have a headache?" Cece asked.

"Not yet," Natalie said, "but by this afternoon, we both will."

Cece laughed, remembering Natalie always had a good sense of humor.

"So," said Cece. "We should get started, right? I mean, I really have no idea what I'm supposed to do."

"Well, a little bit of everything, but I need you to spend most of your time with our Sugar Plum Fairy."

"You mean the girl I met the other day? The one with the attitude?"

"That's the one. Dawn Redmond. Fifteen years old, smart as can be, dances like a dream, and a little bit, ah, bitchy. I tried having Kendall work with her, you know, my new instructor, but she and Kendall weren't a good fit."

"Wow. I see." Cece was growing more nervous by the second.

"I think they're too close in age, and Kendall is a very young twenty-two. She's great with little ones but not the teenagers. Anyway, don't worry. You'll be fine with Dawn."

"If you say so."

"I say so."

Natalie showed Cece a list of all the dancers and their roles in *The Nutcracker*. Cece remembered the ballet well. She had danced one part or another every Christmas from the time she was five, working her way from mouse to soldier to snowflake. At nine years old, she danced Clara, and she and Natalie shared that role, among others, for the next five years. In high school however, Cece surpassed her best friend.

"Do you remember," said Natalie, "the fight we had when my mother picked you to be Sugar Plum Fairy?"

"I'll never forget it. I said something so awful to you that I still have nightmares over it."

Natalie laughed. "All I remember is that I shoved you into the wall and got grounded for two weeks."

"You had good reason."

"Why?" Natalie asked. "What did you say?"

Cece hesitated, but decided what the hell, it had been fifteen years. "I said: 'Your Mamma loves me more than she loves you because I'm a better dancer.'"

"Is that what you said? Really?"

Cece nodded. "I did. Took me years and a few therapy sessions to understand why I said it."

"Oh? And why was that?"

"Jealousy," Cece said. "By the time we were fourteen, my mother was hardly ever around, off with one of her affairs probably, and she left me and my brother to fend for ourselves." Cece scratched her lower lip. "And there you were with the most attentive mother in the world. For years, I wished I were you."

"Well, we're even then. I can't tell you how many times I wished I were you, you with your sexy, wavy hair and sparkly blue eyes."

"Oh, right, and you were the ugly duckling?"

"Damn right I was," said Natalie. "All nose and braces and gangly limbs—it took me forever to grow into these feet!" Natalie held out a size ten foot to accentuate the point.

"I guess that's the plight of the teenage girl—always wishing to be somebody else."

The door opened and Robby came in with the coffees. "Here you go, boss." He put them on the desk. "Anything else?"

"That's it for now. I'll track you down if I need you."

"Want me to mend those tutus?"

"Oh, yeah, could you?" Natalie said. "And be sure to let Brittany's mom know when they're done. She'll be moving all the costumes over to the theater next week for dress rehearsal."

"Gotcha," Robby said. "Oh. Thanks for the snack."

After he left, Cece said, "Kind of adorable . . . straight or gay?"

Natalie sipped her coffee. "I'm not sure. But he follows Kendall around like a lost dog, so I'm thinking straight. You know, teenagers are different these days. Very unconventional."

"Really?" Cece said. "We were pretty out there in the nineties."

"It just seems things are harder for them. And the girls? Oh my God, if you think we saw drama in high school, these kids have . . ."

Cece zoned out, thinking about her own drama over the past two days, and how she had to keep her heartbreak locked inside.

"Cece? Are you okay?"

Cece's head snapped up. "I'm sorry, what?"

"You look like you're about to cry. I don't care if it has been ten years, I can tell when something's wrong."

Cece straightened her back. "My boyfriend and I broke up the other night. That's all I can say—it's too hard for me even to talk about it." Somehow she managed to keep the tears at bay.

Natalie gave her a sympathetic smile. "Hey, I get it."

"Anyway," said Cece, "being here is what I need right now. Distance and distraction will keep me from thinking about it."

"All right then, good, because the only thing you have time to think about now is dance, dance, dance."

CHAPTER 18

By 2:00 that afternoon, a dozen little girls in tights and tutus were scurrying around the studio. Kendall Pakuri, a petite cheerleader type with long black hair and captivating black eyes, clapped her hands, trying to get the girls' attention.

Cece watched, wondering if she'd made a terrible decision. What on earth made her think she had the stamina to be a dance instructor?

"They do have a lot of energy, don't they?"

Kendall nodded. "Yes they do. And gathering them up is like herding cats."

A little Asian girl with a long braid down her back, dressed in pink from head to toe, ran to Kendall and hugged her around the waist.

"Olivia, how are you?"

"Fine!"

"This is our new dance instructor, Miss Cece."

Cece leaned down toward the little girl. "Hi Olivia," she said.

Olivia grinned, revealing a large gap where her two front teeth used to be. "Hi Mith Thee-thee!"

Cece was smitten. "Are you missing some teeth?"

Olivia opened her mouth wide. "Theseth two," she put her finger into the open spot. "Thsanta will bring my new onesth for Christhmasth!"

"Wow, that's exciting!" Cece said.

Kendall put a hand on Olivia's back. "Let's go, cutie pie. Time to get started."

Olivia raised her hand. "Bye Mith Thee-thee."

"Bye." Cece looked at Kendall. "Are they all that cute?"

Kendall made a sour face. "Not by a long shot."

In a whirlwind of dancing bodies and Tchaikovsky music, Cece immersed herself in learning who was who, who did what, and what needed to be done by when. She even had a moment or two, brief snips of time, when she didn't think about Doug. They were fleeting, however. As soon as thoughts of him returned, she felt a painful jolt.

It was nearly 3:30 when Cece glanced at the clock on the wall and realized that Dawn was late.

Natalie shook her head. "If she's not here in ten minutes, I'll try her on her cell. She's usually . . . oops, there she is."

Dawn Redmond sauntered into the studio. She had on the same black cap that she was wearing the day Cece met her and her iPod in her hand.

Natalie put her hands on her hips. "You're late."

Cece flinched. How many times had she heard Ilana say that over the years?

"Sorry," the teenager mumbled. She pulled her earphones out.

"Dawn, this is Cece Camden. She's going to work with you on your solo."

Dawn shifted her dance bag to her other shoulder. "Whatever. I have to go change."

Cece inhaled nervously as she watched Dawn walk away. Natalie patted her shoulder. "Don't worry, her bark is worse than her bite."

Cece waited for Dawn in a smaller dance room connected to the main studio. It had mirrored walls all around except for the outer wall with windows. In one corner there was a table and on the table was portable CD player connected to a speaker. Cece popped open the player. Inside was a CD with *Dance of the Sugar Plum Fairy* written in black marker.

Cece pushed play. The familiar melody of her favorite dance in her favorite ballet filled the room. She closed her eyes and smiled. When she opened them, Dawn Redmond was standing in front of her.

"Oh, good," Cece said. "You're ready."

Dawn said nothing, and Cece tried not to stare at the tiny gem on the side of one of her nostrils. *It must really hurt to poke a hole there,* Cece thought.

Cece looked at Dawn's feet. "Where are your toe shoes?"

A shoulder went up. "I forgot 'em."

Cece chewed her lip. Kids forgot their essentials all the time. She didn't want to make a big deal out of it. "Well then, we'll have to work without them. Try and remember them tomorrow though, okay?"

Dawn looked at her as if she had just said the stupidest thing ever. "Uh, yeah."

Sweat dripped down Cece's chest into the band of her workout bra. She was trying not to be intimidated by a fifteen year old. "Start from the left so I can see your entrance."

Dawn went to the far left side of the room, and Cece pushed 'play.'

For thirty seconds, the teenager danced, and her talent surprised and delighted Cece. Even in her ballet slippers, her pirouettes were precise and balanced, her allegro smooth and light.

Without warning, Dawn stopped. "I need to start over."

"Okay, that's fine." Cece was about to push 'play' again, when another tune interrupted them. It was coming from Dawn's bag.

Dawn jumped. "That's my cell." She ran to get it. Cece sat down and looked at her watch. She tapped her ballet-slippered feet while Dawn carried on her conversation, her back turned to Cece and her hand over the mouthpiece. When she finished her call, Dawn dropped her cell on top of her bag.

"Maybe you should turn that off until we're done," Cece said.

Again, Dawn gave her a look that Cece interpreted as, *are you kidding me?*

Cece let it go. "Okay, let's start over."

This time Dawn got through about a minute of the number, again startling Cece with her graceful dancing. Then she stopped. "I really can't do it without my pointes."

Cece wanted to say something snide, but she resisted. "We'll practice hands and arms then."

Dawn leaned her head back and rolled her eyes. "Fine."

The cell phone chimed again, and Dawn ran for it. Cece sighed. She sat down and waited.

Dawn finished the call, leaned over and picked up her bag. "I have to go."

"Excuse me?"

"My, um, my boyfriend's waiting outside."

"Dawn, we have to practice."

"I usually take Thursdays off, so . . ."

"But this is crunch time. The show opens in two weeks," Cece said, her voice squeaky.

Dawn gave her an exasperated look. "I'll try to come tomorrow." She turned her back on Cece and walked toward the door.

Cece's mouth hung open. She had never been treated with such disdain by a kid. She followed Dawn out into the hallway and shouted after her, "Remember to bring your toe shoes next time!"

Cece spent the rest of the day helping Kendall with the younger kids. It was dark outside when she and Natalie finished up their day. They were in the office putting on their coats.

"Oh, please, if I had a dollar for every time a teenager was rude to me..."

"But what if she refuses to rehearse? I mean, what'll I do?" Cece asked, buttoning her peacoat and wrapping a muffler around her neck.

"I'll call her parents tonight. They're pretty good about kicking her butt when she gets lazy." Natalie took out her keys, and they walked outside together. "But if she doesn't get it together soon, I'll have to give the role to somebody else, somebody not nearly the dancer that Dawn is, though."

Part of Cece wished for that to happen right away. Working with a younger, less skilled dancer, but one who was at least willing to dance, would be so much easier. Besides, this was just a small town studio production. Who would even care if the Sugar Plum Fairy couldn't do a perfect *pas de bourre*?

Natalie locked the door. "This town is very demanding, too. Ever since you were Sugar Plum Fairy, they expect us to put on a professional level production."

That's who would care, Cece thought, only the entire town.

"But I have to say, you did a great job with the little kids. Boy, did they love you."

Cece smiled. After Dawn left, she helped the mice and snowflakes with their numbers. She even worked with the two boys who were sharing the role of Fritz.

"Are you sure I'm not better suited for working with the younger kids? I mean, other than my stepbrother, I don't even know any teenagers. They're real enigmas to me."

"Let's see how it goes tomorrow, this was just your first day."

The walked down the block toward their cars. "I guess you're right," said Cece, opening her car door. "Have a good night."

"You too, Cece. Oh and by the way, in case I haven't said it enough, I'm really glad you came back."

"Thanks. Me too."

Cece got in her car. She waved to Natalie as she drove away. At the corner, she turned onto Main Street. The Christmas lights glimmered from every direction, and the windows in all the restaurants, shops and storefronts glowed with decorations. Cece shook her head. "This town sure loves Christmas," she said aloud.

CHAPTER 19

Cece's cell buzzed next to her ear, waking her up.

"H'lo?"

"You forgot to call me yesterday. You said we'd talk every day, remember?"

Cece sat up and stretched. "Patty?"

"Duh."

"I was sound asleep. I worked my ass off yesterday."

"No excuse, you promised me."

"You're right. Sorry."

"So, how'd it go?"

Cece propped her pillows and sat up. "Ok. Some good, some not so good. My project is the Sugar Plum Fairy, and believe me, she's a project." Cece told Patty about her all-too-brief rehearsal with Dawn.

"Wow, no wonder you're so tired."

"What's going on at home?" Cece asked.

"Not much . . . oh, I got a temp job at The Main Frame on 3rd."

Cece felt a sense of relief that Patty was gainfully employed, at least for now. "That's great, when do you start?"

"Today. They tell me I'll be framing tons of those giant family portraits. Very popular gift item this year. Can you imagine all the hideous Christmas sweaters I'll have to stomach? God, I hate those perfect-looking families."

"Somebody sure is a Scrooge today."

"It's lonely here without you," said Patty. She paused. "Speaking of lonely, how are you doing?"

"I'm not talking about him. I cried so much for two days I almost dehydrated. Anyway, I've got the perfect job for avoiding the harsh realities of my life—working with a teenager. Nothing more distracting than that."

"I've got to get going Ceece. You'd better call me every night."

"I will," Cece said. "I promise. And be a good girl at work. Follow directions and do your best."

"Don't I always?"

"Uh, no."

"Bye-bye." Patty made kissing noises into the phone.

"Good-bye."

Cece hung up and scooted to the edge of the bed. She turned, dropped her feet onto the floor, and reached for her purple robe. As she put an arm through a sleeve, she gazed at her cushy pillows and thick down comforter still warm and inviting. She threw off the robe and crawled back into bed. She closed her eyes and tried to go back to sleep, but all she could think about was Doug—his smile, his laugh, his smell, his touch. Cece pulled the blanket over her head. *I will never get over this,* she thought. *Never.*

Cece walked from snowflake to snowflake, positioning their arms correctly. "There we go," she said. "Now, make a big circle over your heads. Remember we're in second position now. Olivia, feet apart sweetie."

"Like thith Mith Thee-thee?" Olivia spread her feet and pointed her toes outward.

"Exactly! Good job!" Cece grinned. To her relief, the eight sweet little girls were keeping her mind off of Doug. "Now let's bend our knees into a plie', keep it smooth, straighten, and up... good, do it again... and, excellent!" Cece clapped her hands. "Good work girls! Five minute break then hurry back. Lots of work to do this afternoon with Miss Kendall."

The tiny ballerinas scattered, and Cece went to get a drink of water. As she filled a paper cup from the water dispenser, she felt somebody standing very close. "Cece, do you have a minute?"

She looked up. It was the woman in the minivan who had stopped Natalie the day Cece visited Ilana. "Sure. You're Brittany Hemmerling's mom, right?"

"Yes! Very good, you learn names quickly."

"I'm trying."

"And my younger daughter is Emily. She's one of the snowflakes."

Cece pictured a chubby little girl with rosy cheeks and blond ringlets who held hands with Olivia whenever they weren't dancing. "Oh sure, Emily. She's adorable."

"Adorably fat, you mean. But she'll slim down. Eventually. I hope . . ." she leaned in close to Cece's ear. "Could we talk in private?"

"Um, okay," Cece said. They went down the hallway past the restrooms and stood behind a rack of costumes.

"It's about Brittany," Wendy said, her voice just above a whisper. "You know that she and Jennifer, her best friend by the way, are sharing the role of Clara."

"Yes, I did hear that."

"And you know we have only one matinee, right?"

Cece cringed. "Uh-huh."

Wendy put a hand on Cece's elbow. "So I have a little favor to ask you, but please don't tell anyone that I asked."

Here it comes, Cece thought. "Okay . . ."

"I want you to make sure that Jennifer gets to be Clara for the Sunday matinee performance."

Cece thought she misunderstood, or perhaps Wendy misspoke. "Excuse me?"

"Jennifer's grandparents are elderly and quite frail. I know the only performance they'll make it to is that one, and Jennifer's mother would never dream of asking."

"Oh, wow, okay . . ."

"I'd have spoken to Natalie directly, but she's so busy."

Cece nodded. "Don't worry, I'll mention it to her."

"You're a sweetheart." Wendy squeezed her shoulder. "Oh, and good luck with that Dawn Redmond. If my Brittany ever turns into a surly teenager like that, she'll be lucky if I don't pack her up and ship her off to boarding school!" Wendy laughed and pushed the costume rack back into the closet. "See you later!"

Cece tracked Natalie down in the office. She told her about her conversation with Wendy Hemmerling.

"There's something about that woman I can't figure out," Natalie said. "She's always out there making sure that Brittany stands above the rest, but then she turns around and does something totally thoughtful and sweet."

"Must be the Christmas spirit," Cece said. She studied the chart that Natalie was working on. She had colored post-it notes stuck all over it, indicating who would dance what role in which performance.

"Would you look at that," Natalie said. "I already had Jennifer in the matinee spot, anyway. And a good thing too, because it's really too late for us to start making changes."

Cece scanned the names. "Boy, I never realized how much work went into figuring all this out."

Natalie rearranged some of the sticky notes. "My mom used to sit at the dining room table late into the night with charts just like this. She'd rearrange over and over."

Cece leaned on the table, trying to put faces to some of the names. She pointed to one. "Who's Gabe Martin?"

"Our best male lead, sixteen years old and fabulous."

"Good for Cavalier, huh?"

"He's just right, and it'll help with Dawn. We have a better chance of getting her to rehearsals if she's dancing the *pas de deux* with Gabe. They've been friends for years."

Cece hoped Natalie's plan would work. The dance of the Cavalier and the Sugar Plum Fairy was one of the most intense and artistic numbers in the entire ballet. It would be a shame if they had to cut it.

Cece she looked at her watch. "Dawn should be here soon, I'd better get ready. Did you call her parents?"

"I did. I think they're going to come by during rehearsal." Natalie chewed her cheek. "They know she's causing a problem for me."

"All right, well, I can't wait to meet 'em." Cece tightened her wrap skirt around her waist.

They went together into the studio where little ballerinas were practicing with Kendall. Brittany and Jennifer and their clique of friends were stretching on the bar and giggling with one another. Cece looked around.

"I don't see Dawn yet," she said to Natalie.

"Do you mind working with Brittany and Jennifer until she gets here? You remember the music, don't you?" Natalie smiled.

"Like it was yesterday."

Brittany Hemmerling was a classic Clara, with her straight, blond ponytail and a splash of freckles over her nose and cheeks. At ten years old, she could have passed for eight. Her friend Jennifer was the opposite, an exotic, mixed race beauty, with golden skin, green eyes, and black hair down to her waist.

Both were excellent dancers, and Cece enjoyed teaching them. They followed her every instruction, and imitated her positions and movements. As their lesson ended, Cece wished she could pass Dawn off to somebody else and coach the younger girls. In spite of that, she kept checking the clock, worried that Dawn had decided to blow off rehearsal.

"She's an hour late," Cece said to Natalie during a break. "You want to call her?"

"Yep." Natalie got out her cell and dialed Dawn's number. Cece watched Natalie frown as the call went to voicemail. "Hi Dawn, it's Natalie, it's after three and we're here waiting for you. Hope you're on the way. Call me."

Cece shook her head. "What time are her parents coming?"

"Soon," Natalie said. "Probably around four. I tell you, this is the part I hate, chasing after teenagers and telling their parents what problems they cause. I'll come get you when they arrive."

CHAPTER 20

Cece was working with Brittany and Jennifer in the smaller dance room practicing their pirouettes.

"Your weight needs to be on your front leg like this." Cece demonstrated what she wanted the girls to do. "And remember, you always have to have a good spot so you stay balanced."

The girls looked past Cece and started to giggle. Cece turned around to see Robby in the doorway. He had strings of tangled up white lights wrapped around his neck and arms.

"Are you our Christmas tree?" Cece asked.

"I'm in the middle of decorating the front studio," Robby said with a frustrated look, "and look how I found the lights."

"We'll help you untangle them, Robby," Brittany said. "Can we Miss Cece?"

"Absolutely not," Cece said. "We have work to do. Is Natalie looking for me, Robby?"

"Yup, she's in the office."

"Okay, tell her I'll be right there."

"Will do," Robby said. He left with yards of lights trailing after him.

"He's so cute," Brittany said, hopping from foot to foot. She pulled on her friend's shoulder. "Don't you think he's so cute?"

Jennifer smiled shyly. "Super cute," she whispered.

"Okay you two, no more drooling over Robby," Cece said. "I have to meet with Miss Natalie, so I want you both to practice Clara's dance with *The Nutcracker* until I get back."

"Again?" they said in unison.

"Yes, again. And then again and again and again . . ."

Cece left Brittany and Jennifer and walked down the hallway to the office. The door stood open, and she tapped lightly on it as she entered. A man and a woman sat in chairs in front of the desk, their backs to the door.

"Oh good, here she is," Natalie said.

The couple turned. Cece's stomach dropped. She felt heat permeate her body, from her chest, through her neck, and all the way up her face. Dawn's father was the man who spilled her coffee at Nutmeg's.

"Hi." Cece managed to squeak out the one word. It only took a second for her to notice that the stunning woman, dressed in snug black slacks, a gray silk blouse, and expensive looking, high-heeled pumps, was wearing a substantial diamond on her left hand.

The man's face drained of color as he recognized Cece, but he recovered quickly. He was in work attire—a dark suit, white shirt, and sky blue tie loosened around his neck. His face was clean-shaven, and Cece was unnerved by the fact that she found him even more handsome than she did a week ago. He stepped forward.

"Brad Redmond," he said, "and my ex-wife, Pam. We're Dawn's parents."

Ah, ex-wife. Boy, Cece thought, *he slipped that in smoothly.* "Nice to meet you," Cece said, shaking both their hands.

"Let's all sit over here," Natalie said, gesturing to the couch.

Natalie's chart was on the wall, and Pam stepped toward it. "May I take a look?" The former Mrs. Redmond had short blond hair, and she finger-combed the wispy ends at the back of her neck.

"Of course," Natalie said, standing in front of the chart with her.

Brad Redmond sat on the couch, and Cece sat down in the chair across from him. He gave her a slight smile, his eyes curious. "Pleasant surprise," he whispered.

Gripping the arms of her chair to keep her breathing steady, Cece returned the vague smile.

Pam pointed to the chart. "I see you have only Dawn as the fairy at all performances. "I feel terrible that she's become so unreliable."

"We need her, Pam," Natalie said. She and Dawn's mother sat down. "If she doesn't step up, I'm, well . . . we have no back-up plan. Cece, how much have you worked with her?"

"Only that one time. And just for a few minutes. She left when her boyfriend called."

"Her boyfriend?" Brad Redmond looked at his ex-wife sitting beside him. "What boyfriend?"

Cece swallowed. Already she had spoken out of turn. "Um, maybe it wasn't a boyfriend . . . it could have been a school friend, I'm really not sure."

"It's all right," Pam said, smoothing her hair again. "There is no boyfriend."

Brad frowned. "Are you sure about that, because . . ."

"Brad," his ex-wife interrupted him. "Let's discuss this privately, okay?"

Brad stretched his neck and tightened his jaw. "Fine."

Pam's cell vibrated in her hand. She looked at it. "Dawn's here," she said, holding up the text.

"Good. We might as well get this settled right now." Brad put a hand on his ex-wife's upper back. "Let me handle this, Pam."

Dawn walked through the door with the same scornful face she had the first Cece laid eyes on her. Her expression changed when she saw her father. "Daddy? What are you doing here?"

Brad looked at his watch. "The question is what are you doing showing up over an hour late?"

Dawn's shoulders rose, and Cece sensed that she felt trapped.

Brad walked over to his daughter and looked down at her. "This is very simple, Dawn. You either want to dance in the show or you don't. Tell us now, because if you choose not to, Natalie needs to find a replacement."

Brad paused, and Cece glanced at Dawn's mother, her face red and worried looking. "Daddy's right, sweetie. You can't leave them hanging."

Dawn hung her head and picked at her black nail polish.

"On the other hand," her father continued. "If you choose to stay in the production, you will show up to every rehearsal on time, dressed and ready to go. You will give a hundred and ten percent. And if you don't do what's expected of you, I guarantee that the consequences will be very, very unpleasant."

The room was silent, and Cece could hear her own heartbeat.

"Can I have a day to think about it?" Dawn asked, looking at her mother.

Her mother's mouth opened. "Well maybe that's a good . . ."

"No." Brad did not raise his voice. "I'm not going to lecture you Dawn, you already know how I feel about commitments."

"But I . . ." Dawn started.

"Nah-uh." Her father stopped her. When he tightened his lips, Cece noticed the dimple near his mouth.

"Here's what is going to happen. Your mom and I will step out so that you can talk to your instructors. We'll be back in five minutes. If you have not decided by then, I'll decide for you. And I'll do it by flipping a coin." Brad motioned to his ex-wife, and they went to the door. He turned. "I highly doubt that you want to leave such an important decision to chance."

Cece exhaled when Dawn's parents left the office. She didn't realize that she'd practically been holding her breath ever since she'd walked in and seen Brad Redmond. It was almost too much to absorb.

Cece took a deep breath and turned her attention to Dawn and Natalie, who were standing side by side. Natalie's height allowed her to look down at Dawn with an intimidating stance.

"Do you have any questions, Dawn?" Natalie asked.

"Can I see the rehearsal schedule again?"

Natalie went to the desk and pulled out a packet of papers stapled in the corner. It outlined every rehearsal down to the smallest detail. Cece knew that Dawn was expected to be at the studio almost every waking minute that she was not at school. Natalie handed it to Dawn and passed a hopeful look in Cece's direction.

Dawn turned the pages slowly. Cece watched her, intrigued. Dawn's expression had gone from impertinent to almost earnest. It gave Cece a flicker of hope that she might not be so difficult after all.

At the five-minute mark, Brad Redmond and his ex-wife reentered. "Have you decided?" he asked his daughter.

"I think so. Can I talk to you outside for a second, Daddy?"

They stepped out. Pam sat on one of the chairs. She folded her hands and smiled uncomfortably. "So Natalie, how's Ilana. Still fighting that bug?"

Natalie shifted. "Feeling better Pam, thanks. She should be back tomorrow or the next day."

"Good to know." Pam looked around the office as they all waited, the clock on the wall ticking.

Dawn and her father came back. Their expressions gave nothing away.

"What did you decide, honey," Pam asked.

"I'll dance," Dawn said quietly.

Cece could see relief wash over Natalie's face.

"I'm glad," Natalie said. "Now go get ready."

Dawn nodded. She glanced at Cece then picked up her dance bag and walked out the door.

CHAPTER 21

After rehearsing with Dawn until after dark, Cece drove home in an exhausted trance. Only two days in Clearwater, and already she was overwhelmed.

Meeting Brad Redmond, or re-meeting him, made her edgy. What if he thought she had lied about going back to LA after Thanksgiving? She would have to explain why she was back. Although why? She had no obligation to explain anything to him or to anybody. On the other hand, part of her wanted to make it known that she was only in Clearwater to help Natalie produce the Christmas show, and then she'd be leaving right after the last performance.

Already people were gossiping about the return of Cecilia Rose. The mothers in the dance studio figured out who she was in less than two days. She had heard whispers in the locker room about 'Miss Natalie's old rival.' And when she went to get a coffee at Nutmeg's one afternoon the teenager stopped her.

"Hey," he had said, passing her a paper cup with a lid. "I hear you're hanging out for a while."

"And where did you hear that . . ." Cece peered at his nametag, "Trevor?"

"Hello? I'm the assistant to the assistant manager at the busiest business in Clearwater. I hear everything."

"Do you now?"

"Yup. You're an old friend of Natalie's."

"That's right." Cece picked up her coffee. "See you next time." Cece turned to leave.

"Oh, hey," Trevor called after her. "Do you know if Natalie would be, uh, up for, you know, a Mrs. Robinson kinda thing? I sure could use a few *lessons*, if you know what . . ."

Cece rolled her eyes and pushed open the door with an exaggerated shove.

Phil put a grilled cheese sandwich and a mug of tomato soup on the kitchen table in front of Cece. "Here you go."

"My favorite comfort food, how'd you remember that?"

"You have any idea how many years you survived on nothing but grilled cheese? The soup I could change up now and then, but not the grilled cheese."

Cece took a bite and savored the smooth, gooey mouthful. "Oh, so good." She hadn't realized how hungry she was until she started eating. "Sorry I kept you up so late."

"Don't mind at all." Phil sat across from her, his hands wrapped around a cup of hot tea. "Thought we'd get the tree tomorrow. Real big one, you know? I'm thinking Blue Spruce."

"Sounds nice." Cece sipped at her soup and felt the hot liquid run down her throat.

"Julia and Ryan'll decorate with us, okay?"

Cece looked at her father. "Of course they will. Why are you telling me that?"

Phil scratched the back of his head. "I don't know. I just want everything here to be the way you're used to it, make you feel like you're sixteen again."

Cece choked. "Dad, the last thing I'd ever want to be is sixteen again." She thought about what Natalie had said about all the current drama around the dance studio. "I have no desire to relive any part of my teen years."

Phil patted Cece's hand. "I understand. You want more soup?"

Cece stretched, cracking her neck and back. "No. Thanks for dinner." She got up and went to stand behind her father, leaning over his shoulders. "I am so happy to see you happy, Dad. You deserve it more than anyone."

Phil squirmed a bit. "Now don't you get all mushy on me, hear? Most important thing in the world to me is still my kids, no matter how big you and your brother are."

Cece kissed her father's scruffy cheek. "I know that. I've known that my entire life."

The bubbles in the tub floated to the edge. Cece put one toe in to check the temperature. She stepped in and sank into the water.

"Ahhh," she said. She leaned her head on the terrycloth pillow, closed her eyes and imagined the music. She was the Sugar Plum Fairy once again, dressed in her favorite lilac tutu and satin bodice with white tights and pointes. Her hair was fastened into a bun so tight that it pulled her eyebrows back. The last time she had danced the part, she was sixteen years old, but in her dreams, time melted away . . .

"Oh shit!" Cece woke when her head dropped forward, and she inhaled a nose full of soapy water. She sputtered and jumped out, shivering, and wrapped herself in a towel. Her fingers and feet were crinkled up like road maps. *Jesus,* she thought, *I'm freezing.*

Cece got into bed, snuggled under her covers, and passed out. She'd been asleep only few minutes when her cell chimed.

"You forgot about me again."

"No, no I didn't. I was just going to call you." Cece glanced at the clock. It was almost midnight.

"Liar," Patty said.

Cece sat up. "You will never believe what happened today." She fluffed up her pillows and regaled Patty with the whole story about her surprise encounter with the man from the bakery and whose father he turned out to be.

"No! Mr. Sticky-buns is that nightmare teenager's father? Unbelievable!"

"Don't call him that. Yuck."

"I'm callin' him that. Live with it. Sheesh, you weren't kidding about that small town business. Not safe for a minute there, are you?"

"I know. It's crazy," Cece yawned. "I can't keep my eyes open, Patty. Talk tomorrow?"

"Wait," Patty said. "I have something important to tell you."

Cece's heart skipped. "Oh no, did we get another rent increase?"

"No, nothing like that. It's about Doug. He came by today."

"He did?"

"He did. He left his camera here the other night."

Cece closed her eyes and pictured Doug's camera bag sitting on the entry table beside her front door. It contained thousands of dollars' worth of equipment, and he never let it out of his sight. Whenever they'd gone anywhere, if it was in his truck, he took it with him—into restaurants, movie theaters, friends' houses. For him to forget it somewhere, he must have been . . .

"He was a mess, Ceece. I'm sorry to tell you, but I just feel like I have to."

Cece felt her eyes sting. "It's okay. Did you talk?"

"Just for a sec. He looked like he hadn't slept in days. Anyway, and this was really weird, he went and stood in the doorway of your room for like five minutes."

Cece squirmed. That was strange. "Do you know why?"

"Not really. I've never seen anyone look so sad."

Cece thought she had no tears left, but found she had plenty. "Then what happened?" she asked, wiping her eyes.

"He lifted his camera bag and put it on his shoulder, you know, the way he always does, with a little twist of his neck?"

A sob caught in her throat. She could picture the exact movement Patty described.

"I think he was about to leave, but then he stopped, like something occurred to him all of a sudden, and he went back into your room and picked up your painting of the ballerina face.

"Rea . . . really?"

"Uh-huh. And he took it with him."

Cece felt a chill run down her back.

"I hope you're not mad, Ceece. He told me to ask you if it was okay, and if it's not, he'll bring it back. Do you want me to tell him to bring it back?"

Cece wiped her face. She reached for a tissue and blew her nose. The tears slowed. She was surprised how content she felt knowing that her painting was with Doug. And that he was with it. "No, no it's fine. It's good."

"Are you sure?"

"Yeah. Actually, I want him to have it."

Cece didn't pay attention to the rest of the conversation. She said goodnight to Patty, got out of bed, and padded to her dresser. She opened the drawer and removed the picture in the Tiffany frame. In the dim light, she studied the beloved photograph. She smiled at the way her body folded into Doug's, her back against his chest. Cece closed her eyes. She could feel Doug's arms around her, his lips on her neck, his kiss on her shoulder. An inkling of hope lit up inside her. The fact that Doug wanted her painting meant that there was still a chance. She knew it in her heart. They loved each other, and maybe this time apart was what they both needed to realize that their relationship was worth saving. She would call him in a day or two. They would talk everything over, and then, as soon as the show ended, she'd go home.

Cece fell asleep knowing that she and Doug would be reunited in time to celebrate Christmas together.

CHAPTER 22

"Dawn, you're welcoming Clara into the Kingdom of Sweets. Show the audience what kind of queen you are."

They had been rehearsing for hours, and Dawn's talent continued to impress Cece. However, she had no warmth in her smile, no glint in her eyes. Her facial expressions were non-existent.

Dawn stopped dancing. Her hands flopped to her sides and her shoulders drooped. "How am I supposed to do that?"

Cece sighed. She herself had wondered the same thing the first time she had the role. "You have to figure out what you want to convey, just like every dancer who has ever danced this part. I only know how I did it."

Dawn frowned. "You danced this part?"

Cece studied Dawn for a moment. "Yes, and that's why Miss Natalie asked me to coach you."

"I don't know. Guess I hadn't thought about it."

Cece turned off the music. She opened two bottles of water and handed one to Dawn. "I grew up dancing here, and Miss Ilana was my instructor."

"She was?"

"Uh-huh."

Dawn sipped her water. "We don't see much of Miss Ilana anymore. She used to be here all the time, but she's been sick or something."

"I know," Cece said. She tipped her head back and drank some water.

"She scares me," Dawn said.

Cece licked her lips. "Hey, she used to scare me, too. Dance instructors have to be intimidating. I think I need to work on that."

Dawn laughed. It was the first time Cece had heard her laugh, and it sounded sweet and a little bit girly. "Yeah, you really aren't intimidating at all."

"Guess I'm going to have get tougher."

"Oh my God!" Dawn's eyes grew wide as she looked past Cece.

Cece turned. A teenage boy stood in the doorway. His lip was split, and blood dribbled from a gash near his eyebrow.

Dawn ran to the boy. "Gabe! Again?"

Cece was taken aback. Her Cavalier had arrived. Even with a damaged face, he was perfect—tall, muscular, dark skin, and piercing eyes. "What happened?" Cece walked toward him.

Gabe looked at her. He tried to smile but winced when it stretched open the cut on his lower lip. His tongue touched the blood.

"Gabe, this is our new instructor, Cece, the one I told you about."

"Hi," he said, touching the back of his hand to his lip.

"Were you in an accident?" Cece asked.

"Guess you could call it that," Gabe said. "I accidentally ran into a couple o' assholes."

"We'd better get you cleaned up," Cece said. "Stay here."

She headed down the hallway and ran into Robby. "Oh, Robby, do we have a first aid kit somewhere? And an ice pack?"

"Yeah, right over here."

Cece followed Robby as he got the first aid kit out of a cabinet and an icepack from the freezer. "Thanks."

"Who's hurt?" Robby asked.

"Gabe."

"Gabe?" Robby went with her into the dance room. "Whoa, they got you good this time."

"Hey Robby," Gabe said. He wiped some blood off his chin with his shirt. "Yeah, they did."

"What happened?" asked Robby.

"Same bullshit. Cornered me and Johnny, called us fu.... freakin' faggots." Gabe glanced at Cece. "Sorry."

Cece gave him a sympathetic smile. *Some things never change,* she thought.

"That's so not cool," said Robby. "And you're not even gay."

"Yeah, but Johnny is, and we both dance, so they just figure we're fair game either way."

Cece opened the first kit and dabbed the cut on Gabe's eyebrow with antiseptic.

"What about Johnny," Dawn asked. "Is he okay?"

Gabe laughed without smiling. "Better than that. He got douche bag McNulty right in the balls. Classic."

"Man, wish I could go back to school and, you know, be like your bodyguard."

"Thanks Robby, but I got at least 20 pounds on you, and the last time you showed up there you almost got arrested. Besides, I have Ryan on my side."

Ryan? Cece thought. My brother Ryan?

"Yeah," Dawn said. "Ryan'll be there."

Things were getting more interesting with every word. They talked like Cece wasn't even in the room.

"Listen to you talking about Ryan," Robby said to Dawn. "You still like him, don't you?"

"Kind of." Dawn said. A shy smile crept over her face, and she lifted a shoulder toward her chin.

Jesus Christ, Cece thought, *no mistaking that body language. My Sugar Plum Fairy has a crush on my little brother!*

"Here Robby," Cece said, handing him the ice bag and changing the subject. "Throw this out. Gabe, Dawn, back to the dance room."

"You're making Gabe rehearse? He can't dance."

"Yes I can," Gabe stood up. He looked in the mirror. "I look pretty tough with this scrape by my eye, don't you think?"

Cece smiled. Maybe coaching teenagers wouldn't be so bad after all.

CHAPTER 23

The sun was almost down. Dawn and Gabe were fading, and Cece's feet felt like she'd been walking on rocks. But her mood was uplifted. Ever since she learned that Doug had taken her painting, she felt a sense of relief. They would be good. They would work everything out. They would be back together.

Cece stood. She put a hand on Gabe's shoulder. "You are a trooper, Gabe, and a great dancer. Good work you two."

"Are we done?" Dawn asked.

"Done for today," Cece said.

Gabe yawned and then yelped. "Is my lip bleeding again?"

Cece looked. "Just a bit. You'd better ice it more when you get home."

"Can we have tomorrow off, Cece? It's Sunday." Dawn stretched her shoulders, arching her lithe body.

"No, but I'll tell you what. Let's sleep in. We'll start at eleven, how does that sound?"

"Okay," Dawn said. She picked up her bag. "Oh, hi Daddy."

Cece turned. Brad Redmond was standing in the doorway. "Hi sweetie."

Cece smiled casually. "Hello," she said.

Dawn's father gave Cece a little nod. "Nice to see you again." He turned his attention to the kids. "Gabe, do you need a . . . Jesus! What happened?"

"It's nothing Mr. Redmond, just a scrape."

Brad lifted Gabe's chin. "You'll have a fat lip there, son. Looks to me like a right hook caught your face."

"He's fine Daddy," Dawn said. "You can drive Gabe home, right?"

"Of course." Brad put a hand on Gabe's shoulder. "Hope you got in a few hits yourself."

"Yes sir, I did."

Brad winked. "Good for you. Go get your stuff kids, car's out front."

"See you tomorrow," Cece said as the two teenagers left.

"So," Brad said, putting his hands in his pockets.

Cece picked up some CDs, averting her eyes from Brad Redmond's handsome face.

"So . . ." she repeated.

"So," he said again. "I had Chinese for lunch yesterday, and my fortune said that I should *prepare for an unexpected event.* I believe your appearance might be that."

Cece brushed some hair off her face. "Have to admit, you were quite a surprise as well."

They both smiled awkwardly.

"Dawn did well today," Cece said, breaking the uncomfortable silence. "We finally connected, I think. I hope. She's a lovely dancer."

"I agree, but of course I'm biased."

Cece picked up her jacket.

"I, uh, hope you don't mind my asking, but weren't you going back to LA?"

"Oh, I did. But I came back . . . obviously, here I am." Cece's hands grew clammy. "I'm an old friend of Natalie's. She's the one I was meeting the other day, you know, the day when we, uh, had coffee."

"I remember."

"Anyway," Cece said. "It's a long story, but I'm here just for a few weeks to help open *The Nutcracker,* and then I'm going home. Again."

"Well then, on behalf the dance families, thank you. The Christmas show is very important around here."

"Yes, I am aware."

Brad smiled. "I'd better go see what those kids are up to. Get 'em home for dinner."

"Okay." Cece recalled Patty's nickname for him, Mr. Sticky-buns, and she suppressed a smile. "See you next time."

Brad nodded. "Hope so."

Cece pulled into the driveway as Phil, Tom, and Ryan were trying to slide the Christmas tree out of the back of Tom's truck.

"That tree is gigantic," Cece said, getting out of her car.

Tom lifted the upper half and eased it off the truck bed while Phil and Ryan caught it and set it on the ground.

Julia came out and stood on the porch. She had on cowboy boots, jeans, and a green, crocheted poncho. "How on earth will that ever fit in the house, Phil?" Julia asked. "It's way too tall!"

Phil put his hands on his lower backed and stretched. "Nope. Eleven feet, ten inches. You think I'd buy a tree without measuring it?"

Cece smiled. Her father never went anywhere without a tape measure. She walked up the steps and gave Julia a kiss on the cheek. "This is going to be fun to watch."

Julia put an arm around Cece's waist.

"You seem better."

"I am." She thought about her plan to go home and reunite with Doug. "I think Doug and I might work things out," she whispered. "I'll tell you about it later."

Julia gave her a quick squeeze. "Can't wait."

Christmas music and the aroma of fresh pine filled the house. They had just finished dinner and were about to decorate the tree.

"Come on, come on everyone," Phil said. "Let's go. Tom, fill the stand with water."

"You want me to get you the corn syrup, honey?" Julia asked.

"Corn syrup?" Cece said.

Phil scratched his head. "I don't think so. I did some research online, and now they're sayin' don't add anything to the water, just keep it filled."

Tom looked at his sister. "Last year Boomer kept drinking the sugar water, and he gained like three pounds."

Cece laughed. "Boomer, come here you silly boy." She rubbed the dog's face and kissed his nose.

For the first time since she arrived in Clearwater three days ago, Cece felt herself unwind. Rehearsals were going relatively well, and she had a definitive plan for fixing the situation with Doug when she got home.

Cece was certain that Doug missed her every bit as much as she missed him. She would call him tonight and apologize for everything—her impatience, her control-freakishness, her hang-ups about money, and most of all, for her outburst the night of her birthday. They both were still young, and there was plenty of time to think about marriage over the next few years.

Phil pulled strands of tiny white lights out of a box and wound them in and around the tree branches, while the rest of them hung ornaments. With the five of them working, it took less than hour.

"Okay, Ry," Phil said. "Light her up."

Ryan inserted the plug into the wall. The tree glowed like a Wonderland dream.

"Oooh," they all said.

"It is so beautiful!" Julia said, sliding in her hand inside Phil's arm.

Cece felt an emotional tug at the sight of her family and their sparkling tree. It stood in front of a tall picture window, and visitors would see it before they even came inside. Phil Camden's Christmas tree was always perfect. It literally burst with lights, colors, and dozens of ornaments, each one, set in between shimmering gold, ivory, and cranberry ribbons, with a story behind it.

Julia went to the kitchen and came back with coffee and Christmas cookies. "Fresh baked," she announced. The men wasted no time devouring most of the cookies.

"Hey! I want one," Cece said. She was sitting on the floor leaning against Boomer, using him as a backrest.

Ryan picked up a gingerbread Santa and brought it to her. "Here Cece." He sat down beside her. Boomer lifted his head as if to see who had joined the dog pile. He gave Ryan a sniff and went back to sleep.

"Thanks Ry," Cece said, biting off Santa's leg.

Julia started organizing the empty boxes. "Oh wait. What's this?" She opened a small box and removed a pink, blown glass ballerina.

Cece caught her breath. She hadn't seen the ornament in years, not since her mother had left. "Oh my God," she said. "I completely forgot about that one."

Julia handed it to her, and Cece held it up by its string. The delicate ballerina twisted slowly and shimmered in the light. A single tear ran down Cece's cheek, and she quickly brushed it away.

"It's nice," Ryan said. "Where'd you get it?"

"It was a gift," Cece said, trying to swallow an overwhelming rush of emotion. "Given to me the first Christmas that I danced the role of Clara in *The Nutcracker*. I was nine." Cece realized that twenty years had passed. A lifetime.

Everyone sat on the floor beside Cece. She sniffed, willing herself not to cry. "I remember that I was so scared. I'd never danced a solo before." She looked at Ryan. "On opening night I kind of freaked out."

"You did?"

Cece nodded her head. "I did. So my dance teacher, Miss Ilana, asked me what I was afraid of, and I told her I was scared that I'd disappoint her."

"But I thought you were a good dancer," Ryan said.

Cece laughed. "I was good. And I had practiced for months, but I still was really scared.

"So what happened?"

"Well," Cece smiled at the memory. "Miss Ilana said that the only way I could disappoint her would be if I refused to dance. So I just went out there and danced."

"I bet you were fabulous," Julia said.

"Nope. Not even close. I missed steps and even tripped over my own feet at one point, but I kept going." Cece pictured herself pirouetting across the stage. She touched the delicate tip of the ballerina's toe shoe. "Then after our last performance, Miss Ilana gave me this ornament. I can still her saying, in that thick Russian accent, 'Cecilia Rose, you make me proud, so very proud.'"

"That's a good story, sis," said Tom.

"It is, isn't it?" Cece got up and stood beside the tree. She lifted a branch and moved over one tiny light. She found the perfect spot for her ballerina, right next to a little wooden nutcracker.

CHAPTER 24

In the darkness, Cece sat on the couch, snuggled under a blanket. Boomer was curled up next to her, his head resting in her lap. The Christmas tree lit up the room, and the glass ballerina, catching the warm air from a heating vent, danced in the glow of the tiny lights. Cece picked up her cell, put it down, picked it up again. Her palms were damp, and her heart thumped. She hadn't spoken to Doug in four days, not since he'd walked out of her house, leaving his camera behind. She placed the call and held her breath.

I'm being ridiculous, she told herself, I know he wants me to call him, I know he does . . .

"Hello?"

Cece gripped her phone. "It's me."

"Cece. Is everything okay?" His voice was low and a little shaky.

"Yeah," Cece fought back her tears, "everything's fine. I, um, I just wanted to talk to you. I miss you, Doug." Her voice cracked, and it was useless to even try not to cry. Good thing she always had a box of tissues with her lately.

"Don't cry, Ceece."

Cece could tell by the raspy tone in Doug's voice that Patty was right. He wasn't doing well.

"I wanted to tell you, that . . . that I'm sorry," she took a trembling breath, "I'm sorry for everything I did."

"Please, Cece, stop. It's okay."

"Patty told me she saw you, and that you're . . . you're not good."

"I'm not. It's been the worst week of my life."

"Me too, Doug. And when Patty told me that you took my painting, I just knew that . . ." she couldn't get the words out between her sobs.

"I'm . . . I'm glad you called."

"You are?"

"Yeah. I . . . I was going to call you."

"Really?" Her shoulders quivered.

"I need to tell you something."

"Okay." Cece's body stiffened. She closed her eyes and willed him to say the words that would bring them back together.

"I'm going away."

"What?"

"I got a job, a photography job, with a nature magazine. You know it's what I've always wanted to do."

That was true. He had told her the very first time they met that he wanted to photograph animals in their natural habitats. "Where are you going?"

"Central America. We're . . . we're starting in Costa Rica."

Cece looked at the lights on the Christmas tree. They appeared to be moving and looked like little white fireflies. She put her free hand across her stomach, feeling ill.

"Are you still there, Ceece?"

She cleared her throat. "I'm here."

"I can't stay in LA anymore, Ceece, it's too hard without you. And I need to figure some things out, you know?"

She wanted to beg him not to go. "How long will you be gone?"

"Couple of months, maybe more. If the publisher likes the series, we'll move to another location. I'm going to see the rainforest, babe, take pictures of insects and birds and . . ."

"Monkeys," Cece said. "You'll . . . you'll see lots of monkeys." She gave up trying to stifle her tears.

"I know you're sad, I'm sorry. But I need to do this."

"I get it. I know you do. It's just that I was hoping that . . . that after I got home, we'd be able to . . . that we could . . ."

"Please don't, Ceece. It hurts too much. The truth is, if we were together I never would've considered the job. So in some twisted way, I don't know, I guess the timing was right."

Cece tried to imagine what her life would be if only she could turn back time, undo one thing, change one decision.

"You'll miss Christmas."

"I know, but without you . . ." Doug stopped, and Cece could tell that he was unable to finish the sentence.

She took a deep breath. "It's great that you're doing this, Doug. I mean it. It's always been your dream." She tried to keep her voice steady. "I'm . . . I'm happy for you."

"Cece?"

"Yeah?"

"About the painting. I, um, I'm sorry. I shouldn't have done that, but for some reason when I saw it in your room, I . . . I just felt like I needed it. I watched you paint it, and I loved the story that inspired it, you know?"

"I do know."

"I'll drop it off before I leave. Give it to Patty, or maybe I should leave it by the back door."

"No. Don't do that."

"You want me to mail it?"

"I want you to keep it."

"You do?" Doug sounded shocked. "Are you sure?"

"Yes. I'm completely sure." Mae's words swam in Cece's mind. She wanted her work to matter, and it mattered to Doug. "Take it with you."

Cece could hear Doug's shaky breaths, and she pictured his face fighting back tears. Her handsome, masculine man was as heartbroken as she was, maybe more. "Thank you," he said, his voice barely audible.

"You stay safe now, you promise me," Cece said, her tone firm.

"I will. I promise."

"I hope you have an amazing time, Doug." She sniffed and dragged the back of her hand under her nose. "I really do."

"God, Ceece, this hurts. It hurts so much . . ."

"I'll always love you.

"Me too . . ." Doug's voice broke.

"Bye," she whispered, ending the call. Cece shut her eyes, and, in her mind, she saw a door close, leaving her in darkness.

CHAPTER 25

Cece walked into the office and fell into a chair across from the desk. Natalie gave her a crooked smile. "Are you hung over?"

"I wish," Cece said, sipping on her third cup of coffee Sunday morning. She had been awake most of the night, and her head felt like it was made of brick.

"Bad night?"

"Didn't sleep, that's all," Cece said. "I'll be fine."

Natalie gave her a worried frown. "Are you sure?"

Cece nodded. "I just want to work. Rehearsals are at eleven, and I don't want to think or talk about or do anything else. Just work."

"Okay then. Look at this calendar." Natalie turned her laptop around to show Cece what December looked like. Every day was jammed. "Today's December 4th, and the show opens on the 16th. It's crunch time."

Only twelve days until opening night. Cece shook her head and tried to clear it. "Not much time, is there?"

Natalie rubbed her forehead. "Shit. No. If only my mother could help. Did you see her when you came in?"

"No. I came through the back door."

"She's probably in the front," Natalie said.

Cece leaned on the desk. "Does she know I came back? That I'm working here?"

"I've told her every day, several times a day, so she should."

Cece hoped so. She hadn't seen Ilana since her visit the day after Thanksgiving. The door opened, and Ilana walked in.

"Vhere is my record, Natalia?"

"I have it, Mamma." Natalie took a vinyl album out of a drawer and handed it to her mother. It was in its original cover, the same one that Cece remembered from when she was a little girl.

"Look who's here Mama," Natalie said. "It's Cece."

Ilana turned.

"Good morning, Ilana," Cece said. She stepped forward and kissed Ilana on both cheeks.

Ilana looked confused.

"Mamma," Natalie said. "I told you Cece was working here, remember? She's come to help with the Christmas show."

Ilana nodded her head slowly, a slight smile formed on her lips. "Ah, yes, I remember. You are Sugar Plum Fairy dis year, Cecilia."

"Not exactly, Ilana. I'm coaching Dawn Redmond. She's our fairy this time." Cece felt her headache worsen. "She's a very good dancer. You'll be pleased."

"But I put Cecilia Rose on de board," Ilana said. She went to the chart and began rearranging Natalie's post-it notes.

"Let's get the record player, Mamma, so that we can listen to the album." Natalie gently took her mother's hands off the chart and put the post-it notes back where they belonged. "Cece would love to hear the old record we used to use, wouldn't you, Cece?"

"Sure."

They went into the main studio. It was empty, and their footsteps echoed on the hardwood floor. Natalie opened the door of a closet on the back wall. She pulled out a cart that held the old turntable and speakers and rolled it across the room. As she passed by Cece she whispered, "Don't worry. She'll snap out of it."

Cece wasn't worried, just exhausted. She'd had three hours sleep, maybe, and those were on the couch, sandwiched between the cushions and Boomer. She wondered where she could find Natalie's supply of headache remedies.

One of the French doors opened, and Wendy Hemmerling walked in followed by Kendall, who was holding a white costume wrapped in plastic.

"Good afternoon everyone!" said Wendy. "Oh my goodness, Ilana, how nice to see you. Did you have a nice trip?"

Ilana looked at her daughter. "Vhere did I go?"

Cece's eyes darted from Wendy to Natalie. Ilana looked confused.

"Nowhere Mamma. You had a bad cold and stayed home for a while."

Wendy frowned. "Didn't you say she was out of town? Somebody said she was out of town."

"No. She just had a stubborn cold, that's all," Natalie said.

Kendall coughed loudly. "I think I'm catching it, too."

Bad actress, Cece thought, but at least she's trying to help.

Natalie flashed an appreciative smile in Kendall's direction. "Thanks for getting the costumes, Wendy. How did they turn out?"

"Fabulous!" Wendy said, easily distracted. "I brought in one of the snowflakes to show you." She took the costume from Kendall, lifted the plastic, and shook it out. Then she fluffed up the edges of the sparkly, white tutu attached to a long sleeved, white bodice adorned with sequins. "How darling is this? I sequined all the tutus!"

Cece imagined little Olivia and all her friends dressed in glittery white from head to toe. They'd be adorable.

The door opened again and Dawn Redmond came in. Cece was surprised, and pleased, to see her arrive a half hour early. Except for the fact that she did not look happy.

"Hi Dawn," Cece said. "You look tired."

Dawn scowled. "So do you."

No point in fighting with this girl, Cece thought. "I am. Didn't sleep well."

Dawn shrugged as if to say 'tell someone who cares.'

Natalie lifted her head. "You're early, Dawn."

"My dad had to drop me off on his way somewhere." Dawn's caustic tone made Cece's head throb even more. "And he had to drive me because my mom couldn't, because she had to go to my brother's soccer game." The teenager rolled her eyes and slumped into a chair.

"Sit up straight!"

Dawn jumped to her feet when Ilana appeared in front of her. "Oh! Miss Ilana, I didn't see you. How are you feeling?"

Ilana stepped close to Dawn. "I am well, tank you. Must I remind you again de importance of proper posture? You are ballerina."

"I know, Miss Ilana. I'm sorry."

Cece and Natalie grinned at each another, hearing Ilana scold Dawn the same way she used to scold them.

"Ilana," Wendy interrupted, "do you want to see the snowflake costumes?"

Ilana harrumphed. "I do not. I must instruct my prima ballerina, much work to do."

Dawn looked nervously at Cece. "Oh, okay, I'll get ready."

"Not you, my dear. Cecilia." Ilana put the record on the turntable and carefully placed the needle. The dance of the Sugar Plum Fairy music began. She clapped her hands twice. "Cecilia Rose, vhere are your pointes?"

Wendy stared wide-eyed at Ilana. Dawn stepped back. Cece raised her eyebrows and looked at Natalie for help.

"Mamma," Natalie said, putting an arm around her mother. "Cece's not dancing, she's . . ."

"Natalia!" Ilana interrupted her daughter. "I am sorry, but Cecilia Rose is the better dancer, and she will be Sugar Plum Fairy. You are disappointed. I am sorry."

Cece tried to scoot Wendy, Kendall, and Dawn out of the studio. "Natalie needs a few minutes," she whispered. "Let's go into the dance room and let her . . ."

"Cecilia! Vee must rehearse! I spoke vith your mother. Did she not tell you scouts from San Francisco come to see you dance?"

Dawn stepped closer to Cece, frightened. "What's she talking about?"

Cece put a hand on Dawn's back.

"Natalie," Wendy hissed. "What's going on?"

Ilana marched to the record player. She started the number over and turned the volume up. The dance of the Sugar Plum Fairy blasted from the speakers. "Cecilia Rose," Ilana shouted. "Dance!"

Cece didn't know what came over her, but without thinking, she followed Ilana's orders. The music filled her head and pushed away every thought about Doug and her broken heart. She thought about nothing except becoming the Queen of the Land of Sweets once again.

The music halted without warning. Cece stopped. She was out of breath. Natalie was standing beside the record player holding the disconnected plug.

Cece jolted back to reality. "Natalie, I'm sorry, I just . . . "

Natalie put her hand up. "It's okay."

"Natalia, vat are you . . ."

"Mamma," Natalie said, her voice soft and soothing. She took her mother's arm and guided her toward Cece. "Cecilia is twenty-nine years old, and so am I. We aren't teenagers, and we're not your students anymore. We're all grown up." She took a few steps with Ilana to the side of the room where Dawn and Wendy stood. "Now, this is Dawn, you remember her, right? She's danced with us for years. And she's our Sugar Plum Fairy. Do you understand?"

Ilana closed her eyes for a few moments. She opened them and looked at Cece. "I am sorry, Cecilia. I am sometimes confused, and I do not . . ." she stopped and looked at her daughter. "I should rest now, yes?"

Natalie nodded, blinking back tears. "Come Mamma, I'll help you."

Ilana and Natalie walked out.

Cece looked at the other three, disbelief on their faces. "Excuse me a minute."

She ran down the hall into the bathroom and stood in front of the mirror, just like she had done the day she had seen the letter. Leaning over the sink, Cece splashed her face with cold water. One of her recurring nightmares, dancing for a furious Ilana, had just come true. She looked at herself in the mirror and took a deep breath. "Pull yourself together," she said. Cece grabbed a few paper towels and dried her face. Whatever was about to happen, they might as well get it over with.

She returned to the studio. Kendall and Dawn stood against the wall, while Wendy was seated in a chair, her jaw tight and pulsating.

"Listen Wendy, Natalie will explain everything."

Wendy nodded, her mouth a thin, tight line.

Cece stood in front of Dawn and put her hands on the teenager's shoulders. "Are you okay?"

Dawn looked at Cece as if she had just sprouted wings. "You're an amazing dancer, like, wow, totally incredible."

Before Cece could reply, Natalie appeared. "We need to talk," she said to everyone.

"Yes, we do," said Wendy.

The five of them sat down in the row of folding chairs reserved for dance parents. Natalie leaned her elbows on her knees. "My mother isn't well."

"Clearly," Wendy said. "And my guess is she hasn't been for some time."

Natalie chewed a fingernail. "You're right, Wendy. I was trying to keep my mother's, um, condition private. I guess, well, now that you all saw . . ."

"Nobody," Wendy interrupted Natalie and pointed a finger at all of them. "Absolutely nobody can know what happened here today."

Natalie's head snapped up.

Cece was so shocked she bit her tongue.

"We five are going to be a team," Wendy said. "We have a mission, and that is to get *The Nutcracker* opened on time and without a hitch. Every one of us has to be part of the plan. Agreed?"

Dawn nodded. "I can keep a secret. I promise."

"Me too. I haven't told anyone, and I've known for a long time," said Kendall.

"Good." Wendy looked at Natalie. "You need somebody to look after Ilana, at least until after the show closes. Do you have anyone?"

Natalie shook her head.

"No problem. My housekeeper's aunt needs a job, and she has experience in elder care." Wendy reached into her purse for her smart phone and started sending messages. "I'll take care of blinging and repairing costumes, and taking them to the dress rehearsal at the theater, and any other logistical items."

Natalie's head bobbed up and down. "That's good. I'll tell Robby that he reports to you for now. As far as my mother goes, I don't know. What should I tell everyone?"

"Pneumonia," Wendy said. "Very common in people her age, and treatable, but serious."

Cece's head was spinning with Wendy's take-charge skill and her no nonsense approach. Within minutes, the plan was set. The five of them held hands.

Wendy's face was stern. "We have eleven days until the show opens and eighteen days until it closes. After that we'll sort out the rest of the situation. But until then, our sole objective is to put on the best Christmas show this town has ever seen."

CHAPTER 26

Cece began to feel a sense of order in her life. Her days were scheduled from early morning until late at night. *The Nutcracker* ballet filled her mind every waking moment and most of her sleeping ones as well. She ate when food was put in front of her and didn't care when or what it was. The only things she wanted to do were teach dance and sleep.

On Friday night, five days after Wendy's plan was put into action, Cece got home from the studio especially late. She found Julia and Phil alone in the kitchen lingering over hot tea and dessert.

"Hi," Cece said as she walked in.

"Hey baby-girl," Phil hugged her. "You hungry?"

"Just tired." Cece trudged through the kitchen toward the stairs.

"Don't you want some dinner, honey?" Julia followed her. "I made a pot roast."

"Maybe later."

As Cece walked slowly up the stairs, she could hear the whispers.

"I'm getting very worried about her," Julia said.

"Me too. I've never seen her so . . ."

Cece went into the bathroom and closed the door, shutting out the sound of parental concern.

Cece sat on the couch in the dark and stared into the fireplace. A small fire still burned, and she was mesmerized by the orange and gold embers. She felt numb. She closed her eyes and pictured Doug hiking in the rainforest, cameras hanging from straps around his neck, bug spray glistening on his tanned skin.

Julia came and sat down next to Cece. "Hi sweetie." She handed her a bowl with a small serving of pot roast, vegetables and potatoes. "Just eat what you want."

"Thanks." She took a bite, but couldn't swallow. She had to force the mouthful down.

"I wish there were something I could say to help, Cece, but I know what you're feeling, and I know there's nothing anybody can say to make you happy right now."

Cece appreciated Julia's understanding. "I'm so tired, and I'm so tired of being miserable."

"I know," Julia said.

"The other night when I called him, I really thought we'd . . . we'd get ba . . ." she hiccoughed, "back together." A sob jolted her body.

"Oh honey," Julia said.

"I just want to go to sleep and never wake up."

Julia rubbed her back. "Maybe it's a good thing that you're so preoccupied with the show. Keeps your mind busy. And in a few weeks, you'll be better able to, well, adjust."

"If only I'd never said anything about getting married," Cece said. "That's what started the whole problem, that and my . . . my crazy, controlling, plan-for-everything obsession!"

Julia put her hand on Cece's leg. "You're not being fair to yourself, honey. Sure, you might be a little, oh, uptight you could say, but you did nothing wrong by letting Doug know that you wanted to marry him."

"You don't think so?"

"I don't. Perhaps your timing and method were a little awkward, but it's never wrong for a person to let someone know what she, or he, wants. Especially when you've been together for a while."

Boomer pushed his head onto Cece's lap and sniffed at her bowl. She plucked up a piece of meat with her fingers and fed it to him.

"I guess." Cece scratched Boomer 's ears. "I just need to get through the next couple of weeks. But I hate it that I'm so unhappy, especially around the kids."

"Then don't be."

Cece gave Julia a curious look. "What do you mean?"

"Just what I said. Be happy when you're around the kids."

"But I'm not happy. I'm more sad than I've been in years."

"Doesn't matter. Act like you are. Pretend."

Cece almost laughed. "That's impossible."

Julia looked at Cece with a stern, motherly expression. "It's difficult, yes, but not impossible. And frankly, you owe it to those children. Listen, seven years ago when my husband took off with a younger, prettier version of me, I forced myself to put on a happy face for Ryan. I struggled with it for months, and there were days it nearly killed me. But as time passed, it became less of an effort. And as more time passed, it became less of an act."

A log in the fireplace cracked and fell, sending sparks up the chimney. Cece stared into the red-orange glow. Maybe Julia was right. She leaned into Julia's shoulder and cuddled against her. "I wish my mom had been more like you."

"That's sweet, thank you."

"And I hope that someday, if I ever get to be a mom, that I'm the kind of mom you are."

"Oh goodness," said Julia, working Cece's damp hair into a braid. "There is no doubt in my mind that you will be a mommy one day. And you will be fabulous at it."

CHAPTER 27

Little girls dressed as snowflakes giggled and danced in place as they lined up for inspection. It was their first time trying on their costumes, and they were so excited they could not stand still. Wendy and Robby herded them together.

"Hey, hey, hey!" Robby shouted. "Careful there, you're gonna get 'em dirty! Brooke, Whitney! Don't sit down on the floor!"

"Mith Thee-thee look at me," Olivia broke away from the group and ran into Cece's legs. "I'm a thnowflake!"

Cece knelt down. She held Olivia's hands and spread out her arms. "Let's see your pirouette."

Olivia turned in her little slippers, her wide smile showing off tiny teeth buds breaking through her gums.

Cece laughed. "Excellent, Olivia, just perfect." She stood and clapped her hands at all the snowflakes. "Costume check. Everyone hold still!"

Kendall came in followed by six gray mice. "Come on guys," she said, trying to herd them. "Follow me!"

"Quit pulling on my tail!" a little boy shouted.

The studio erupted in chaos with all the activity. Opening night was in less than a week, and Wendy had recruited a group of mothers to help her check and fit every costume.

It took all weekend to complete the work. But Wendy had organized the schedule and assigned the tasks as expertly as a CEO running a Fortune 500 company.

By mid-afternoon on Sunday, the last of the parents and kids were gone. The costumes safety-pinned with nametags and hanging on four rolling garment racks, billowed on both sides like huge, colorful clouds.

Cece found Natalie in her office. "You want to get some coffee?"

"Oh wow, yes!" Natalie stood and stretched. "Two days of costume fittings, I am exhausted. Thank God for Wendy. She's an organizational genius."

They put on their jackets and stepped out into the cool, afternoon air. The sky was clear and sunny.

"What a beautiful day," Cece commented.

Natalie glanced in her direction. "You seem better.

"I'm working on it." Cece put her hands in her pockets as they walked toward Nutmeg's.

"Have you spoken with your boyfriend?"

Cece bristled at the word 'boyfriend.' "I don't think I would call him that, I think he's officially my ex-boyfriend now. I haven't talked to him since we broke up . . ." Cece sniffled.

"It's okay, Ceece. You don't have to talk about it."

Two boys sped past them on skateboards, and they stepped to the side. "It's not that I don't want to tell you. I'm just sick to death of crying, you know?"

"Yeah, I know," said Natalie.

"But," Cece said, forcing her voice to sound chipper, "the good news that I'm really enjoying the kids. Some of them are pretty special."

"They are, aren't they?" The sound of chirping birds came from Natalie's bag. "Hold on, that's my cell." She rummaged in her purse and pulled out her phone. "Hello?"

Cece stepped away to give Natalie a little space. The afternoon sun was setting in an orange and purple sky, and the Christmas lights all over Main Street twinkled. There wasn't a pole or street lamp or store window that wasn't decorated. Green wreaths adorned with cranberries, colorful ribbons, tiny ornaments, and twinkling lights hung on every door.

"Cece, I'm sorry," Natalie said, "but I've got to go. It's Maria, the caregiver Wendy sent me. She can't find my mother's medicine."

"Don't worry," Cece said. "You go on. I hope everything's okay."

"It'll be fine. I'll see you tomorrow. Have a good night."

"You too." Cece watched Natalie jog back toward the dance studio. She stood still, not sure which way she wanted to go. She had listened to Julia and forced herself to act happy around the children. But nobody said she couldn't wallow when she was by herself. Cece took a few steps toward Nutmeg's. She turned around. Maybe she just wanted to go home. She looked at her watch. It was almost three, and she hadn't eaten since breakfast. Her stomach growled at her.

"Pecan sticky bun, heated, and large hot chocolate, please."

"Whipped cream?" said a cute girl with purple fingernails, dark skin and short, black hair. Cece was relieved to avoid the lustful, teenage boy who usually served her. She and Natalie had shared a good laugh over his request that Natalie play Mrs. Robinson to his Benjamin Braddock.

"Yes, please," Cece said. "Whipped cream on both."

Cece carried her snack to a table in the corner and sat down, relieving her tired legs and feet. She lifted the oversized mug of hot chocolate to her mouth and closed her eyes as she drank.

"Do you know that you got the last sticky bun again?"

Cece's eyes flew open at the sound of Brad Redmond's voice. She put her hot chocolate down.

Brad pointed to his upper lip. "You have some whipped cream on your, um, lip there."

Cece felt her face heat up. She grabbed a paper napkin, wiped her mouth, and tried to contain her discomfiture. "Hello," she said.

"May I sit?" Brad asked, motioning to the empty chair beside her.

"Um, sure," she said, regaining some composure. She moved her plate over a bit.

"Don't worry, I won't knock it over."

Cece laughed. "It's good that you showed up."

Brad's eyebrows rose as he set his coffee on the table. "Really? Why's that?"

"To prevent me from eating this entire thing all by myself. Still carrying silverware in your pocket?"

Brad laughed. "You," he said pointing at her, "have a wicked sense of humor."

"Thank you, I think."

"Absolutely meant as a compliment." Brad went to the counter for a knife and fork then rejoined Cece at the table. "I think I'll search the attic for my old boy scout mess kit with the folding cutlery. Something tells me that it could prove useful."

Cece took the knife from him and cut the sticky bun into pieces. "Number one rule of scouting—be prepared."

"Don't tell me you were a girl scout."

"Of course I was. Little green dress and a sash covered in badges."

"Prima ballerina, girl scout, and straight A's I'll bet," Brad said, taking a bite of the pastry. "Can't imagine your SAT score."

"Very, very high, I assure you." Cece smiled with false bravado. "Quintessential over-achiever and stressed out perfectionist. It's exhausting to be me."

He grinned, and the dimple near the corner of his mouth appeared. "I know the feeling."

Cece was enjoying the banter with Brad Redmond, and she realized that she wasn't forcing herself to act happy at that moment. She actually felt, if not exactly happy, at least not sad. Julia was right—it did get easier.

Brad took a sip of coffee. "I finally figured out, kind of, who you are."

"Who I am?" Cece replied. "What does that mean?"

Brad rested his chin on his fist. "Years ago, the day we signed Dawn up for lessons at the studio, Ilana asked her to dance. Wanted to see if she had any talent, I guess. She put on some music, and my sweet little girl started dancing. I was standing right next to Ilana, and under her breath she whispered, 'just like my Cecilia Rose.' For some reason, what she said stuck in my mind."

Cece looked away. "Ilana was the only person who ever called me that. My mother sometimes called me Cecilia, but only when she was mad at me."

"It's a beautiful name."

Cece lifted a shoulder. "I never liked it. I was so happy when my little brother started talking. He pronounced Cecilia as Cece, and because it is also my initials, it just caught on."

Brad leaned back in his chair and crossed his legs. "Well then, I will call you Cece, or do you prefer Miss Camden?"

"Cece will be fine."

"Good." Brad took another bite of the pastry. "I have to tell you, when you walked into Natalie's office last week, I was, damn, completely stunned."

"Imagine how stunned I was to see you with your lovely wife. And what? Less than a week earlier you had . . . had . . ." Cece stumbled over the words.

" . . . asked you to dinner, as I recall. But I believe I made it clear that Pam is my ex-wife."

"Yes you did. And quite effortlessly, I must say." Cece slid her hand smoothly over the tabletop. "Just slipped it in there without missing a beat. I was impressed."

"Impressed? Good." Brad toyed with his coffee cup. "You've impressed me, but you probably already know that."

Cece looked away. "I'm not so sure." Her heart beat rapidly, and she felt a twinge of guilt, although that seemed ridiculous. She didn't have a boyfriend anymore. She was allowed to be attracted to another man. And Brad Redmond was particularly attractive.

Brad put his elbows on the table and folded his hands. They were large, masculine hands with clean, neatly trimmed nails. "I'm sure about it. Very sure in fact."

His eyes were hazel green, clear and intense, his smile alluring. Cece could feel his gaze on her. She shifted in her seat.

"I'm sorry, I've made you uncomfortable."

"Not at all," Cece fibbed. "I'm just fine."

"Cece," Brad said. "I'm going to take a leap here, which I may regret, but I get the feeling that your situation, your personal situation, may have changed." It was a question hidden in a statement.

Cece swallowed. She tilted her head and began twirling a curl at the base of her neck. "Very perceptive of you."

"So it did?"

She tightened her lips. For a brief moment, she felt her eyes burn, but thankfully, the feeling passed.

The seriousness of Brad's look disappeared, and his eyes softened. "There I go again. The first time we met I ruined your breakfast, and this time I've spoiled your, what is this? Lunch?"

Cece looked at him out of the corner of her eye. "Maybe we should avoid accidentally running into each other."

"Then why don't we run into each other on purpose? Have dinner with me Monday night."

Cece rubbed her palms on her legs and tried to keep her nerves in check. "Monday? Isn't that tomorrow?"

"Yes."

"Um, I don't know if . . . "

"It's just dinner. Nothing more."

Cece lowered her eyelids. *Why the hell not?* "Okay." She looked up at him. "I'll have dinner with you."

CHAPTER 28

"Oh my God, are you kidding me?" Patty shouted through the phone. "Where's Mr. Sticky-buns taking you?"

"Quit calling him that, his name is Brad, and I have no idea." Cece snuggled under a blanket on the couch sipping a cup of tea.

"What are you going to wear?"

"That is a serious problem. I hardly brought any clothes, and I can't exactly go in a leotard and ballet skirt."

"I don't know, that is a good look on you."

Cece laughed. "Right."

"No, I mean it. Accentuates your assets."

Cece rolled her eyes. "I have skinny jeans and boots, and Julia said I could borrow a top from her."

"I hope she has something besides than those flowery, pleasant blouses."

"I do too, otherwise I might end up in one of my brother's flannel shirts."

On Monday night, after spending the entire day and part of the night at the studio, Cece rushed home and cleaned up for her dinner with Brad Redmond. She leaned toward the mirror above her dresser and dabbed on pink lip-gloss. The last time she primped for a date in her childhood bedroom, it was senior prom. She put on the butterfly necklace that Mae had given her. It went well with the dark blue Burberry sweater that Cece selected from the more than ten tops Julia had pulled out for her. It had a simple scoop neck, long sleeves with signature cuffs, and fit just snugly enough to hint at her curves. At first Cece hesitated to borrow something so expensive, but Julia had insisted.

"Don't be silly," Julia said. "It looks amazing on you. Besides I've waited half a lifetime to share my clothes with someone!"

Later the sound of a knock on the door made Cece jump. "I can't believe I'm nervous," she mumbled as she headed downstairs. In the foyer, Cece looked in the mirror, fluffed her hair, and checked her makeup one more time before opening the door.

"Hi." Cece tried to look relaxed as her eyes fell upon Brad. Her thoughts turned to Doug but she shook them away. The man standing in front of her was gorgeous.

"Hello," Brad said. He wore jeans, a white button down shirt, and a charcoal gray North Face jacket. He smiled and presented her with one long stemmed, red rose. "I know it's cliché, but . . ."

"How sweet, thank you." Cece took the flower from him. "Come in."

Brad stepped inside. "Wow, that is one impressive Christmas tree," he said, looking at the giant tree with twinkling white lights and dozens of ornaments.

"I know. My family is really into Christmas."

Brad followed her to the kitchen. "It's been a long time since I picked someone up at her parents' house."

Cece laughed. "Now that I believe." She filled a vase and put the rose in it.

"Do I, uh, have to meet your father or anything, you know, hear the, 'have my daughter home by midnight' speech?"

"Well, hold on a sec . . . Daddy!" Cece leaned on the banister and called upstairs. "Daddy, come down and meet my date!"

Brad's face turned a bit pale, and Cece cracked up.

"Oh, are you an easy target! Nobody's here. They went for pizza."

Brad smirked. "Good one. But just so you know, fathers generally like me. And besides, I make Dawn introduce me to all her suitors."

Cece picked up her coat. Brad took it and held it for her. She slipped her arms in and looked over her shoulder at him. "I'm sure you do," she said, wondering if Ryan ever had been one of them.

They went outside and crossed the driveway. Brad opened the passenger door of his car, a small, black SUV, and Cece slid into the tan leather seat. Her heart beat a little too quickly, her palms grew damp, and she chided herself for feeling like a teenager.

"So where are we going?" Cece asked as Brad started the ignition. "I hope I'm dressed okay."

Brad looked at her out of the corner of his eye and smiled. "You're dressed perfectly." He put his hand on top of hers—the gesture was at once both reassuring and scintillating. "And I hope you're hungry. I'm taking you to a place that serves the best steak in California."

Her nerves began to settle. She leaned back against her seat and tried to relax as they chatted all the way to the restaurant.

"Oh my God, I'm stuffed." Cece pushed her plate away. "That was the most delicious steak I've ever had."

They sat next to each other at a small table close to a fireplace. The restaurant was just outside of Clearwater in a small shopping center with exclusive, expensive looking shops. Inside, the high ceiling boasted exposed beams and massive, iron light fixtures. The fire flickered and popped, and it filled the intimate corner where they sat with a warm, yellow glow.

"I'm glad you liked it," Brad said. He wiped his mouth with a white, cloth napkin.

Cece lifted her wine glass. After two glasses of cabernet, her anxiety had vanished. "And this wine is sensational."

"Comes from a winery right up the road. One of my favorites." Brad tapped his glass against hers. "So tell me more about the gallery—your friends sounds like real characters."

Cece shook her head. "I have talked non-stop this entire meal—it's your turn."

Brad tore a roll in half, buttered a piece and ate it. "Okay. What do you want to know?"

"I want to know," Cece said, taking another drink of wine. She chose her words carefully. "About your family, Dawn and the stunning Mrs. Redmond."

"Ex-Mrs. Redmond," Brad corrected.

"That's right." Cece tightened her lips. "I just have to say, you two look pretty perfect together."

"We were perfect for a while, but things got complicated."

"Long story?"

"Got a few days?"

"I might." Cece said, tilting her head.

Brad refilled the wine glasses. "I'll give you the Cliffs Notes version. But not until we order dessert." He motioned for the waiter. "One apple dumpling, heated, with lots of whipped cream." He winked at Cece. "And extra on the side, please."

When the waiter left them, Cece raised her eyebrows. "You do know how to please a girl, don't you?"

Brad leaned toward her and put a hand on her cheek, his thumb near her lips, his fingers lightly touching her neck. "You have no idea." His kiss was like melted chocolate—smooth, sweet, warm. Cece was unnerved by his move, but she closed her eyes and allowed herself to enjoy it, the first kiss from a man other than Doug in a very long time.

The Cliffs Notes version took only a few minutes. "We met in college, UC Santa Barbara. We were only twenty-one when Pam got pregnant, but completely crazy about each other, so of course we did everything in the wrong order. Had the baby, then finished college, and then got married. Somewhere I fit law school in there while working two jobs. It was insane."

Cece pictured his little family fifteen years ago—the handsome husband, beautiful wife, and darling baby girl. "How'd you end up in Clearwater? Not exactly a mecca for lawyers."

"Pam grew up in Oakland. When Dawn was born, we moved there so her mother could help out while we went to school. One weekend we went on a family outing, got lost, and stumbled into Clearwater. Looked like it'd be a great place to raise our family." Brad sighed. "We were happy then, when Dawn was little and everything revolved around just the three of us. But things change sometimes, even if you don't want them to."

Cece almost said, *don't I know it?* but she stopped herself. "It's sad when the fairytale doesn't end up happily ever after, isn't it?"

"I don't much believe in fairytales," Brad said. "Sorry if that makes me sound cynical."

Cece looked down at her lap. "Yeah, well, me either." She leaned her arms on the table. Her eyes met his. "So what happened, if you don't mind my asking, to your happy ending?"

Brad rubbed the back of his neck. "You know, too much, too soon, too young. We were kids. And, well, we made mistakes."

Cece was not sure what that meant, but she had an idea.

"Anyway, Pam is a good mother. And we work things out, even if we don't agree on everything involving Dawn."

"Parents never agree on everything. Mine sure didn't."

"Exactly. But we both put Dawn first no matter what. Our marriage was over for a long time before we finally split."

The apple dumpling arrived—a big, round crust stuffed with warm, spicy apples—surrounded by mounds of whipped cream. Cece opened her eyes wide, feeling like a child walking into a candy store.

"That looks divine." She picked up her spoon. "May I?"

"You may," Brad said, flashing his smile. Cece liked the way he responded to her, as if she charmed him with every word.

"You know," she said, her mouth full. "Now I can't have a sticky bun all week, not after this dinner."

"Too bad. I was going to accidentally run into you there tomorrow."

"Nuh-uh," Cece said, taking another bite. "Remember we agreed, no more accidental run-ins."

"Oh, that's right. I certainly don't want to spoil any more of your meals."

"Or snacks." Cece put a large bite of apple dumpling loaded with whipped cream in her mouth. "Or desserts."

"Or desserts," Brad said, pushing his spoon into the dumpling. "Do you like this?"

Cece ran her tongue over her lips, licking off the cream. "What do you think?"

"I think you do." Brad touched her hand. "How could you not?"

A shiver ran up Cece's back. Whether it was the wine or the attention, she did not know, only that she loved the feeling. Brad filled her glass again.

"If you keep pouring me wine, I won't be able to walk out of here."

"Then I'll have to carry you."

"And park me on my father's porch in a shopping cart?" she asked, referring to a classic movie scene from the '70s.

"Right!" Brad laughed loudly. "God, you are funny."

"Laughter's good, isn't it? Some days I think that I have to laugh, or else I'd just have to cry."

Brad's face grew serious. "Is that how you feel right now?"

Cece allowed her eyes to wander for a moment, then she looked at Brad. "A little bit." She wondered how a man could be sweet, sympathetic, and sexy all at once.

Brad toyed with the tips of Cece's fingers. "I like you, Cece. A lot. I liked you the very first time we met."

Cece pulled her hand back. "Ah, yes, the time you spilled my coffee. Did I tell you about the really cute dog on the sidewalk that day? He came up and . . ."

"Cece," Brad said, his voice gentle, "I can tell you're not ready for anything . . . serious. That's okay. I'm not going to push you. I just want to spend time with you while you're here, as long as you want that, too."

Cece blinked. She slid her hand back to where it was and touched the tips of his fingers. "I do," she said.

CHAPTER 29

Eight little snowflakes danced their way across the floor in front of the mirror. "Arms up everyone. Bend your elbows! Come on, we've done this a hundred times!" Cece tried to stay upbeat, but she was exhausted. "Brooke, Olivia, Taylor, and Emily, come up front through the middle and then turn. That's right!"

Every day, the studio was in pandemonium with dancers and parents coming and going from mid-morning until seven or eight at night.

Cece helped Kendall with the younger kids every day until Dawn showed up after school, when they would disappear to rehearse the dance of the Sugar Plum Fairy.

Natalie and Wendy had their heads together constantly, juggling every detail of the show while keeping Ilana's situation under the radar. Ever since the day Ilana had her breakdown, the five of them had bonded over the conspiratorial scheme.

Cece picked up a towel and wiped her face. The studio was hot with all the bodies, and she had demonstrated the same *petit fouette'* at least a hundred times. "We need a little break, huh?" Cece said, turning off the music.

"Yeth," said Olivia. "I have to thinkle."

"Me too!" said another tiny snowflake whose name Cece could never remember.

"Okay," Cece said. "But hurry back! Show opens in two days!"

The snowflakes disappeared down the hallway, and Cece went to get water. She bumped into Robby, who was pushing a cart loaded with more than a dozen poinsettia plants.

"What are you doing with those?" Cece asked.

"Natalie wants them all over the place. Not enough that we have the tree and all the lights out front and fake snow sprayed on the windows," Robby said. "Now I have to take care of these." He picked one up and put it close to Cece's face, as if to accentuate the extent of his burden. He put it down. "After I put these around, I'm going to Nutmeg's. Do you want anything?"

"Oh my gosh, yes, you're the best. Get me a large coffee, extra-large, giant size. Thank you, thank you!" Cece gave Robby a sideways hug. She had grown fond of him.

Robby backed away, blushing.

"Did you offer to get Kendall anything?" Cece teased him. "Maybe she'd give you a kiss on the cheek if you did."

His mouth opened. "Wha . . . why'd you say that?"

Cece put a hand on his shoulder. "Oh please, you follow her around like a mouse after cheese, just ask her out already. It's Christmas—everyone wants to be in love this time of year."

Robby's face brightened. "You think she'd go out with me?"

"Never know 'til you ask, Robby. Now please, hurry back with that enormous coffee."

Natalie was sitting at the desk when Cece walked in with two coffees.

"Oh, thank you," Natalie said.

"Thank Robby. He ran to Nutmeg's . . ." Cece looked out the window . . . "in the pouring rain."

Natalie took a long sip. She crumpled something up and dropped it into the wastebasket.

"So how are you doing?" Cece asked.

"Okay." Natalie shuffled some papers on the desk. "Just paying bills. Honestly, I don't know how my mother did it, teaching dance, running her business, taking care of my dad."

Cece recalled how Natalie's father had been sick off and on for years. He died shortly after Cece and Natalie finished high school.

"I don't know what I would have done if you hadn't come back, Cece. Probably would've had a nervous breakdown by now."

"I know," Cece smiled. "How does your mom like the caregiver? What's her name, Maria?"

"Half the time she thinks Maria is her cousin Mary who lives in Scottsdale. So yes, thankfully, she likes her a lot. This whole situation would be almost funny if it weren't killing me. I don't know what's going to happen when everyone around here finds out what's really going on."

Cece understood, and she worried about Natalie and the stability of the dance studio without Ilana. She felt a twinge of guilt. Pretty soon she'd be leaving Natalie and going back to LA.

"If we lose students, I'll be in . . ." Natalie stood up. "I'm sorry, Cece. I don't want to burden you with my worries; you've been a lifesaver already. How's our Sugar Plum Fairy doing?"

"Good, really good. Dawn's an incredible dancer. I think the fact that she's in on the secret about Ilana has made her more, I don't know, committed maybe?"

"I've noticed that, too. And Wendy, wow, talk about rising to the occasion."

"I guess that's another silver lining." Cece said.

Natalie came around the desk to Cece and gave her a big hug. "Listen. Thank you for coming back to work this month. I know I keep saying it, but it's true. To me you're the angel who saved Christmas."

"Hey, you're doing me a favor too, you know. If I weren't working here, I'd be in the unemployment line."

"I'm glad it worked out," Natalie said. "Oh by the way, Pam Redmond called this morning."

Cece's pulse quickened. Just hearing the name Redmond made her think of Brad. Cece found his attention to be a welcome distraction from her heartbreak over Doug, and, admittedly, she enjoyed being with him.

"Pam had compliments for you."

"Really? What did she say?"

"Just that Dawn likes you a lot. I guess she told her mom that you're a great instructor. Nice, huh?"

"Wow, yeah, very." Cece toyed with the lid on her coffee. "I'll tell you this, I sure have a new appreciation for your mother. I never realized how much work it was for her to mold and teach and train us. Ilana really was incredible."

Natalie sighed. She looked beyond Cece to the chart on the wall with all the colored slips of paper stuck to it. "She certainly was."

Dawn and Cece rehearsed alone for over an hour before Gabe showed up. Then they worked together perfecting the *pas de deux*. Cece felt like she could watch them forever, they danced so elegantly, the regal Sugar Plum Fairy and her handsome Cavalier, in one of the most romantic and captivating dances known to ballet.

It was dark when Cece shut off the music. "Great work you two. Don't forget, tomorrow come right from school, and then Thursday is dress rehearsal."

"Okay, Miss Cece," said Gabe, using the younger kids' name for her.

Dawn stuffed her pointe shoes into her bag and shook out her jacket. "Gabe, can you drive me home?"

"My brother took the car. Thought you said your mom was picking up."

"I never said that. I guess we could walk, but it's freezing. Cece, can you drive us?"

Cece looked up. "Sure. Where are you going?"

"Just to my house," Dawn said. "We have to study for a calc test tomorrow."

Cece hesitated a moment. She had no idea if Dawn meant her mother's or her father's. She lived part-time in both. "Um, okay, that's fine. Let's go."

Gabe rode in front with Cece, while Dawn gave her directions from the back seat. She drove up Main Street, past Nutmeg's, and then north, heading in the opposite direction of the Camden house.

"Gabe," Dawn said. "Did you talk to Ryan?"

Cece's ears perked up at the mention of her stepbrother's name. She looked in the rearview mirror at Dawn, who was texting with very fast thumbs.

"I saw him after school." Gabe said.

Dawn raised her head. "You did? He wasn't with that girl again, was he?"

Cece saw Gabe's chest go up as he inhaled. "Nope." His tone was crisp.

"I don't know why he ever hung out with her in the first place, you know?" Dawn said. "She's kind of a skank."

Gabe didn't respond. He looked straight ahead. Cece caught a flash of annoyance in his face. *Oh no,* she thought, *my Cavalier and my Sugar Plum Fairy. And my stepbrother. This can't be good . . .*

"Oops," said Dawn, "we were supposed to turn back there. Sorry."

"No problem." Cece turned the car around. She turned right on a small street lined with attractive, newer homes.

"End of the street," Dawn said pointing in front of her. "Gray house on the left."

Cece pulled into the driveway of a two-story, shingled house at the end of a cul-de-sac. From the outside it looked spacious and well-kempt. She saw Brad in the garage, his head in the trunk of his car. He turned around, looking confused, until he saw Dawn hop out.

"Hi Daddy. What's for dinner? Me and Gabe are starving."

"Gabe and I," Brad said, correcting her grammar. He took a step toward Cece's car. "I'm going to pick up Chinese. How does that sound?"

"I like Chinese," Gabe said, pulling his bag off the back seat. "See you tomorrow Miss Cece, thanks for the ride."

"You're welcome."

Dawn thanked her, threw her ballet bag over her shoulder, and walked into the house with Gabe in tow.

Brad sauntered over to the driver's side window, leaned an arm on the roof of her car and looked in. "You have an uncanny ability to show up at just the right time."

"I do?"

"Yes. I was just thinking about you. Would you like to come in?"

"That might be weird."

"Right. Well, have you had dinner?"

"Not yet."

"Meet me at Ming-Loo's. Do you know where it is?" Brad raised his eyebrows.

"Of course. I've been eating there since I was a kid."

"We'll grab a quick bite, then I'll bring home food for the kids. Go on ahead, I'll be five minutes behind you."

"Um," Cece hesitated. They'd just had dinner together the night before. Two in a row? "Okay."

In the dark glow of red lanterns that lit up the Asian Christmas decorations, Cece sat in a booth with her face behind a tall plastic menu. She hoped no dance moms would see her, because she didn't want anybody to know that she was having dinner with Brad. Not that it was any big deal. Who cared if she went out on a few dates with a handsome man? Besides, Brad Redmond's attention might help to soothe her wounded ego and repair her broken heart.

The waiter came and filled her water glass. "You dine alone?" he asked.

"Oh, um, no. There'll be two of us." Cece motioned to the second glass. The aroma of fried wontons and hot sauce stimulated Cece's taste buds. "Could I have an order of egg roll, please? Just until my friend gets here. Then we'll order dinner."

The waiter disappeared, and Cece texted her father that she'd be home late. Twenty-nine years old, and she was back checking in with Daddy. The egg roll arrived along with hot tea. Cece poured a cup, and sipped.

"Starting without me?"

"Oh," Cece almost burned her tongue. "You startled me!"

Brad scooted into the booth across from her. He picked up an egg roll, dipped it into the sweet, orange sauce, and took a bite. "How'd you know these were my favorites?"

"Because Ming-Loo makes the best egg rolls in all of Northern California." Cece ate hers in three bites.

The waiter took their order, and Brad placed the to-go order at the same time.

"What did you tell Dawn?"

"Just that I had to make a couple of stops first, so it might take me a little longer than usual."

"Guess that's the truth. Sort of."

"Course it is. I didn't say where I was stopping, so this table here counts as a stop, doesn't it?"

"I'd say so." Cece poured Brad some tea.

He picked up the little white cup. "To impulsive acts."

"Impulsive acts?" Cece lifted hers. "What's that about?"

"Well . . . It's about me impulsively asking you out tonight, impulsively canceling a meeting in hopes of seeing you again, impulsively saying things to you without considering the ramifications."

"I don't think you've said anything impulsive."

"Yet."

"Uh-oh. Are you about to?"

"Thinking about it."

"Well then," Cece lifted her shoulders, trying to sound nonchalant, "go ahead."

Brad looked around. He smiled, and Cece caught a glimpse of his dimple.

"I think," he said, "that you're something special, and whenever I see you, even if it's just for a few minutes, I want to be with you more."

Cece looked down into her tea.

"And since I'm being impulsive tonight, I'm just going to put something out there. I haven't been this attracted to somebody in a very, very long time."

Cece's heart raced. Even with his hint of humor, the intent of his words pumped adrenaline into her bloodstream. She swallowed. "You canceled a meeting?"

Brad leaned back and rested an arm over the pink leather seat. He smiled. "A little too impulsive, wasn't it?"

"Canceling a business meeting? Maybe."

"You know what I mean."

Their food arrived—shrimp chow mein, broccoli beef, spicy chicken with green beans.

Cece smiled at the waiter. "Thank you. This looks delicious." She put a small amount of everything on her plate, avoiding Brad's eyes. He seemed almost too good to be true—charming, attentive, and sexy. But she still missed Doug as much as ever.

"Cece, I . . ."

"I really," Cece interrupted, "really enjoy being with you, but it's a little bit, uh, I'm not sure how to put it."

"Too soon?"

"I think so. Yes."

"Okay, I'll keep my impulsive statements to myself."

"Sorry." Cece smiled and started eating.

Brad rubbed his chopsticks together. "However, I still do want to take you to dinner again. I'm thinking Thursday night. I have a place in mind that I know you'll like a lot."

Thursday was only was only two nights away. That would be three dinners in one week. Cece looked up. "It's dress rehearsal night."

"That's okay. We can go when you finish."

"The rehearsal will run until at least 8:30 or 9:00."

"No problem. Dawn will be with her mother that night, so I don't care how late it is. Do you?"

Cece lifted some chow mein noodles with her chopsticks, and looked at Brad. He had on a tight, black cotton shirt that accentuated his strong, broad shoulders. An inkling of desire stirred inside her. "Actually, I don't mind a late dinner." She put the noodles in her mouth.

Brad scooped a serving of broccoli beef onto his plate. "Good. I'll meet you at the dance studio, and we can go from there."

The waiter arrived with the to-go order for the kids, and Brad handed him his credit card.

"This was a real treat tonight," said Cece. "I haven't been here in so long. I'd forgotten how good it is."

"I'm glad you enjoyed it." Brad kept his eyes on her while she continued to eat.

Cece glanced up at him. "Stop, you're making me nervous."

"Okay, okay, sorry," Brad said, returning to his own plate.

The waiter brought the credit card and receipt back to the table with two fortune cookies. Cece finished her dinner and picked up a cookie.

"Do we dare?" she asked.

"What the hell. Live dangerously. You go first."

"No you go first."

"Fine." Brad cracked open his cookie. He ate the broken pieces and straightened out the little slip of paper. "Uh-oh."

"What's it say?"

"It says . . ." Brad frowned in mock seriousness. "*Advancement will come with hard work. Pay close attention to business relationships.* Maybe I shouldn't have cancelled that meeting."

They laughed. Cece opened her cookie and looked at the fortune. She glanced at Brad. "It says: *a tall, dark, handsome stranger will turn your life upside down.*"

"Really? That's your fortune?"

"No silly, I made it up!"

"Guess I deserved that."

"Yes you did," Cece said, smoothing the tiny slip of paper. "Here's what it really says: *Big changes lie ahead, open your heart and mind to something or someone new.*"

Brad's eyes sparkled in the red lantern light. "Now that is one intriguing fortune."

CHAPTER 30

Cece drove home in a quandary. She didn't understand how she could be so attracted Brad when she still was pining for Doug. It made her feel somehow disloyal . . . to both of them.

She entered through the back door and saw Phil, Tom, and Julia sitting at the table finishing dinner.

"Hi guys." Cece sat with her family. "Tommy, do you really have your own apartment?" She flashed a smile at her brother.

"Yeah," Tom said. "But when I moved out of here three years ago, Julia said I could come back for dinner anytime I wanted."

Julia put a hand on Tom's arm. "And we love having you here, honey."

Tom looked at Cece. "See?" he said, his mouth full.

"Tom," Phil said. "Get Cece a wine glass, would you?"

Tom stood. He went to the kitchen and returned and put the glass in front of her.

"So, Ceece, I hear you had dinner with Brad Redmond last night."

Cece frowned. It sounded like an accusation.

"Who had dinner with Brad Redmond?" Phil asked, pouring wine into Cece's glass.

Tom took a large swallow of Corona. "Cece did."

Phil looked at Cece. "You did?"

Cece ignored her father. "How do you know about that, Tommy?"

Julia got up. "Phil, I need some help in the kitchen."

"Huh? But I'm still . . ."

Julia squeezed Phil's arm. "I need you in the kitchen, honey."

Phil gave Julia a confused look, but he followed her as instructed. Cece was grateful they had left her and Tommy alone.

"What's going on with you?" Cece asked.

"Nothin'. I just think you've been in LA for so long you forgot what it's like to be in a small town."

"Believe me," Cece said. "I have not forgotten."

Tom filled his mouth, chewed and swallowed. He looked at his sister. "Friend of mine tends bar at the restaurant you were at. She texted me."

Cece shook her head. "So big deal, we went out to dinner. He's nice."

"Nice . . . suppose you could say that." Tom licked his fork. "And here I thought you were nursing a broken heart. Typical."

Cece eyed her brother. "What's that supposed to mean?"

"Like you don't know?"

Cece tried to think of a sharp retort but came up empty. She studied her brother's face. "You know, when we were kids I figured something out about you. Whenever you act like an ass, like you are now, it's because of something that has something to do with something else."

Tom shrugged. "All I'm saying is, what about Doug?" His tone dripped with disapproval.

Cece felt her temper flare. "What about him, Tom?"

"Is that all it takes to get over the love of your life? Some good-looking guy in a suit, buying you dinner?"

Cece sat for a moment and said nothing. A slight smile formed at the edges of her lips. "Wait. This isn't about me. It's about you and what's her name, isn't it? The hot little waitress you used to date. Moved on, has she?"

Tom's jaw tightened. "You could say that."

Cece laughed. "Holy shit, got herself a new boyfriend already?"

"Fiancé," said Tom.

"Fiancé?" Cece sobered. "Jesus, you guys only broke up a few months ago."

"Yup." Tom stretched his arms. "Ran into her yesterday. She couldn't wait to flash her diamond at me; even thanked me for breaking up with her, said if we were together they never would've met. She made a point to tell me she's going to be a doctor's wife." Tom shook his head.

Cece winced. *Doug had said something similar. If we were together I wouldn't have taken the job . . .*

Cece patted her brother's hand. "Sorry about that."

Tom shrugged. "Oh well, never would've worked out anyways. And all I'm saying to you is . . . small town, be careful."

Julia and Phil came back to the table.

"We didn't really like her." Julia whispered in Cece's ear.

"I heard that Julia," Tom said.

"Well we didn't; she was too . . . too controlling. Right Phil?"

Phil sat. "Her, um, looks kinda made up for that."

"Phil!"

Tom finished his beer. "I gotta go. My landlord asked me to help him hang his Christmas lights."

He kissed Julia's cheek, hugged his father, and punched Cece's upper arm. "Listen, sis, I won't tell anyone about Brad. But if you are trying to keep it quiet, good luck with that. Everybody knows everyone's business around here, that's just how it is."

Julia handed Cece a stack of plates from the dishwasher, and Cece put them in the cupboard. "Do you think it was wrong of me to go out with someone?" she asked. "Like it's too soon or something? I mean, should I be wallowing more?"

"Absolutely not." Julia wiped the table with a towel. "Going to dinner with another man doesn't mean you've forgotten Doug, or that you don't still love him. It's just a distraction."

Cece leaned against the counter and twisted a ringlet of hair. "But I do like Brad Redmond."

"Of course you do. He's charming. And gorgeous."

"You know him?"

"Not really, but I've seen him around. And I think his daughter has a crush on Ryan."

Cece went to work on another curl. "Yeah, I heard something about that the other day. How do you know about it?"

"I'm a cyber-stalker. Ryan leaves for school and never logs out of his profile page. It is so easy for a clever mother like me to snoop online—those kids have no idea."

"I guess." Cece shook her head. "Does Ryan like Dawn?"

"That, I'm not sure about." Julia filled a kettle with water and put it over a flame. "Get the tea, honey."

Cece looked through the boxes of tea bags in the pantry. She turned back to Julia. "I haven't forgotten Doug, you know. Not at all."

"Of course you haven't. And you probably never will. We remember our first loves forever."

Cece looked at her stepmother. "Are you talking about Ryan's dad?"

"Heavens no, my high-school sweetheart. I was crazy about him."
She laughed. "Ancient history now. Anyway honey, you'll have Doug
in your head for a long time. Even when you're attracted to other
men."

Cece chewed on a chipped fingernail. "I am attracted to Brad, I
mean really attracted. Does that, I don't know, make me shallow?
Maybe Tommy's right, how can I still love and miss Doug, which I do,
but have these feelings for someone else?"

"Because nothing compares to new."

"What do you mean?"

Julia opened the tea bags. "Attention from a man is so . . . so
flattering and fun, especially somebody different. Gets all those crazy
hormones pumping."

Cece recalled how she felt the first time she met Brad at Nutmeg's.
She was attracted to him even then. And she and Doug were still
together at the time. "So I shouldn't feel guilty going out with him?
That's what you're saying?"

The kettle whistled, and Julia poured the boiling water into the
mugs. She bobbed the tea bags up and down. "That's what I'm saying.
For heaven's sake, you had one dinner."

"Two."

"Two?" Julia said.

"We had dinner tonight, kinda last minute." Cece blushed. "I
drove Dawn home, and he was there. Asked me to meet him at Ming-
Loo's. It was great."

Julia waved a hand. "Okay, two dinners then." She set the mugs of
tea on the table, and they sat across from each other. "You are a
young, beautiful, single woman, and you don't have to explain
anything to anyone. Go out with Brad while you're here, and have a
wonderful time with him. He does know that you're going back to Los
Angeles, doesn't he?"

"Yes, he knows."

"So it is what it is—a little romp for the both of you. Sort of like a
summer fling, just at holiday time."

Cece sipped her tea. *A holiday fling.* What Julia said made perfect
sense.

CHAPTER 31

For two days, Cece and Natalie could barely come up for air as the countdown to opening night began. On Thursday afternoon, dress rehearsal started early, went for hours, and ended in chaos.

"Kyle! What are you doing? Let go of Travis!" Cece rushed onto the stage to pull apart two young boys—one of the mice and one of the soldiers.

Robby wrapped a long arm around Kyle's middle and pulled him off of Travis.

"He pulled my tail!" Kyle cried.

Robby unhooked the tail from Kyle's backside and put him back on the floor. "I'm taking this before the entire costume is ruined."

"Dammit Travis! Leave your brother alone!" Their mother jumped into the fray, wrangling her two sons and dragging them away.

"Cece!" Kendall hollered. "Can you come here and help the snowflakes?"

Cece looked back stage to see a dozen little snowflakes squirming, some of them crying, some of them giggling.

"Mith Thee-Thee, I'm sthuck!" Olivia had herself twisted up in the sequined bodice of her costume, as did several others.

"It's scratchy!" another little snowflake cried.

"Hold on girls," Cece said. "We'll help you. Don't pull or you'll tear the costumes."

Cece, and Kendall went to work getting the girls undressed and the costumes on hangers. Robby helped the boys on the other side of a curtain, while Wendy was careful to safety pin the nametags back on before hanging the costumes up. Natalie stood with a clipboard in the middle of the room talking to the two Claras. As the dancers left one by one, the theater cleared out until only Natalie and Cece were left. They collapsed into front row seats.

"Well," Natalie heaved a sigh of relief. "That went better than I thought it would."

"Really?" asked Cece. "I thought it was kind of hectic."

Natalie shook her head. "You should've been here last spring when we did Peter Pan. Somebody knocked the whole box of Tinkerbell's magic fairy dust out of the rafters, and it gave half the kids on stage sneezing attacks. What a disaster that was."

Cece laughed. "I can imagine. Well . . . tomorrow's our big night. Think we're ready?"

"You know? I think we are."

"Me too." Cece checked her watch. She was meeting Brad at the studio for their late dinner date.

Natalie looked at Cece with an expression of curious amusement. "Is there some reason you keep checking the time?"

"Oh, no, not really, I'm just, well, I have a . . ."

"Date with Brad Redmond?"

Cece felt like she'd been caught with her hand in the cookie jar. "This is why I love Los Angeles. Nobody knows anything about you, and if somebody does know something, they're much too self-absorbed to care."

Natalie stretched out her long legs. "Hey, it's okay with me. I'm thinking he might be just the thing that keeps you in Clearwater."

"Keeps me in Clearwater? What are you talking about?"

Natalie gave Cece curious look. "Don't tell me you haven't heard. Everyone's asking if you're our new assistant director."

Cece had heard, but she ignored the gossip. "That's ridiculous. I'm going back to LA."

"Can't blame anyone for wondering," Natalie said.

Natalie got up. She walked onto the stage and over to the Christmas tree, a thick, six-foot Douglas fir decorated with old fashioned candles, huge red bows, and swooping rows of silver garlands. She leaned over and unplugged the fake candles.

"I hope I don't seem unappreciative, Natalie." Cece looked up at her friend. "I've loved working with you."

Natalie gave her sad smile. "No, of course not." She walked down the three steps on the side of the stage. "It's just that, to be honest, I'd love it if you did stay. My mother, even if she does get better, will never be what she used to be."

"I'm sorry." Cece felt terrible. "But . . . but my life is in LA."

"I know it is."

They went out the back exit into a misty night.

Natalie tucked her hand into Cece's arm and bumped into her like she used to do when they were young. "But if you change your mind, the job is yours."

She said it with a laugh, but Cece knew that she meant it. They stopped at the corner to let a car pass. Cece looked at the fresh pine wreaths with twinkling white lights that hung on the street lamps up and down Main Street. Clearwater at Christmas was a magical sight.

"And as far as your dating Brad Redmond . . ."

"I'm not dating him! We've just gone out a couple of times."

"Okay," Natalie said, putting an arm over Cece's shoulder. "I'm just reminding you what it's like here. Small town gossip is unavoidable. That's why my love-life is far away."

Cece turned to her old friend as they crossed the street. "Your love life? You have one?"

Natalie laughed. "I do, and it is in the city, far away from the gossip mill in this town."

"Do tell," Cece said, intrigued.

"He's older, divorced, grown children. Very uncomplicated and low maintenance."

"Sounds perfect."

"Perfect? Nothing is ever perfect. But it works for us."

They went into the office where Natalie unlocked a cabinet, which housed a small refrigerator.

"You do have a few secrets, don't you?" said Cece.

"Doesn't everyone?" Natalie lifted the cover on the mini freezer and pulled out a bottle of vodka.

Cece smiled. "Stolichnaya? Nice."

"I am Russian, you know." Natalie poured the ice-cold vodka into two cut crystal glasses. She handed one to Cece. "To Tchaikovsky."

"To Tchaikovsky." Cece clinked her glass against Natalie's, and the crystal made a tinkling sound, like the ringing of a bell.

Brad pulled up in his SUV as Cece was putting her dance bag into her trunk. She locked her car and jumped into his. "Woo, it's freezing out there," she said.

Brad smiled and looked at Cece with warm eyes. "Hi," he said, his voice low and relaxed. "You look nice."

"Thanks." Cece had changed into jeans, flat black boots, and a white, nubbly sweater.

"So, how did rehearsal go?" Brad asked.

"Good. Exhausting. The Beckwith brothers got into it again." Cece pulled her seatbelt over her shoulder. "Pretty chaotic, but I think we're ready for tomorrow night."

"And my daughter? Did she show up on time?"

"She did. Danced beautifully, as expected."

"Good." Brad leaned toward her. His lips touched hers, and she felt the warm, moist softness of his mouth. "You," Brad licked his lips, "have had a drink. Vodka maybe?"

"Stoli." Cece giggled. "It's Russian."

"It certainly is," Brad said. "I like it." He kissed her again, leaving Cece short of breath.

Brad backed his car out of the parking lot, turned the corner, and headed down Main Street. "I'm taking you clear out of Clearwater tonight, okay?"

Cece leaned back against the leather seat. "Absolutely."

They drove for over a half an hour, deep into Napa Valley. Brad parked and looked at her. "This will be fun."

They got out of the car. He took Cece's hand and guided her into a noisy, crowded bar inside of a renovated barn. There was a band on a small stage in the front playing "Hotel California."

"I love this place," Brad shouted. "Great food, and I never run into anybody I know!"

Cece squeezed Brad's hand. How did he know that Cece needed to disappear? The hostess seated them at a round table tucked into a dimly lit corner. Large candles burned on every table and in sconces on the walls.

"Kinda like a haunted house." Cece looked around, as she scooted into the single, curved, dark red leather booth.

"Are you scared?"

"Me? No way, I love haunted houses. My favorite ride at Disneyland."

"No kidding? Mine too."

The waiter came, and Brad ordered.

"Two vodka martinis, please, dry with extra olives." He looked at Cece. "Okay if I order your dinner for you?"

She nodded. "That'd be great."

Brad looked back at the waiter and shouted. "Two classic burgers and a side of sweet potato fries."

It sounded delicious, and Cece felt her stomach gurgle. "You must think I eat enough to feed a horse."

He leaned closer. "What? I didn't hear you."

She repeated it.

Brad put an arm over the back of the booth. "It's refreshing. Do you have any idea how boring it is to take a woman out and all she orders is green salad with dressing on the side?"

Cece laughed. "Can't say that I do. I come from a long line of very big eaters."

The waiter came with their drinks, cool, clear liquid filled to the edges of large, frosty martini glasses. Cece leaned over and took a sip. "Oh yum," she said. "So good."

Brad tapped his glass to hers. "To opening night," he said.

"Ah, yes," Cece said, returning the tap. "To opening night."

They drank and talked and sang with the band until the waiter brought them their enormous hamburgers and a bucket of fries.

"This looks fabulous!" Cece ate a fry. Then she had a few more. "These are the best. It is so hard to find good sweet potato fries in LA."

Brad ordered a glass of Pinot Noir for them to share.

Cece ate, and drank, with abandon.

"How do you like it?" Brad asked.

She looked up, her mouth full. "So . . . so, so good!"

The band returned from a break, and the female vocalist took the mike. She had blond hair cut short and wore tight jeans, a red tank top and cowboy boots.

"Isn't she cute?" Cece asked.

Brad gave the singer an appraising look. "Not nearly as cute as you."

Oh Jesus, Cece thought, *did I set him up for that?*

She bumped him with her shoulder and drank some wine.

"We've had a request!" the singer said. She had a strong voice and a southern drawl. "From this gentleman right here in front. He and his lovely wife are celebratin' their anniversary!"

Everyone applauded.

"How many years y'all been married?" the singer asked, holding the microphone out in front of her.

"For twenty-two years," the man said, "I've been married to my high-school sweetheart, the love of my life!"

"Isn't that the sweetest thing ever?" Cece said.

Brad nodded. "Pretty sweet."

"Twenty-two years! How 'bout that folks," the singer said. She stepped back. "And she is "still the one!"

The music swelled behind her. The band played "You're Still the One." It sounded as if Shania Twain herself was singing.

Cece swallowed hard.

You're still the one that I love, the only one I dream of . . .

The pain in her gut caught her by surprise, and she put a hand over her mouth.

"Going to the bathroom!" Cece shouted to Brad above the music.

She scooted out of the booth and maneuvered through the crowd of drinkers and dancers singing the song that made her heart ache. The thought of Doug and how much she missed him made her feel dizzy.

The bathroom was crowded, and she waited in line for a stall. A large woman bumped into her, a young girl stood too close, two teenagers argued with each other . . .

Cece went into the stall. She stayed put until her stomach settled. When she felt certain that she wouldn't be sick, she exited and washed her hands. The icy water made her hands cold, but she liked the feeling of something going numb. In the mirror, she saw that her makeup was smeared. She wiped underneath her eyes with the corner of a paper towel and applied a touchup of black eye pencil. Then she freshened her blush, and lipstick. There was no way she would let Brad see her upset.

As she made her way back, the band was playing *"Oh What a Night."*

Cece smiled. "Much better," she said aloud.

Brad looked up as she approached. She gave him a confident smile, picked up her martini, and drank. She sat.

"Almost empty," she said, putting the glass on the table.

"You want another?"

"Yes, please," she said.

"Want to share a bowl of chili, too?" He motioned to the server to bring two more drinks.

"Oh my God, no, I couldn't eat another bite." She picked up a couple of fries and held them out. "You have to finish these." He ate them from her hand.

"Wait," Brad said, taking hold of her hand. "Ketchup." He licked the tip of her finger, his tongue lingering. It sent chills up the back of Cece's neck. She picked up her martini, downed the last drop of it, and turned her face toward his.

He leaned in and kissed her. She felt the tip of his tongue brush over her lips. Whether it was the vodka, the sensuality of his kiss, or both, Cece didn't care. She pushed Doug out of her head. Her lips parted, and Brad responded, putting his hands on her cheeks and gently pulling her toward him.

The sound of throat clearing interrupted them. "Here you go," the server said as he put two fresh martinis on the table."

"Ah, great," said Brad. "Thank you."

They laughed, clinked their glasses, and drank.

"This is the best drink I've ever had," Cece said. She took a big swallow of it.

"You're kinda supposed to sip it," Brad said.

"That so? What if I prefer to gulp it?"

Brad's green eyes reflected the candlelight. "Then you can do that, too. Whatever pleases you . . ." he rested his hand on her thigh, "pleases me."

Cece caught her breath and drank more, feeling the cold, spicy vodka fill her mouth and run down her throat. She gazed at Brad over the rim of her glass.

"But maybe you ought to slow down just a little." Brad's expression held a hint of concern.

"I don' think so," Cece said. Getting drunk was working just fine. It made her carefree, uninhibited. "I can sleep late t'morrow."

"That's good," Brad said. "'Cause you'll need to."

Cece moved closer to him. "You . . . you're nice."

Brad rolled his eyes. "Oh, that's just great."

"What?"

"Come on, you know nice guys finish last."

Cece ran a finger around the edge of her martini glass. "That's not necessarily a bad thing."

"No?" Brad's smile looked tempting, seductive. "How's that?"

"Depends wha' they're doin'." Cece realized her words screamed innuendo. She drank again.

Brad rested his chin in his hand. "You're killing me, Cece. You have no idea."

She placed her hand on his knee. "Di' you know tha' you are a good kisser?" Cece could hear her words slurring.

"You think so?"

"Uh-huh," she said, stretching the word.

"Would you like more kisses then?"

"Uh-huh," she said again.

Brad lifted her chin with one finger. He put his mouth next to her ear. She felt his breath on her skin. "Good," he said.

She shivered as his fingers moved her hair out of the way and his lips brushed over her ear to the soft skin behind it. He kissed her there, and she felt the light touch of his tongue, cool and wet. Cece leaned her head to the side and allowed his kiss to trail down her neck as his hand slipped underneath her shirt and around the curves of her back.

CHAPTER 32

Cece woke up with a headache that reminded her of her 21st birthday. Boomer, snoring loudly, was sprawled over more than half the bed. She glanced at the clock—only a little past nine, and she didn't have to be at the studio until three. Cece turned over, threw an arm around Boomer, and went back to sleep.

At noon, her cell phone rang. Cece grabbed it and opened one eye to see that Patty was calling.

"Hey."

"Hey yourself. Did I wake you?"

"Kinda. It's okay, I gotta get up."

"How was last night?"

Cece put a hand over her eyes to shield them from the light. She felt nauseated. "Oh yeah, last night. It was . . . good."

"Drank too much, did you?"

"I did. Way too much."

Patty laughed, and it made Cece's head throb.

"So tell me, did he sweep you off your feet?"

Cece sat up. "Kind of." She pushed back her covers, disturbing Boomer, who jumped off the bed and trotted out.

"Did you . . ."

"No Patty. He did drive me all the way home, though."

"Do you really like him?"

"Do I like him?" Cece pinched her eyebrows together to relieve the pain, but it didn't work. "Yeah, we have a great time together."

"I hear a 'but' coming," Patty said.

Cece sighed. "But it's not going anywhere, Patty. I'll be home in a couple of weeks, so there's no point in getting all excited about a few dinners."

A fleeting memory made Cece shiver. She recalled the feel of his lips on her neck and his hand on her back.

"Oh, hey," Patty said, interrupting her thoughts. "I almost forgot— Barbara called. It's looking good for the gallery to reopen in January."

Cece perked up. "Really? That's great. You think Mae got things figured out for her?"

"That, and I'll bet Barbara talked her sister into another infusion of cash."

"Probably," said Cece.

"Come January," Patty said, "everything goes back to normal. I can't wait."

Well, Cece thought, not quite everything . . .

She stood up. Then she sat down. "I'm a little hung-over."

"I can tell," Patty said. "Jealous. I wish I were. I'm bored to death without you."

"Are you going to Texas for Christmas?"

"Still figuring that out."

The sound of hammering hit Cece's ears. "What the hell is that?"

"Someone's building a frame behind me."

"Oh, are you at work?"

"Yeah I'm at work," Patty said. "And shouldn't you be? Doesn't the show open soon?"

"Tonight."

"Tonight? Wow, good luck! Are you excited?"

"Actually, I am."

"Take pictures. And get one of Mr. Sticky-buns and text it to me."

"Yeah, right. Talk to you later. Love you."

"Love you more. Bye!"

After a long shower, many Dixie cups full of water, and some extra-strength Tylenol, Cece got dressed. She tugged her dance pants up, and felt herself having to shimmy into them. *Shit*, she thought, *a little too much holiday cheer.*

Cece headed downstairs. "Hello?" she called. "Anybody here?" She went into the kitchen where Boomer was lying on his bed. He lifted his head.

"Too bad you don't drive, big boy."

Boomer whined as if he agreed. Cece picked up the phone and called her brother.

"Hey Tommy. Where are you?"

"I'm doing a job just east of town. Why?"

Cece squirmed. "I . . . I need a ride to the studio."

"You got car trouble?"

"Um, kinda."

She heard Tom laughing. "I'll be there in twenty minutes."

The cast assembled at the theater three hours before curtain call. Cece looked around for Dawn. She stopped Kendall, who was sitting on the floor painting whiskers on the mice.

"Have you seen Dawn?"

Kendall looked up at Cece. "You know, I did see her, but not in a while. Maybe she's putting on her make up somewhere."

"I just saw her," one of the mice said. "I think she left."

"Left?" Cece felt a surge of panic.

"She went out that way." The little mouse pointed toward a side door that let out into a courtyard.

Cece ran toward the door and threw it open. Outside, she saw Dawn sitting on a bench. She had her arm wrapped around a crying boy. He couldn't have been more than six or seven.

"What's wrong?" Cece asked. The boy was wearing the top half of a soldier costume.

Dawn looked up. "Henry's scared."

Cece exhaled with relief.

"Henry's in my little brother's class at school," Dawn said. "And this is his first show."

Cece's heart melted. She hardly recognized the little boy, but she recognized his fear. "Dawn, why don't you go on in and finish getting ready? I'll take care of Henry."

Dawn stood and smiled at the young dancer. "Don't worry, Henry. Miss Cece will know exactly what to do. She can fix anything."

If only . . . Cece thought.

Henry wiped his eyes with the backs of his hands. Cece sat next to him. She rested a hand on his thin arm.

"Why are you scared, Henry?"

"I . . . I'm scar . . . scared I'll mess up."

"Really?" Cece said. "You know, I totally get that."

"You . . . you do?"

"Sure I do. Let me tell you about the first time I was Clara."

"You were Clara? But you're so old."

Cece laughed. "Well, it was a really, really long time ago . . ."

Cece lost herself in a flurry of kids, costumes, and nervous anticipation. Everyone had poured their hearts into Clearwater's

162

annual Christmas production of *The Nutcracker*. Cece thought about Natalie and how much she had riding on it. If the performances went well, it would make things much easier for her when the situation with Ilana became public knowledge.

A horrible cry coming from the dressing room sent Cece running. Behind the partition, Little Olivia, dressed in her white-as-snow snowflake costume, had blood dripping down her chin onto the front of the sequined bodice. The adorably chubby Emily stood next to her biting down on a trembling lower lip.

"What happened?" Cece tried to hide her horror at the condition of the costume.

Olivia extended her hand and held out a tiny, bloody tooth. "Mith Thee-thee," she sobbed. "Emily crashed into me and . . . and . . . "

"And my hand hit her in the mouth." Emily started to cry, too. "And knocked out her tooth!"

"Look at my costh-tume Mith Thee-thee." Olivia's face scrunched up like she'd eaten a lemon. "I'm thso thsorry!"

"It's okay, honey," Cece said, kneeling down. She hugged Olivia, smearing the little girl's blood on her own white shirt.

"Miss Cece," Emily said. "She can have my costume."

"Oh, Emily, sweetie, don't you worry. We'll get Olivia fixed up. Now, this is important, can you go find Kendall and let her know that everything's okay? Would you do that for me?"

Emily nodded, her face serious. "Yes, Miss Cece." She turned and ran off to complete her mission.

"Robby!" Cece shouted. "I need you!"

Robby, with a mouth full of safety pins and yards of royal blue tulle wrapped around his neck and shoulders, appeared. When he saw Olivia, he spit the pins into his hands. "Oh fu . . . fudgy-wudgy!"

At the sight of the tulle on Robby, Cece momentarily forgot about Olivia. "Oh no, is that . . . "

"Yup, Mother Ginger's skirt tore, but I've got it under control," Robby said. "I'm a magician with safety pins."

"Wha . . . what about me?" Olivia asked.

"Oh, yeah, Olivia," said Robby. "It's all good. I'll work my magic and *poof!* you'll have a fresh snowflake costume." He turned and trotted away, dragging a train of blue tulle behind him.

Cece sat on the floor and looked at Olivia. "Come here, sweetie."

With her shoulders still quivering, Olivia sat in Cece's lap.

"Where's your tooth?"

Olivia opened up her fist.

"Wow. Is the tooth fairy going to come for it?"

"Uh-huhhh," Olivia sniveled.

"Then we don't want to lose it. How about I hold it for you until after the show, okay?" She plucked the little tooth from Olivia's palm.

Olivia nodded. "Do you think Robby will make me a new costhtume?"

Cece boosted Olivia off of her lap and got up. "I'm sure of it!"

Olivia smiled her toothless smile.

Behind the heavy velvet curtains, stage left, Natalie and Cece stood together. The first dancers, comprising of the Party Guests, the Maid and Butler, and the Stalhbaum family, lined up in order, chirping excitedly.

"Okay, you guys," Natalie whispered, fixing Fritz's twisted suspender. "This is it, almost curtain time. You all look fabulous. And I'm so proud of you!" She had tears in her eyes as she turned to Cece. "Thank you. I could never have pulled this off without you."

Cece's eyes burned. "I'm glad I'm here, Nat. I really am."

The overture swelled, the curtains opened, the lights came up, and as her dancers took the stage, Cece realized that she felt happy. Truly happy.

CHAPTER 33

One performance ran into the next. Each show was thrilling, nerve-racking, and heartwarming. There were mistakes, mishaps, and missed cues, but far more triumph and joy than anything else.

For three days straight, Cece and Natalie lived between the studio and the theater. Following each performance, they reviewed performance notes like football coaches after a game, making changes and adjustments.

"Let's tell the Mouse King to touch the Nutcracker with his sword," Natalie said. "It looks too fake when he just puts it near him."

"Agreed," Cece said, adding the memo to her "To Do" list.

On Sunday afternoon, after the matinee, they sat on the couch in the office with their feet up.

"I may never move again," Natalie said.

"Me neither, three shows in two and half days. Was it this hard when we were younger?"

"God no," Natalie said, kicking off her shoes. "We're just old now."

Cece leaned her head back and looked at the ceiling. "Could you believe Dawn's dancing? She was spectacular."

"Thanks to you."

"Yeah, well." Cece laughed. "I'll take a modicum of credit."

Natalie pulled her legs underneath her and turned to Cece. "When Dawn first started dancing with us, like five or six years ago, my mom was watching her. She took my arm and said, *'Natalia, one day dat one vill be our Sugar Plum Fairy.'*"

165

"Whoa, you sounded exactly like her. Kinda creepy."

Natalie gazed toward the old armoire that held Ilana's memory books. "I really hope her doctor can give us some kind of pill that helps. I don't know how I'll keep the studio going without her."

"You'll be fine, Natalie. You're smart and talented, good with the parents, definitely good with the business side of things. And the kids practically worship you."

Natalie took a deep breath. "It's just so much work. And without my mom, I feel like the magic is missing."

Cece wanted to say that it wasn't so, but it was. The Lurensky Dance Academy was not the same without Ilana.

"And you know, she's my partner, the only one who truly understands what this place means to me."

Cece squeezed Natalie's hand. "I think I understand."

Natalie gave her sad smile. "You know, I think you do."

The clock on the wall chimed. It was six. "You want to go get some dinner together?" Cece asked.

Natalie stood and stretched her arms and back. "Actually, I'm going to the city."

"You are?"

"Yeah, just for dinner . . ."

Cece gave her a sidelong glance. "How long have you been seeing this mystery man?"

"Three years."

"Really? That's a long time." It was the same amount of time that she and Doug were together. "And no plans to, you know, take the next step?"

Natalie went to the desk and thumbed through a stack of mail that had piled up over the last week. She pursed her lips. "No. He won't ever marry again."

"But you stay with him?"

"I do. We broke up one time, because he thought I shouldn't give up the dream of marriage and babies."

Cece leaned forward. "And now you have?"

"Maybe. I don't know. Not sure I'm even cut out to be a mom." She tossed a few envelopes in the trash. "I'm not like you that way."

"Like me? What are you talking about?"

"Remember your stroller?"

"My stroller?"

"Yes!" Natalie laughed, a full, joyful laugh. "That play stroller you had? You used to stuff it with dolls and walk down Main Street pretending to be the mommy."

"Oh my God!" Cece said, picturing herself. "I did do that, didn't I? What an idiot I must've looked like."

Natalie sobered. "No. You didn't at all. Actually, it was . . . it was so you."

"So me? Come on."

Natalie straightened her back and looked at Cece quizzically. "You don't remember much of our childhood, do you?"

Cece thought about her mother and the havoc her affairs wreaked on their family. "There's a lot I choose to forget."

"Yeah, well, okay. But remember what you always said whenever someone asked what you wanted to be when you grew up?"

Cece looked at the ceiling. She remembered vividly. "I said, 'First I am going to be a ballerina and then I am going to be a mommy.'" Cece could almost hear a clock ticking inside of her. "I blew the ballerina part, didn't I?"

Natalie pushed her feet back into her shoes. "You will be a mommy one day, Ceece. And a freakin' great one, too."

Cece wound her hair up on top of her head and secured it with a large clip. She recalled that Julia had said the same thing. "I hope so."

They got up and put on their coats. Cece put an arm around Natalie's waist.

"I have to tell you, putting on the Clearwater Christmas show has been a lot more fun than I thought it would be."

They walked through the main studio, passing the Christmas tree in the corner, the poinsettias placed all around the room, and the windows framed with twinkling white lights.

Outside on the porch, Natalie locked the door, and they headed back toward the theater where their cars were parked. On the corner, as the street lamp flickered and a cold wind whipped around them, Natalie turned and faced Cece.

"I want you to know something," Natalie said.

"Okay," Cece looked at her friend. "What?"

"I was never the dancer you were. I worked my ass off trying to make my mother as proud of me as she was of you. I'm not saying this to make you feel bad, Cece. You had more talent, the perfect ballet body. Jesus, even your feet were the right size."

Natalie laughed, but Cece could see tears clinging to her long, black lashes.

"And when we were, what, sixteen, and you quit dancing, part of me was happy. Finally, my competition was gone. And I could be the star."

Cece shifted her feet. A deep confession was not what she expected.

Natalie looked to the sky. "But you know what? It didn't happen. When you left, my dancing diminished, and it wasn't because I got lazy without the competition. I just felt . . . uninspired." Natalie wiped the tears off her cheeks with her hand. "I'm sorry, I know it sounds ridiculous."

"It doesn't," said Cece. She thought about how she had no desire to paint anymore. Not since Doug. "It doesn't at all."

"Anyway, these last few weeks with you here, I have a feeling inside that I haven't felt in a long time, a renewed energy. It's like that old glimmer is back."

"Maybe it's the Christmas lights all over town," Cece said, trying to lighten the mood.

Natalie pursed her lips and shook her head. "Nope. Christmas decorations come out every year. The only thing I have that's different this time is you."

CHAPTER 34

"I'm home," Cece shouted as she walked into the kitchen Sunday evening. Her entire family had attended the matinee, and were waiting for her.

"There she is!" Phil, wearing an old apron, swooped her into a big bear hug. "We are so proud of you. The show was spectacular!"

Julia rushed her as well. "Oh my God, best Nutcracker we've seen in years honey, and I'm not just saying that."

Cece swelled with pride. Her family had watched it on Sunday so they could all be together, and it had been the best performance so far.

Tom walked in, his face red from the cold. "Hey sis. Show was great. Really great, congratulations." He gave Cece a big bear hug. "And Ryan, how about that Sugarplum? You've got good taste." He gave Ryan playful slug on the arm.

"She's not my girlfriend," Ryan said, his mouth full of potato chips. "I keep telling you that."

Phil put a fatherly arm around Ryan. "You know, Tom can help you out with that if you want. He's got quite a way with the ladies."

"Stop it you two, you're embarrassing him," Cece said, trying to stifle a laugh.

"We are not." Tom put Ryan in a headlock. "Are we Ry?"

"Go away," Ryan said wriggling free. "I'm hungry, Mom. When's dinner?"

Julia pulled a pan of lasagna from the oven and placed it on a trivet in the middle of the table. "Right now, honey."

The five of them sat down to the family meal.

"So," Julia said, "no show tomorrow?"

Cece blew on a fork full of hot lasagna. "Right. We take Monday off. Then we'll have a full dress rehearsal again on Tuesday, to rehearse a couple of changes, and then shows the rest of the week."

"All the way through Christmas?" Phil asked. "That Natalie's a real slave driver isn't she?"

"The last show's on Friday, Daddy, the day before Christmas Eve."

Julia served Ryan a second serving of lasagna. "That's right. And I have tickets for the closing show. We're all going again, including you, Tom."

"I have to go again?"

Cece punched him. "Don't you want to?"

"Do you have any idea how many times I've sat through *The Nutcracker*?"

Phil put down his wine glass. "Not as many as I have, son."

Cece gave her father a look.

"But I've enjoyed it every time, baby girl, every single time."

It was after ten when Cece awoke. She meandered into the kitchen wearing her purple robe and a pair of sweat socks she found in the clean laundry pile. She poured herself a cup of coffee. It appeared that nobody was home, which she appreciated. A lazy morning was exactly what she needed.

She made herself a piece of toast and jam and sat down with her Christmas gift list. She had gifts for almost everyone thanks to the items Barbara had given her. Only a few things left, and she would pick those up today. Her cell chimed. It was Natalie calling.

"Hey there."

"Good morning. I didn't wake you, did I?"

"No, I'm up. What are you doing?"

"I'm heading out to the dry cleaner's with a few costumes that need stains removed. I wonder if you could do me a favor."

Cece drank some coffee. "Sure," she said, thinking it had something to do with the show.

"Could you run over to my mother's house?"

Cece gripped her phone. "Um, yeah. Anything wrong?"

"Probably not, but Maria, you know the caregiver? She just called and said my mom's disoriented."

"More than usual?" Cece asked. Ilana was confused most of the time now.

"I'm not sure, but it makes me nervous. Anyway, I'm almost to the cleaner's. I'll drop off the costumes and come right back. I'd just feel better if Maria had some help until I get there."

"No problem."

"Thanks Ceece."

"You're welcome." Cece stood and took her dishes to the sink. "I'll leave here in ten minutes."

"You're a lifesaver. Oh, and I hope I didn't flip you out last night, you know, with my confession."

"Not at all, Natalie."

"Good. Thanks Cece. See you in a bit."

"Right. Bye."

Cece put down her phone. She took a deep breath and went upstairs to get ready for her visit to Ilana Lurensky.

Cece knocked on the door of the yellow, ranch style house. She couldn't remember the last time she'd stood there.

Quick, heavy footsteps approached. The door opened a crack, and a slightly built, older Hispanic woman greeted her.

"*Bueno?*"

"Maria? I'm Cece, Natalie asked me to stop by."

Maria pulled the door open and ushered Cece in. "*Si, gracias.* Senora not so good today."

She followed Maria into the living room where Ilana sat wearing a pink, silk robe and staring blankly at the wall. Cece approached her. She wondered if it was more serious than Natalie had thought.

"Ilana? How are you feeling?"

She looked at Cece, and her face lit up. "Cecilia, you are here. Natalia!" she called loudly. "Cecilia here to play. Come!" She turned back to Cece. "Cecilia, you should vant to eat. I make you a grill cheese, yes?"

"No thank you, Ilana," Cece looked at Maria. "How long has she been so disoriented?"

"One hour, two maybe. This morning she tired. Now she confused. She think I her cousin."

"Has she had her medication?"

"*Si.* I give her this morning."

Ilana stood. "Petrov? Vhere are you?" She began speaking Russian.

Cece could not understand a word, but she could tell that Ilana was searching for her dead husband, Petrov.

"Maybe she need to see doctor," Maria said, standing beside Ilana with a worried frown.

Ilana stepped toward Cece, still rambling in Russian. Then she switched to English.

"Cecilia Rose, vhere is your mamma? I call her to talk but I not hear back. Too busy vith all those men, I tink!"

Cece cringed. Even the confused Ilana remembered her mother's affairs. "Maria, do you have the doctor's number?"

"*Si*, I have right here." Maria picked up a pad of paper. "I go call from other room."

Cece took Ilana's arm and coaxed her back to the couch. They sat next to each other, their legs touching. Ilana had stopped looking for her dead husband, and her face took on a grave expression. She picked up Cece's hand and looked at her with penetrating eyes.

"Cecilia, you vill go to San Francisco. You vill dance vith the company. Then vee send you to New York, maybe London."

Ilana's voice was calm. She smoothed Cece's hair and cupped her cheek with a cool hand, and Cece felt herself transported back half a lifetime ago.

"I vill miss you, my dear, but your talent is too much now, you grow beyond vat I can do." A single tear rolled down Ilana's cheek. "Cecilia Rose, you vill be a shining star."

Cece tried to stop her own tears, but she couldn't. What would her life have been like if she hadn't quit ballet?

"Yes, Miss Ilana, I'll go. And I will make you proud of me."

Ilana moved Cece's hair out of her eyes and kissed her forehead. "My dear, you make me proud every day, every dance, since you vere a little girl."

Cece hugged her beloved teacher and mentor. She felt Ilana's arms around her. Ilana, who seemed frail and thin, held her with an embrace full of strength and comfort.

Maria returned and tapped Cece's shoulder. "The doctor say to bring her," she whispered.

Cece disentangled herself from Ilana's arms. She looked into the woman's watery blue eyes.

"Ilana," she said softly. "You need to get dressed. Natalie is going to take you to see the doctor."

"Vhy?"

"Just to check your medication. Make sure everything's right."

"Very vell. Ve go to see de doctor. But first I must give Petrov his lunch."

Oh no, Cece thought, *she's really losing it.*

They stood up, and Cece felt something swishing around her ankles. "Holy shit!" She nearly jumped out of her skin.

A huge, white Persian cat looked up at her. "Meowwwww..."

"Petrov!" Ilana's voice was cheerful. "Dere you are, my boy." She scooped the cat into her arms and carried him into the kitchen, speaking to him in Russian the entire way.

CHAPTER 35

Cece and Natalie sat at Nutmeg's on Tuesday afternoon before rehearsal. With only three performances left, Friday's closing show sold out, and Christmas in five days, Cece could be back in LA in less than a week.

She sipped at her steaming black coffee. "So how'd it go with your mom and the doctor yesterday?"

"Pretty well," Natalie said, lifting her foamy latte. "He changed her prescriptions again. I'm hoping they'll work better than the last regimen she was on."

"Well, it's only been one day. Probably takes some time."

Natalie nodded. "Right. But she does seem a little better to me already. Maybe I'm just being overly optimistic."

"Can't blame you. She certainly made perfect sense once I realized she was talking to the cat and not to your dad."

Natalie laughed.

Cece shook her head side to side. "Can't believe she named her cat Petrov. A little bit eccentric, don't you think?"

"My mother is many things, and eccentric tops the list. Her explanation is that she missed saying my father's name after he died." Natalie shrugged.

Cece stretched her back and shoulders. Her return to the world of dance was straining her muscles.

"So, what's happening with you," Natalie asked. "Any more late night dinners with the handsome Mr. Redmond?"

Cece glanced around Nutmeg's, half expecting Brad to pop up. "Actually I haven't heard from him." Cece thought about their last dinner together—the drinks and the kisses and his hand on her back. "I might've freaked him out though. Drank a teensy bit too much last time, might've said some embarrassing stuff."

"It would take a lot more than that to scare him off. He's into you."

"What are you talking about?"

"Didn't you see him at Sunday's show? Whenever Dawn was off-stage, he was staring at you."

"How do you know?"

"I know because I saw him. You were sitting between the wall and the curtain directing the snowflakes, and I was further back. I was at the perfect angle to see him. And he was at the perfect angle to see you."

Cece brushed it off. "That's ridiculous. And if that were the case, why haven't I heard from him?"

As if in answer to the question, Cece's cell vibrated. She glanced down. "Speak of the devil."

Natalie winked at her. "Told you so."

His call was an apology for not calling sooner and an invitation to dinner that night.

As she shampooed her hair, she calculated the number of times they'd been out. The fabulous steak, the impulsive trip to Ming's, and the bar where she drank too much. Three dates, not counting the times they bumped into each other at Nutmeg's.

Cece soaped her legs and started to shave. *Dinner number four,* she thought. *He probably expects me to sleep with him by now.* She smiled and switched legs. *Might have done it the other night if I hadn't gotten so drunk.* She shaved under her arms. *Maybe tonight, maybe, maybe, maybe.*

There was no denying that she found Brad Redmond desirable, and sleeping with him would probably be amazing, but she was a relationship kind of girl. Every man she had been with, and there hadn't been very many, had been her boyfriend first.

She stood, closed her eyes, and enjoyed the feeling of hot water running through her long hair, over her shoulders, and down her back.

She got out of the shower, grabbed her towel, and looked at herself in the medicine cabinet mirror. "You're twenty-nine," she said to herself. "What are you waiting for?"

Her cell buzzed. She answered and put it on speaker.

"Hi Patty."

"Hi Ceece."

"What are you doing?"

"Stalking this really cute guy on online. He ordered a frame the other day, so I snagged a copy of the receipt to get his name. I'm looking at all his Facebook photos."

Cece laughed and dried her feet. "You're dangerous."

"I know. Oh, wow, just found a link to his webpage. He must be a model or something . . . shit, he's a god . . . I'm sending you the link."

"So that I can stalk him, too? You and I are going to end up in jail together someday."

"I hope so," Patty said. "What are you doing?"

"Getting ready to go out."

"Really? Another date with sticky-buns?"

"Dinner number four."

"Hope you shaved your legs." Patty teased her.

"Yes . . . I did."

"Pits, too?"

"Patty, Jesus . . ." Cece laughed.

"Well, I'm just trying to figure out where you're going with this. So, are you planning to . . . "

"I don't know." Cece wrapped the towel around her body and went to her room, taking the phone with her. "Maybe, if the opportunity arises.

"Believe me, it's gonna *arise* for sure," Patty laughed.

"You are a sick little girl, missy. I gotta go."

"Call me after. I don't care what time it is."

"Maybe."

"Fine. And look at that link I sent. His pictures will get you going for sure."

"You're disgusting."

"I try. Talk later. Bye."

Cece tossed her phone onto the bed and got dressed. She put on a pair of black jeans and another shirt borrowed from Julia—a cream colored, gauzy thing with long sleeves. It was funky, but sexy with a low cut, scoop neck that showed a generous slip of cleavage. She stood in front of the full-length mirror on the back of her bedroom door. A slight smile formed around the edges of her mouth. *Not bad,* she thought. She spritzed a touch of cologne and went downstairs.

Phil was at back door putting on his jacket.

"Where are you going?" Cece asked.

"I'm meeting Julia at the hospital. We're delivering Christmas presents to the children's wing."

Cece put her coat on a chair. "That's so sweet."

"Yeah, it's nice." Phil looked at Cece. "You going out?"

She grinned at her father. "Out to dinner."

"Uh-huh . . . " Phil smiled at his daughter. "Good. I'm glad you're having some fun. And you look very pretty." He kissed the top of her head. "Oh, don't lock the door when you leave. Ryan'll be back soon, and he never remembers his key."

"Okay. See you later."

"G'bye, baby girl."

Cece stood at the counter and organized her oversized purse into a small, red leather Crossbody bag. She dropped a lipstick on the floor and bent down to pick it up. As she stood, Ryan's laptop caught her eye. It was sitting open on the kitchen table. She finished organizing, closed her purse, and sat down at the computer.

It had been weeks since she'd done anything online. She logged in so that she could take a peek at Patty's latest obsession, but when her profile page appeared, a photo jumped out at her. It was from a party she and Doug had gone to over a month ago, and the picture was of the two of them standing with another couple and laughing as if someone had just told a joke.

Her fingers hesitated over the keyboard as she contemplated opening the album their friend had posted. She turned to look at the clock on the wall. Fifteen minutes until Brad would get there. With a shaking finger, she clicked.

Scrolling through dozens of photos, Cece took deep, calm breaths. Three weeks had passed since the night they broke up. Cece couldn't even remember who broke up with whom or who was at fault or how everything unraveled so quickly. But seeing the pictures reminded her of how much they both had lost.

Part torture, part catharsis, she continued. She and Doug were in the background of dozens of pictures, holding hands, leaning against each other, smiling at one another. She stopped on a candid in which she was talking to somebody, and Doug was standing off to the side. He was looking at her, although she didn't know it at the time, with a slight smile and adoring eyes, soulful, brown eyes that Cece knew so well. Eyes that revealed every emotion, from love to heartache.

Her throat felt like it was closing, and Cece almost choked. "This is so stupid," she said "Why are you doing this?"

She shook her head and closed the laptop with a slap of her hand. "Shit."

Cece grabbed a tissue, and held it to the corners of her eyes. For the next five minutes, she chastised herself for even looking at the pictures. She went to the refrigerator to see if there was an open bottle of wine. None. She opted for a glass of Ryan's chocolate milk. By the time Brad arrived, she had her emotions in check.

They walked down a quiet, tree-lined street in St. Helena, a small town in Napa with old inns, wineries, and spas. They had just eaten at a romantic French bistro.

"You okay?" Brad asked.

"Of course, why?"

"You seem kinda quiet tonight."

Cece looked up at him and smiled. "Just tired. I think all these rehearsals and performances are a little draining for me."

That much was true. Cece felt like she was running a marathon that she hadn't trained for in advance.

It was cold and windy outside, and the air smelled of fresh pine and fireplaces burning.

Brad picked up Cece's gloved hand. He pulled her glove off slowly, deliberately, finger by finger. He lifted her hand to his lips and kissed it. Then he wrapped his own hand around hers and tucked it inside his coat pocket.

"Is there any chance you'll stay through New Year's? I have to go to this party, one of my clients throws a huge bash every year, and I, uh, need a date."

"You need a date?"

"Not really. I want a date. And I want that date to be you."

Cece moved her hand around in his pocket, feeling his warm skin against hers. "I don't know yet."

Her tentative plan was to leave right after Christmas. But being in LA alone for New Year's would be miserable. She and Doug had had a tradition. They would go to his brother's house in San Diego for a clambake. Afterwards they always spent the night at a cozy bed and breakfast near the beach.

"I might still be here."

"Just keep it in mind and let me know later."

They turned the corner, and an older couple bundled in heavy coats passed by slowly.

"Evening," the old man said. "Nice night."

"Yes sir," Brad responded. "Merry Christmas."

"Merry Christmas," the husband and wife replied together.

The brief interaction touched Cece. How romantic it must be to grow old with the love of your life. Doug's face flashed through her mind. She untangled her hand and pulled it out of Brad's pocket.

"What's wrong?"

"Um, where's my glove?" The red, cashmere gloves, a gift from Doug.

"Right here." Brad handed it to her. "I wasn't going to lose it."

"I know. I . . . I just wanted to put it back on."

"Okay." They continued walking. Stars sparkled in a cloudless sky.

"Are you cold?" Brad put an arm around her shoulder. He pulled her close, and her body involuntarily stiffened.

Brad stopped and turned to face her. He furrowed his brow. "What just happened here?"

Cece forced a smile. "Nothing."

"Really? I might be a guy, but I'm not completely dense."

Cece bristled. "It's nothing, Doug—" she caught herself, "Brad."

Brad said nothing for several seconds. "Did you just call me Doug?"

Cece felt hot in spite of the freezing temperature. "I can't believe I did that. I'm so sorry, it's just that I was . . . I wanted my glove because . . ." tears filled her eyes, and she turned away.

"Hey, hey." Brad wrapped his arms around her. "It's okay. Doug's a good name."

Hearing Brad say Doug's name only made her cry more. "I . . . I'm so embarrassed."

He turned her around. Cece looked up at him.

"Did you know you cry black tears?" Brad teased.

Cece laughed and cried at the same time. "Oh, I must be a mess."

"If I were a true gentleman, I'd have a handkerchief in my pocket to give you."

Cece fished through her purse. "I don't even have a tissue." She wiped her eyes with her glove, smearing mascara onto the red cashmere.

Brad pulled her toward him and wrapped her inside of his black, wool coat. "Come on, let's get inside."

Cece sniffled against him like a child, while he guided her toward an espresso bar down the block. Brad opened the door, and warm air greeted them. They walked past an old-fashioned Christmas tree garlanded with strings of popcorn and fresh cranberries. A guitarist sat on a stool singing "White Christmas."

Brad pulled out a chair. "Sit," he said. "Coffee or tea?"

She sat and slipped off her coat. "Tea."

Brad went to the counter, and Cece dropped her head into her hands. She pulled a few napkins from the holder and blew her nose. With another napkin, she wiped underneath her eyes to remove the mascara smears.

"I must look like shit," she said to herself.

"Not really."

She looked up to see Brad standing over her holding a teapot and two mugs.

"If there were a hole full of quicksand here, I'd jump in."

"Then I'd just have to rescue you. And I'm wearing my good shoes."

Cece laughed, even though it hurt. Brad set the tea on the table and poured. The waitress brought over a large lemon square and placed it between them.

"No sticky buns here," Brad said. "I hope you like lemon bars."

Cece nodded and sniffled. "I love them."

Brad took a sip of tea and put it down. "You want to tell me who Doug is? Although I probably can guess."

"I can't believe I cried in front of you."

"Don't worry, I'm used to it. I have a teenage daughter, you know."

Cece straightened her back, forcing herself to pull it together. She did not want to be reminding Brad of his daughter.

"I feel the need to review," he said.

Cece blew her nose again. "What do you mean?"

"If I recall correctly, the first time we met, you said you were in a relationship. Then a week later you were back in Clearwater and, evidently, not in a relationship."

"Yes," Cece said, avoiding his eyes. "That pretty much sums it up." She nibbled a bite of lemon bar.

"So what happened?"

Cece circled the rim of her cup with one finger. "We, we just weren't on the same page about some . . . some stuff."

"That's vague."

Cece lifted her shoulders and brushed a strand of hair out of her eyes. "There's nothing more to say. We just . . ." Cece closed her eyes. Her hands were shaking. "We weren't in agreement about something. Something big."

"I see." Brad took a bite of the lemon bar, and Cece watched him chew. She could see him ruminating. He crossed his arms and leaned them on the table. "I'm going to guess, then, that one of you wanted to take it to the next level, and one of you didn't."

Cece took a deep breath. She wiped her mouth with a napkin. "Right." There was an edge to her voice that she hadn't intended.

Brad scooted his chair back and turned to the side, crossing his legs. His laugh was almost cynical.

"I don't want to play games, Cece. I'm too old for that." His dark eyes focused on hers.

Cece looked at him directly. "I'm not playing games, Brad. It was a horrible breakup, and I . . ." she cleared her throat. "I don't really want to talk about it."

"Do you want to get back together with him?"

Cece swallowed hard. There was no good answer to that question. "Why . . . why would you ask me that?"

"Because I want to know."

Cece took a breath. She considered telling Brad that she was sorry, but it was none of his business. She licked her lips and spoke softly. "You know I'm going back to LA, so what difference does it make?

Brad looked away. He inhaled through his nose, and a Cece caught a fleeting look of irritation, or hurt perhaps, in his expression. She felt awful.

"Brad," she picked up his hand. "The show closes in two days. I need to go home. I have to get back to my life."

Brad squeezed her hand. He opened his mouth as if to say something. But then he closed it, changing his mind. He smiled, and his relaxed, confident face returned. He stood. "Do you mind if we leave? I have an early appointment tomorrow morning."

CHAPTER 36

Cece balanced the phone against her shoulder, pulled on her pajama pants, and got into bed.

"And then we left," she said to Patty.

"Just small talk the whole way home?" Patty asked. "That was it?"

"Pretty much. And some very awkward silence." Cece said. "It was like he just flipped a switch. But come on, why would he ask me about Doug?"

"Because he really likes you, that's why."

Cece could not deny that he did. She was the one with ambivalent feelings.

"And because he needs to know his competition. It's a guy thing. Just like those elephant seals you told me about."

True, Cece thought. She pictured the gigantic male bellowing and attacking the other males to keep them away. "Are you saying Brad is like an elephant seal?"

"I hope so. It's very masculine and gladiator-like."

Cece laughed. "All right missy, simmer down. Unless you're expecting a visitor."

"Unfortunately I'm not. Oh, hey, you'll be home for New Year's, right? One of my new buddies at the framing place invited us to a party."

Cece shifted the phone to her other ear. "I'm not sure. Brad asked me to go to a party with him. Although now . . ."

"No! Please come home. I miss you so much."

Cece sighed. "Maybe—let me see how the next few days go. I'm too exhausted to make any decisions right now. Call me from Texas, okay."

"Shooore thang," Patty said in her best southern drawl.

Natalie was distressed that Wednesday night's performance was not well attended. Cece noticed that many parents did not attend, including Brad.

Cece and Wendy were sitting next to each other on the sofa in the office going over ticket sales, while Natalie reviewed her notes from the performance.

"I wonder if I scheduled too many shows," Natalie said.

Cece shook her head. "It's probably just a middle of the week lag, Nat. And tomorrow's the last day of school before Christmas break."

Wendy pulled out a spreadsheet. "Look here, Natalie, tomorrow night we're eighty percent full, and Friday's closing show is sold out. We'll be fine."

Natalie gave Wendy a grateful smile. "Thanks Wendy, you have been so much help to me, you have no idea. And thanks for managing the rumor mill about my mother."

"You're welcome, but people know something's wrong with her, Natalie," Wendy said. "She hasn't been at even one of the shows."

Cece listened without comment. It was a delicate subject.

Natalie leaned back in her chair. "Might be time for me address the elephant in the room, huh?"

"I think so," said Wendy.

Natalie looked at Cece. "What do you think?"

"I think," Cece chose her words carefully, "that people imagine things to be worse than they are when they are kept in the dark. Parents need to know that Lurensky Dance Academy is going to be just fine. No matter what."

Wendy pointed a finger at Cece. "I like this one," she said to Natalie. "Can we keep her?"

Natalie winked at Cece. "I wish."

Thursday night was a disaster. The Mouse King rolled his ankle and couldn't finish his dance. The Beckwith brothers got into another fight, and Cece found Dawn backstage crying right before her big number.

After the show, as everyone was leaving, Cece saw Dawn sobbing into her father's shirt. Brad, patting his daughter on the back as if she were a baby, caught Cece's eye and smirked as if to say: "See? Told you I'm used to it."

Cece returned the smile, then looked away. They hadn't spoken in two days, and her embarrassment had not subsided. His New Year's Eve invitation remained unanswered, and Cece wondered if he wanted to rescind it. *What's wrong with me*, she thought as she continued to glance at him with Dawn. *Such a handsome, enticing man, a dream come true for any woman. What am I waiting for?*

Cece glanced back at Brad. Dawn's mother had joined her ex-husband, and the two of them comforted their daughter together. Mother and father whispered to one another, and Cece drew back, feeling like an intruder. She turned and walked toward the exit.

As she reached the door, an arm brushed against her and opened it for her. "May I walk you to your car?"

She jumped and looked over her shoulder to see Brad behind her. "Sure," she said, putting on a smile that belied her discomfort. "Dawn okay?"

Brad sighed. "Crying over some boy again."

"Sorry to hear that," Cece said, hoping it had nothing to do with Ryan.

They took a few steps toward the corner, and Cece noticed for the umpteenth time the town's abundance of holiday decorations. "Did you ever decorate your house?" she asked.

"What?"

"The first time we met at Nutmeg's, we were drinking coffee outside, and the workmen started putting wreaths on the street lamps. You said that you wanted to decorate your house this year."

"I did?"

Cece nodded. She tucked her hands into her pockets. "So did you?"

"No."

"Why not?"

Brad shrugged. "I don't know. Dawn spends most of Christmas with her mom, and I'm, well, I'm not home that much."

Cece looked up at him. She felt a rush of emotion, and this time it had nothing to do with Doug. "I'm sorry about last night."

"Hey, no, I'm the one who should apologize. I . . . I got a little ahead of myself."

They continued walking.

"I'm thinking about staying for New Year's," Cece said. "So if you still want me to go to that party with you . . ."

"I do," he said. "I'd love it."

Cece looked up at him. His profile was perfect. "I just need to find something to wear. And then tell Patty of course. She'll be upset. She's very attached to me."

"I don't blame her," Brad said with a suggestive smile. "Listen, you can let me know. New Year's is still nine days away. "

"I don't want to leave you hanging."

"Don't worry. It's not like there's anyone else waiting to be asked."

Cece laughed. "That cannot be true."

"Well, maybe a few women are pursuing me, but I'm a little caught up with something else right now."

They rounded the corner onto the quiet side street where Cece had parked. Brad leaned against her car. Cece stood in front of him and put her hands on his shoulders. Brad wrapped his arms around her waist and pulled her closer. Looking into her eyes, he slipped his hands underneath her sweater. He rubbed her lower back, and Cece felt the heat of his skin on hers. She leaned against him, her body pressed against his, and felt him adjust his hips.

"Uncomfortable?" she asked.

"That's not exactly the word I'd use."

Cece kissed him, softly at first, then harder.

"Shit," Brad said. "I really wish I weren't such a nice a guy."

"I've kind of been wishing the same thing," Cece said.

Brad kissed her neck, his tongue tracing a line downward to where it curved into her shoulder. His hand slid up her back along the side of her waist and around to the front.

"What are you wearing?" Brad laughed.

Cece laughed, too. "It's my workout bra. Sorry."

"You are adorable." Brad bent her backwards and kissed her like Rhett Butler kissing Scarlet O'Hara. Cece shivered, feeling as if she had been swept off her feet into a romance novel.

Holiday fling, Cece thought, *here I am!*

CHAPTER 37

With standing room only, the theater turned into a flurry of excitement as the entire town of Clearwater poured inside. Nobody wanted to miss the final performance. Backstage in the dressing room the performers darted back and forth as they readied themselves for the closing show. Cece looked around. She grabbed Robby's arm as he ran past her.

"Have you seen Natalie?"

Robby shook his head and sped off.

"Cece!"

Cece breathed a sigh of relief. She turned around to see Natalie hurrying toward her. To Cece's surprise, she had Ilana by her side, Maria trailing closely behind.

"We're here," Natalie said, exhaling audibly, "finally."

Ilana looked tired, but other than that, just like herself. Cece hugged her. "I'm so glad to see you."

"Vell, I could not miss de closing show, my dear." Ilana wandered off as if she belonged there, Maria following her like a protective shadow.

"She seems better, Natalie."

"Yeah, a little, but I brought Maria just in case."

"Good idea."

Cece felt a light touch on her arm. She turned. "Dawn, hi. You look magnificent."

"I'm sorry about last night, Cece. I know I let you down."

Cece rested her hands on Dawn's shoulders. "You did not let me down. Besides, last night's performance is over, and I want you to forget about it. Tonight, beautiful girl, you will be amazing." She kissed Dawn's forehead the exact same way Ilana used to kiss hers.

To Cece's surprise, Dawn threw her arms around Cece's neck and held onto her. "I wish you didn't have to go back to LA. I'm really going to miss you."

Cece felt her eyes burn. "Me too, Dawn."

Dawn released her. "You will be proud of me tonight. I promise."

Cece picked up a few strands of hair that had fallen from Dawn's bun and put them in place. "I already am, sweetie."

Dawn gave her delighted smile. "Thanks." She turned with a fluid, graceful step and pirouetted back to her friends.

"Hey sis!"

"Tommy?" she turned toward her brother. "What's the matter? Don't you have a seat?"

"Yeah, but I need to talk to you for sec. Come here." He motioned with a curved finger, and she followed him to stage left.

Cece's mouth dropped open. "Patty!"

Patty jumped on Cece, practically knocking her over. They squeezed each other until Cece ran out of air.

"What are you doing here? I thought you were going to Texas!"

"I was, but I changed my mind. My parents have five other kids and eleven grandchildren. They won't even miss me!"

"Lucky me!" Cece said.

"That's right lucky you. So here I am!"

Cece gave her best friend a tearful smile. "I'm so happy to see you."

"Me too, Ceece. You know I'm lost without you. And I'm dying to see this show, among other things . . ."

Cece smacked Patty on her little rear end. "Naughty girl. Go take your seat, and I'll see you afterwards."

"But wait, where is . . . ?"

"Come on you, let's go." Tom intervened. He winked at Cece then wrapped an arm around Patty and swooped her away.

Cece stood between the curtains, clinging to the fabric, as Dawn, utterly resplendent in a lilac tutu, satin, strapless, sequined bodice, and sparkling tiara, took her place on stage. She was the queen of the land of sweets, presenting her kingdom to her guests. Dawn danced exquisitely, bringing applause from the audience at several turns. She held herself with regal authority, yet her face portrayed the queen's generosity and kindness.

From her spot just off stage, Cece glanced at Brad. He was sitting next to his ex-wife in the third row, watching his daughter with a proud, beaming smile. Seeing them together reminded Cece of what a beautiful couple they must have been. She turned her attention back to Dawn, who pirouetted *en pointe* with quick, precise steps, her arms as graceful as wings, and a smile that lit up the stage.

Cece felt Natalie standing next to her. She looked at her friend and saw tears in her eyes. "She's spectacular," Natalie whispered.

Cece nodded, wiping away her own tears. "Yes she is."

They put their arms around each other and watched Dawn finish her solo. The audience rose to its feet, and a deafening roar filled the theater. Clearwater hadn't seen a Sugar Plum Fairy so glorious and captivating since the days of Cecilia Rose.

Cece's entire family, including Patty, swarmed around her. With her arms loaded with bunches of flowers, Cece accepted hugs and kisses and congratulations from everyone.

Mothers, fathers, grandparents, and friends of the performers stopped Cece to tell her how wonderful the show was. Off to the side, Ilana greeted all of Clearwater as if she were as lucid as ever. But Cece could see confusion hiding behind the plastered-on smile.

"Excuse me," Cece said to the crowd around her. She handed her flowers to Julia and went to Ilana's side. "You doing okay, Ilana?"

Ilana turned. She blinked, and the blank stare disappeared as she recognized Cece. "Cecilia, de names of all dees people. I cannot remember. I know dem, but . . ." she clasped Cece's hand. Cece turned to Maria. "I'll stay with her," she whispered. "Come with me, Ilana. I'll help you remember."

"Tank you my dahling." Ilana looked up into Cece's eyes, her smile warm. "Ah, Cecilia Rose, you dance like an angel tonight, my dear. An enchanting angel."

CHAPTER 38

"Here, wrap this one." Cece handed Patty another bracelet.

It was Christmas Eve, and the two of them sat on the floor in Cece's bedroom surveying the items that Barbara had given them on the day they had closed up The Art Stop.

"I've got enough bracelets for every little girl at the studio." Cece held up one that was almost all pink. "This one's for Olivia."

Patty glanced at her through slanted eyes. "They're growing on you, aren't they?"

"Who?"

"The kids. Olivia, Gabe, Dawn . . . you haven't talked about anything else all day." Patty pulled a long piece of ribbon off the spool and snipped it with sharp scissors.

"I know what you're thinking, Patty, and I'm not that attached. On January 2nd, you and I are hittin' the road back to Southern California." Cece pinched Patty's cheek.

"Good. 'Cause I won't go back without you." Patty smiled at her best friend. "Hey, did you tell Natalie about what Ilana said last night?"

"Yeah, I did this morning. She wasn't surprised. The doctors said that Ilana's grip on reality would fluctuate." Cece tied a green and red bow. "I'm nervous for her. Some of those dance moms are nuts—when they find out what's been going on, it won't be pretty."

"Girls!" Julia voice floated upstairs. "Lunch is ready!"

Patty's face lit up. "This is the best. I feel like I'm twelve years old again!"

The two of them bounded downstairs like little kids on Christmas morning.

They spent the rest of the day in the kitchen preparing food for the annual Camden Christmas open house. They expected dozens of friends to come by for champagne, eggnog, and Julia's famous cooking.

The sun was just setting when Phil drove up with Tom and Ryan. Tom had a few last minute holiday lights jobs, and Phil, who normally took Christmas Eve off, helped him finish. On their way home, they picked up Ryan from his father's house.

"What's to eat around here, Mom?" Ryan grabbed a few cookies off a big platter that Julia was arranging. She slapped his hand.

"Nah, those are for tomorrow. Didn't your father feed you?"

"Yeah, but I'm hungry again. I'm always hungry."

Tom grabbed Ryan in a great bear hug and pretended to punch his shoulder. "That's what happens when puberty kicks in, big guy."

Ryan blushed. "Puberty kicked in four years ago. How long is it supposed to last?"

"Don't you worry, Ryan," Cece said. "Tommy's only giving you a hard time because his voice squeaked until he was twenty."

"It did not," Tom said, purposely raising his voice.

Phil came in carrying a bottle of wine as if it were a newborn baby. "2006, Silver Oak, Cabernet Sauvignon. Been saving this one for a special occasion!"

The family sat down at the long farm table in the kitchen set with a straw placemats and big white dinner plates. Cece and Patty helped Julia dish up her traditional Christmas Eve spaghetti and meatball dinner. Cece inhaled deeply and sighed. She looked at her family, her amazing, wonderful, wacky family, and her heart swelled. Everyone in the world that she loved was with her, close enough for her to touch, hug, and kiss. Almost everyone.

"There are enough presents under that tree for the entire town," Julia said. "What did you girls do, rob a store?"

Phil and Julia sat on the couch drinking tea with Boomer snuggled between them. Patty and Cece were on the floor beside the Christmas tree arranging the gifts. Ryan and Tom had gone upstairs to watch a movie.

"Let's just say we stumbled into a great sale," Cece said, giving Patty an ironic smile.

Boomer lifted his head and let out a soft bark. He jumped off the couch, padded to the front door, and perked up his ears. At the sound of a knock, the dog barked and jumped up.

Cece stood. "I'll get it." She pushed Boomer aside and opened the door.

"Hi there," Brad said, standing on the front porch holding a big pink bakery box. He smiled his irresistible smile, dimple and all.

Cece stepped outside, closing the door behind her. "Hi yourself. What are you doing here?"

"I tried calling, but I kept getting your voicemail."

"Oh, I'm sorry. My phone's upstairs charging. I didn't hear it."

"No big deal. Just wanted to bring you some sticky buns for Christmas morning." He held out the bakery box.

Cece's eyes lit up. "You do know how to please a girl, don't you?"

Brad grinned. "Didn't you say that to me once before?"

"I believe I did. And I liked your response."

He put the box down on the swing and pulled Cece into his arms. His lips, cold from the night air, pushed against hers. His hand went to the back of her head, and he wound his fingers into her hair. Cece caught her breath, as his smooth, cool tongue slipped around hers.

Brad groaned. "How long are you going to make me wait?"

Cece heard a note of jest in his voice. She leaned back and looked into his expectant eyes. "Rhetorically or literally?"

Brad laughed. "I'll take either."

"Why don't you come in?"

"Nobody's home?" His tone was hopeful

"Everyone's home."

"Well, shoot," he said with exaggerated disappointment.

"Sorry. But come in anyway."

"I shouldn't. I'm heading out to my sister's in Santa Rosa."

"You are?"

"Yep. She feels sorry for me, doesn't want me to be alone on Christmas."

Cece toyed with his fingers. She didn't want him to be alone either. "Just come in for a minute. Nobody's going to bite you."

Brad picked up the box. "I wouldn't mind if you did."

Cece slapped his arm. "Oh, Patty's here. She might bite. She's not very well behaved."

Cece pushed open the front door. Boomer greeted Brad by jumping up and almost knocking the box out of his hands.

"Oops." Cece rescued the box and put it on the side table beside the front door. "Forgot about the dog. He's not so well behaved either."

Patty leapt to her feet as they entered the living room.

"Dad, Julia, this is Brad."

"Hello," Phil got up from the couch, hand extended. "Phil Camden."

"Nice to meet you, Phil," Brad said, shaking his hand.

"My wife, Julia," Phil said.

Julia got up and welcomed him with a warm smile. "I'm so happy to finally meet you, Brad."

"Thank you, Julia, likewise."

"And this," Cece said, extending her arm with a flourish, "is Patty."

The corners of Brad's mouth turned upwards into an amused smile. "Ah, the roommate. I've heard about you."

Patty nearly fell over herself. Her mouth dropped open as she stared at Brad.

Cece rolled her eyes. "Told you—she has terrible manners."

Brad was unruffled. "Very nice to meet you, Patty."

"This is Mr. Sticky-buns?" Patty said, her jaw hanging.

"Excuse me?" Brad said.

"Patty!" Cece wanted to crawl into hole.

"Did she just call me Mr. Sticky-buns?" Brad asked Cece.

"Daddy, would you get Brad a drink?"

"Of course. How about some scotch on the rocks, Brad?"

Brad looked at Phil. "Sounds good. Thank you."

"Come Patty," Phil said, taking her by the arm. "You can help me."

Patty backed away, her mouth still open.

"I'm so sorry." Cece smiled sheepishly at Brad. "We really shouldn't have let her out of the cage tonight."

Julia rested a hand on Brad's arm. "She's a bit of a character."

"I can tell. And I guess I earned that nick-name, didn't I?"

"Well, you did just show up with an entire box of them."

"Brad," Julia said. "I can't believe we haven't actually met before. Clearwater is such a small town."

"I travel quite a bit for work. My firm's main office is in New York, so I spend a lot of time out of town."

Cece didn't know that about him. He'd never mentioned it. Not that it mattered.

Patty and Phil came back, and Phil handed Brad his drink.

"Thank you, Phil," Brad said, accepting the glass. They clinked glasses. "Merry Christmas."

"Merry Christmas," said Phil. "Patty, do you have something to say."

Patty sidled up to Brad. "I must apologize for my rude behavior, Brad. I was caught off guard by your devastatingly handsome face."

Cece gave Patty a light shove. "Go sit on the couch with Julia. You may not speak again."

Brad winked at Patty as she sat down. "Patty, you are beyond charming."

Patty opened her mouth as if to reply, but Julia gently pushed her chin up and closed it.

"Mom!" Ryan's voice could be heard as he came downstairs. "I'm hungry. Is there anything to eat?" He walked into the living room and stopped dead in his tracks. "Mr. Redmond?"

Brad stood. "Yes?"

"What are you doing here?" Ryan asked.

"Ryan," Julia got up. "That's no way to . . ."

"Am I in trouble?"

Brad turned to Cece. "Who is he?"

Cece covered her eyes. "Oh no," she whispered to herself. She took a deep breath. "He's my step-brother, Ryan Bailey."

Brad's face went from utter loss to vague confusion to clarity in a split second. "You're Ryan Bailey? Dawn's b . . . friend?" He looked at Cece. "Ryan Bailey is your brother?"

Ryan's face drained of color. "We're friends, I think."

Julia the diplomat stepped up. "Ryan, Mr. Redmond is a friend of Cece's. He came by to . . . to bring us sticky buns."

Patty got up and stood next to Cece. "You know, people would pay good money to see this."

"Shhh!"

"Why did he bring us sticky buns?" Ryan asked.

"For Christmas, of course," Patty interjected.

"I told you to keep quiet," Cece hissed.

"Mr. Redmond," Ryan said, putting his shoulders back. "Are you here to talk to me?"

Brad gave Ryan a hard look. "I wasn't, but now that I know who you are, maybe we should talk about Dawn."

"Dawn?" Phil said, "Who's Dawn?"

"The Sugar Plum Fairy, honey, in *The Nutcracker*," Julia said.

"Oh, yes. She was spectacular, fabulous!" Phil turned to Brad. "You know her?"

"She's my daughter, Phil."

"Okay," said Phil. "Okay, I think I'm getting this, but maybe not."

"Ryan," Brad said, his voice controlled. "I'd like to know if there is something going on between you and my daughter."

"Nothing, sir, I swear . . . nothing."

"Then why has she been crying over you?"

"Over me?"

"That's right, son."

"Now hold on there a minute . . ." Phil began.

Julia went to stand between Cece and Patty. "Oh God."

"I am so loving this," Patty said.

"Phil," Brad said. "Your boy Ryan here has caused my daughter considerable heartache."

Phil put an arm over Ryan's shoulder. "I'm sure there's a perfectly reasonable explanation for everything. Ryan is a good kid."

"Then why is Dawn crying her eyes out? Do you know what it's like to see the daughter you adore suffering with a broken heart?"

"Well, uh . . ." Phil stammered, "as a matter of fact I do."

Patty put a hand on Cece's arm. "I'm in heaven."

Brad took a swig of his drink. "Yeah, well, my daughter is only fifteen years old. Yours is, what, like," Brad glanced at Cece. "I don't even know how old you are. Thirty?"

"Jesus Christ, twenty-nine, I'm twenty-nine."

"God, I love him," Patty whispered.

Phil turned to Ryan. "Is his daughter your girlfriend? I didn't even know you had a girlfriend."

"I don't!"

"Well then, do you know why she's been crying over you?"

"I don't know," Ryan said. "I like Dawn. I do, but . . . but I can't hook up with her, because Gabe wants to."

"Gabe?" Brad said. "Gabe Martin?"

"Yes, and he's one of my best friends."

Phil looked at Julia. "What does 'hook up' mean?" he whispered.

Julia raised her shoulders and looked at Cece.

Cece looked at Patty. "See why I hate small towns?"

Patty sighed. "I'm never leaving this place."

Brad looked flabbergasted. "Wait a minute. I thought Gabe was gay."

"He's not gay," Cece and Ryan said together.

"Who's not gay?" Tom entered the living room. "Whoa. If it isn't Brad Redmond."

Brad looked at Cece. "Your house is a circus."

Cece felt a headache coming. "You think?"

"So, Brad, I hear you've been making the moves on my sister."

"Who's your sister?"

"Sheesh," Cece said, "I am."

Patty practically jumped up and down. "This just keeps getting better and better."

Tom put his shoulders back and extended a hand toward Brad. "Tom Camden," he said, his voice low and authoritative.

Brad shook his hand slowly. He frowned at Tom, studied his face, and looked him up and down. "That name's familiar."

"Same last name as my sister's."

"No, that's not it," Brad said.

"Maybe we've crossed paths in town. I do a lot of the electrical work for . . ."

"Wait, wait." Brad pointed a finger at him. "Tom Camden. Tommy Camden! You used to play football, didn't you?"

Tom nodded. "Yeah, in high school."

"I used to watch you play! Wide receiver, my God, you were great. I remember your last game, had to be about eight years ago. You caught that Hail Mary pass, came at you from outta nowhere, and you scored the winning touchdown!"

"You were there?" Brad said, his face beaming.

"Hell yeah I was there!"

Brad slapped Tom on the shoulder. "What happened to you, man? Thought for sure you'd get recruited."

Tom lowered his head and swung it back and forth. "Ah, shit, went to Berkeley and blew out my knee out before the season even started."

Brad tightened his lips in sympathy. "What a rip."

"Hey Brad," Phil said. "Come into the den, and I'll show you the photo of my boy catching the ball."

"You still have that, Pop?" Brad asked.

"What are you kidding . . ."

The three men headed into the other room.

"Um, Mr. Redmond?" Ryan said.

Brad turned. "Oh, Ryan, what is it, son?"

"Are we . . . are we, like, done?"

Brad nodded. "I think so. Sure. Did you want me to, uh, you know, to say anything to Dawn about, well, about . . ."

"Oh no. That's okay. I'll just see her back at school."

"Good then." Brad squeezed Ryan's shoulder. "Great. I like you."

Ryan's Adam's apple bobbed in his skinny neck. "Thank you sir."

Brad followed Tom and Phil. Ryan collapsed onto the couch. Cece picked up the bakery box from Nutmeg's and opened it. She looked at Julia and Patty. "Sticky bun?"

CHAPTER 39

"Your family's great, Cece. What a riot it was in there."

They walked down the steps toward Brad's car.

"Uh-huh," Cece said, still embarrassed by the scene, "a regular comedy act."

"I can't believe I used to watch your brother play football. What a small world."

"What a small town," Cece said. "It's one of the reasons I left, everybody knowing everyone else and their business. I could not wait to get out of here and run off to the big city."

Brad put an arm over Cece's shoulders. "See that? I grew up in the big city and romanticized living in a small town. You, the exact opposite."

Cece sighed. "Funny how that works. What we don't have somehow becomes the ideal." The thought sobered her.

"Is living in Los Angeles your ideal?"

"Absolutely," Cece said. "Is living in Clearwater yours?"

"For now, at least until Dawn graduates high school. After that, who knows?"

"Maybe you'll follow your daughter to wherever she goes to college."

"Maybe I will," Brad laughed. "Wouldn't she just love that?"

The sky was clear, the stars sparkled, and Phil's extravagant Christmas lights illuminated the entire front yard.

"This house could win one of those contests with all the lights and decorations." Brad said. "Especially the reindeer."

"My dad loves to decorate. We used to have this Santa and sleigh thing on the roof, but Julia nixed it. Too dangerous."

"That's actually very sweet," said Brad.

"It actually is."

They continued their slow walk down the driveway, gravel crunching under their steps.

"So," Cece said. "How long will you be away at your sister's?"

"Just a couple of days. Will you still be here when I get back?"

"Yes," Cece smiled up at him. "I decided to stay through New Year's."

"Did you, now?"

"I did. And I'll go with you to your fancy party. If you still want me to, that is."

Brad stopped and faced her. He put his arms around her and kissed her. "I absolutely still want you to." He kissed her again, his hands on both sides of her face. She stood on her toes and parted her lips, inviting him into a deep and sensuous kiss.

There was an old picnic table to the side of the driveway nestled in amongst some tall trees. Cece stepped backwards in the direction of the table, bringing Brad with her. She boosted herself up and sat on the end, her legs dangling.

"So what should I wear?" She gave him a flirtatious smile.

"That is a loaded question if I ever heard one." Cece could see a glint in his green eyes.

"Well, I expect some of your colleagues will be there. I would not want to be underdressed."

"I wouldn't mind."

"Then I'd be cold."

"Then I'd warm you up." Brad stood in front of her and looked down, his eyes sexy and mischievous, and removed his heavy jacket.

"What are you doing? It's freezing out here."

"Shhh..." He wrapped it around Cece's shoulders, lowered her onto the table, and leaned over her, his hands underneath her head. He kissed her with an urgency Cece hadn't felt before. He nestled his nose into her neck and inhaled. "You are driving me crazy, Cecilia Rose."

Cece wound her fingers into his hair. His kisses on her neck made her skin tingle and her breaths shorten. The stirring inside her stomach made her think of Doug, but she pushed the thought away. Brad Redmond was here; he was now, and the way he wanted her made her body ache.

She put her hands on his shoulders and gently pushed him up. He lifted his head and looked at her, his eyes questioning. Cece said nothing. She ran her tongue over her lips, and unzipped her jacket. Brad's muscular arms were on either side of her, supporting his weight. She watched him breathe deeply.

"Don't move," she said, her eyes trained on his. She wriggled out of her jacket. "Just watch."

Brad swallowed. "Yes ma'am," he whispered, one corner of his mouth rising, his dimple showing.

She began unbuttoning her shirt. Even on her back, vulnerable and unable to move, she felt in control. She watched his eyes trail downward as she released the buttons one by one. When she reached the last button, she opened her shirt, revealing her lacy, black bra. "You did say you'd warm me up, didn't you?"

Cece stretched and yawned. She could hear quiet whispers floating up the stairs. Patty snored softly next to her. Cece jumped on her best friend. "Merry Christmas, little girl!"

"No. Too early . . ." Patty sat up reluctantly, her spiky hair shooting out in all directions. She opened one eye. "What the hell were you doing outside so late last night?"

"Nothing . . ." Cece sat up.

"You didn't. Or did you?"

"No." Cece shook her head. "Much to his disappointment. Gave him a little preview, though."

"Hey, you know what they say—if you can't be with the one you love . . ."

"Love the one you're with." Cece said the words with a false note of enthusiasm.

"I hear it works wonders at getting someone out of your head."

"Well, that's what I need to do then. I'm not going to think about 'you know who' anymore, not at all, at least not until we go home." Cece got out of bed. "And I told Brad that I'd go to that New Year's party with him."

"That must have made his night."

"That, among other things . . ." Cece scratched her shoulder. "Hey, how is it you got the whole week off work?"

Patty frowned. "Didn't I tell you? I got fired."

"Fired? Why?"

"The assistant manager said I assaulted him with the hot glue gun."

"Did you?"

"No! Well, not exactly. Okay, kind of. He was stupid and incompetent and constantly telling me how to do things."

"So you shot him with hot glue?"

197

"First of all, it was an accident, and besides, it was just one drip! I get that stuff on my hands all the time. Look." Patty held up her hand to show Cece several faded scars. "What a whiny wimp he was!"

Cece pushed Patty out of bed. "You are a scary girl. Come on, I hear the boys scurrying around. Let's go see what Santa brought!"

For Cece, Christmas day unfolded like a scene from a storybook. Her entire family was there—Dad and Julia, her brothers, and her best friend in the world.

Julia had made enormous Christmas stockings stuffed with chocolates, homemade treats, mittens, and matching Santa hats for everyone. They sat for hours in front of their huge, magnificent tree opening gifts, drinking coffee, eating sticky buns, laughing and delighting in every joyful moment.

By the time they finished opening presents, the floor was littered with wrapping paper, ribbons, and scrunched up balls of tape. It was almost noon when Julia stood up. "Okay, everyone, clean-up time. Company's coming in only a few hours!"

Countless friends, friends of friends, and family of friends filtered in and out of the Camden house all afternoon and into the evening. They had a roaring fire in the fireplace, white lights twinkling on the tree, Christmas music playing, and everyone eating, drinking and toasting the holiday and the coming new year.

Cece stood against the wall watching the joyful chaos. She felt a tickle on her back.

"Happy?" Julia wrapped an arm around Cece's waist.

Cece hugged her. "You know what? I am."

"Good." Julia smoothed Cece's hair out of her eyes. It was a sweet, maternal gesture, and Cece liked it. "Did you notice that your brother is paying quite of bit of attention to Patty?"

Julia pointed to the far corner of the living room where Patty was sitting on Tom's lap. Cece smiled. "About time he made a move. I practically wrapped her up and gave her to him for Christmas."

"Well, I just hope the feeling is mutual," Julia said. "I'd hate to see him get hurt again."

A loud clatter in the kitchen sent Julia running. Cece stayed where she was and watched her brother and Patty. She could read Patty as easily as a children's book. Her eyes shined, her head tilted to the side, her smile enticing and coy. *She's interested in him,* Cece thought, *very interested.*

Finally, the crowd started to thin. Cece was about to sit down and relax in front of the fire, but one of Julia's old friends cornered her. "Oh Cece, hello dear, how are you?"

"I'm great. How are you?"

"Good, good. Just wanted to tell you how much we loved the show—it was spectacular."

"I'm so glad. Thank you for coming to see it."

"Of course. I haven't missed a Christmas show in twenty-five years!" The woman touched Cece's elbow. "But I heard disturbing news about Ilana, what a shame, she's gone senile? How's she doing, dear, do you know?"

"Um," Cece did not want to discuss Ilana. "She's, uh, actually doing much better, I think. I'm sorry, but would you excuse me?"

"Oh, of course, I . . ."

Cece didn't listen to the rest. She had to get away. Just thinking about Ilana and the hurdles facing Natalie made her squirm. She was about to sneak upstairs, but Tom stopped her.

"Ceece, got a sec?"

"Sure. What's up?"

"Uh, I just . . . um, I wanted, well, I was thinking . . ."

Cece raised her eyebrows at her brother. "Is this about Patty?"

Tom grinned. "Yeah. I'm thinking about asking her to go out with me on New Year's Eve."

Cece squeezed his muscular arm. "That's a great idea."

"Really? You think she'd want to?"

"Yes I do. And go ask her before you chicken out."

"Thanks sis," Tom said, giving her a quick kiss. He headed off in search of Patty.

Yep, Cece thought, *everyone wants to be in love at Christmas time.*

CHAPTER 40

In the days following Christmas, a sense of calm settled over Cece. The frantic tension leading up to the opening and closing of the show was gone. The news about Ilana had become public, so the pressure of keeping it hush-hush had vanished.

Cece felt sorry for Natalie, however. The show had closed only four days ago, and already some of the dance moms were on the warpath. Natalie Lurensky had concealed vital information, and that was considered unacceptable.

Three days before New Year's Eve, Cece went to see Natalie at the studio. She tapped a fingernail on the office door she as she pushed it open. "Hi."

Natalie stood. She walked around her desk, arms spread wide. They hugged each other. "At the risk of repeating myself for the hundredth time, I couldn't have done it without you."

"Repeat all you want." Cece smiled at her old friend. "I loved doing it. Maybe I'll come back next year and do it again."

"I'd love that. But right now I'm not sure we'll have a show next year."

"What are you talking about?" said Cece.

Natalie went and sat behind her desk and leaned on her elbows. "The Lurensky Dance Academy is going to see a mutiny the likes of which we've never seen before."

"That bad, huh?"

"Oh let's see, they're calling it everything from subterfuge to deceit to fraud. If you hear anyone in town shouting 'off with her head,' call me quick so I can make my escape."

"You've got to be kidding."

"Wish I were. I shouldn't have brought my mother to the closing show. One of the parents started a conversation with her, and I guess she just started talking nonsense. I don't know what she said, but . . ." Natalie's voice trailed off.

"That's awful. What about Wendy? She's a pretty persuasive player in the group, isn't she?"

"Yeah, but there's only so much she can do. The other parents are her friends. I can't expect her to take this on for me." Natalie went opened a desk drawer. She pulled out an envelope and handed it to Cece. "I threw in a little bonus for your incredible success with Dawn. I wish I could pay you more. I really, really mean it, Cece. You saved our town's Christmas show."

Cece felt a familiar knot in her throat. "You're going to make me cry."

Natalie gave her a sad smile. "We can cry together. Listen, I'm going to take my mom to Scottsdale for New Year's. We both need to get out of here. I might not be back before you leave."

Cece blinked. This was it. Time to say goodbye to Natalie. It wasn't like she'd never see her again, but there was a sense of finality to the moment. A tear dropped onto Cece's cheek, and she whisked it away with the back of her hand. "Oh no, here I go again."

"Don't you dare," Natalie said, her voice cracking. "You're going to get me crying now."

The two friends laughed.

"I'm going to miss you a lot, Cece."

"I'll visit. And you come down to LA. We can go to Disneyland. Remember when our dads took us there?"

Natalie nodded. She bit her lower lip and closed her eyes. When she opened them, she lifted her chin and her radiant, confident smile returned. "Oh, I almost forgot, I had this picture in one of my albums at home," she said. She lifted a few papers. "I wondered if you ever saw it."

Cece reached out and took the photograph from Natalie's hand. She caught her breath.

It was her ballerina, the Sugar Plum Fairy. The face Cece had painted, perfected, was staring at her. Standing next to the ballerina was nine-year-old Cece, her wild brown curls wider than her body. In the photo, she was looking up at the dancer, enchanted and reverent. The ballerina was looking at the camera, and smiling just with her eyes.

Cece turned the photo over. On the back, in Ilana's recognizable scrawl, it said:

December 8, 1991, San Francisco Ballet
Cecilia Rose and Sugar Plum Fairy

Cece blinked. She couldn't speak.

"Are you okay?" Natalie asked.

Cece nodded. She turned the photo and looked at it again. "Um, sure . . . of course. I just . . . I just don't think I've ever seen, um, any pictures from that day."

"Do you remember it? My mom took us—I think it was for your birthday."

Cece nodded. "I do. I remember it well . . ."

"You can have that if you want."

"Thank you," Cece said. Natalie had no idea how much the photo meant to her.

Natalie got up and put an arm around Cece. They took slow steps toward the door. "I hate to see you go."

Cece turned. "Good luck with everything, Natalie."

"It'll be fine, don't you worry," Natalie said, her voice clipped. "Good luck to you, too. Hope everything back home works out the way you want it to."

"Thanks," Cece said. She hesitated. "I really . . . I really do feel bad leaving you with . . . "

"Oh please, no. Don't feel bad. I knew from the very beginning that this was just a holiday gig for you. I wish you could, or would, stay, but I understand. LA's your home. That's where your life is."

Cece nodded. She gave up on not crying and allowed the tears to stream down her cheeks. Natalie gave in as well. They hugged for a long time before Natalie pulled away.

"Go on," Natalie said. She stepped back. Her face was red and wet with tears. "This is a . . . a lot harder for me than I thought it would be. I'm sorry."

Cece swallowed. She turned and walked out the door.

Cece leaned down and unplugged the Christmas tree lights. The tree still smelled of pine. Phil Camden was a man of many traditions, and keeping the Christmas tree fresh and on display until January 2nd was one of them.

The house was silent. Ryan was with his father, Phil and Julia had gone out to dinner, and Tom had taken Patty out on their first official date.

After seeing Natalie that afternoon, Cece was drained the rest of the day. But she felt satisfied and content. Something wonderful had been accomplished.

She walked upstairs, the photo of her ballerina still in her hand. She hadn't stopped looking at it all day. In her bedroom, she tucked it into the side of the mirror above her dresser. It looked as if it had been there for twenty years. She thought about her painting. It was somewhere out in the rainforest. It was with Doug.

The sound of her cell phone startled her. She answered it. "Hey Patty."

"Ceece!" Patty yelled into the phone. "What are you doing?"

"Nothing. Why's it so noisy? Aren't you out with Tom?"

"Yeah, and we want you to join us! We're having a blast at the old tavern. Hold on . . . what? Okay! Tom says we'll come get you. Are you home?"

"That's okay. I'm staying in tonight."

"I can't hear you!"

"I'm staying in tonight!" Cece shouted.

"What?"

"Patty! Jesus, go outside or something!"

"Okay! Just a sec . . . there, I'm in the bathroom. We'll come get you, and we can party together. Come on Ceece, it'll be fun!"

"No. I have some stuff I have to do. You two have a good time."

"You sure?"

"I'm sure," Cece sighed. "You and Tommy behave yourselves, hear me?"

"Oh don't worry, we won't! See you later." Patty hung up the phone.

Cece sat down on her bed where Boomer was snoozing. She ran her hand over the dog's soft brown fur. Boomer lifted his head and looked at her, his dark brown eyes full of love.

"You are such a handsome boy, aren't you?" Cece reached under her bed to get her sketchpad and art pencils. "And I think I'm going to draw a picture of you."

She opened her old art box. "Oh," Cece whispered. Beside her pencils was the wooden box that held the red sable paintbrush Doug had given her. She had forgotten it was there.

The hair on the brush was supple and shaped to perfection. Cece studied the tip, gently rounded, not a strand out of place. The handle, long and thin with a maroon lacquer finish, gleamed. She rested it on the palm of her hand. It was the finest paintbrush she'd ever held. She swept the hairs over her dry lips, savoring the sensation. She smiled at the thought of Doug finding the page she had marked in the catalog. To Cece's surprise, her eyes didn't burn, her throat didn't catch.

"For you," she said to Boomer, "I will start painting again."

CHAPTER 41

Patty was perched on a tiny round stool in the fitting room at a Julia's favorite boutique. She pulled the Christmas lollypop out of her mouth with a slurp. "That dress is perfect!"

"I have to agree with Patty," Julia said. "It is stunning."

Cece had tried on at least ten little black dresses. "I don't know," Cece said, turning in front of the mirror. "I've gained weight, and it feels awfully clingy. "

"Perfectly clingy," Patty said. "You look fabulous in it."

It was the quintessential LBD—simple lines, small cap sleeves, exquisite fabric. It hugged Cece's body in all the right places, and the square neckline was just low enough to hint at what was hiding underneath. "You don't think it's too sexy?"

"No!" Julia and Patty sang their answer together.

"Cece," Julia said. "It's the ultimate little black dress, alluring, classy. Very Audrey Hepburn."

"It's so expensive though."

"It's a birthday present from your dad and me. Remember? I said we'd go shopping for your birthday. This is what we want to get you. And the shoes, too."

Patty looked longingly at Julia. "Will you adopt me?"

Julia ruffled Patty's spiky hair. "Anytime. Now, let's do this. You girls have worn me out."

After dinner, Julia and Patty talked Cece into modeling her new dress. She put on the whole outfit, including the shoes, and went downstairs into the living room.

"Whoa!" Phil's eyes opened wide. "Look at my baby girl!"

"I don't know," said Tom, shaking his head. "You could get yourself into some trouble wearing that."

Patty sat on Tom's lap. "I think she looks lovely."

Cece made a little pirouette. "Pretty good, huh?" Cece caught a flash of herself in the mirror. She loved the dress. She gave her father and Julia each a kiss on the cheek. "Thank you so much. It's a wonderful present."

"You're welcome, sweetie," said Phil.

Julia smiled. "You'd better go change before something happens to it."

"Right." Cece stood in front of Patty who unzipped her and then smacked her on the butt.

"I hate having such a pretty best friend,"

Tom squeezed Patty around the waist. "Hey, cute and crazy is good, too."

Cece went upstairs. In her room, she lowered the dress to her knees and stepped out, careful not to trip. She put it on the hanger, and wrapped the cover around it. *It is pretty,* she thought. *Doug would love it on me.*

Cece froze. The thought had come out of nowhere. It surprised her, but did not bother her as much as it would have a week ago. It takes a long time to get over the love of your life, Julia had said. Of course it does. And all you have to do, Cece told herself, is think of something, or someone else. Her thoughts turned to Brad. They hadn't seen each other since Christmas. He had called when he got back from his sister's to tell her that he had to be away on business for a few days. And that he couldn't wait to see her on New Year's Eve.

Cece sighed. She turned to go back downstairs and tripped over Patty's open suitcase.

"Ouch!" Cece grabbed her toe. She pushed the suitcase out of the way and started to close the top, but a pile of white paper caught her attention. She moved aside a few of Patty's things and uncovered an enormous stack of mail.

"Patty!" Cece hollered as she stomped down the stairs. She dropped the mail onto the dining room table. "Where are you?"

"She's outside, honey, with Tom," Julia called from the kitchen.

Cece peered out the front window. She could see them sitting on the swing, Patty's tiny body wrapped up in her brother's arms. She sighed. They were adorable together, but not that adorable.

Cece threw open the door and stepped onto the porch.

"Patty! Get in here."

Patty turned. "Can't you see that I'm busy?"

"Yeah, well, you're going to get a lot busier now. I just found the pile of mail that you didn't bother to open all month!"

"Crap," Patty said. "I totally forgot I brought it."

"Thanks a lot, sis."

"Sorry Tommy, but be forewarned. If you ever move in with her, don't leave her in charge of the bills!"

Cece watched as her brother gave Patty a swat on her behind. "See you tomorrow, cupcake."

Patty giggled as she skipped up the front steps. Cece held the door open for her. *Jesus, cupcake?*

"Oh my God, your brother kisses like—"

"Aaack! Stop. Don't say it!"

" —an animal. All luscious lips and swirly tongue and . . ."

"Patty! Don't make me think about how my little brother kisses. It's disgusting." Cece closed the door. "Wanna tell me why you brought a suitcase full of unopened mail with you?"

"Because it needs opening?"

"So you ignored it all these weeks?"

"You know I don't do mail, Ceece. That's your job."

It was true. Cece did handle all the bills. The two of them operated like an old married couple.

They went to the table and looked over the paperwork.

Patty tore open the envelopes, pulled out the bills, flattened them on the table and pushed them toward Cece. Cece checked the dates and sorted them into stacks: 'past due,' 'pay soon,' and 'deal with it when we get home.'

"Put all the trash and junk mail over here for recycling," Cece said, pointing to the far end of the table.

"I hate mail," Patty complained. "So boring."

"Yeah, well. Lucky for you I take care of it. Keep going. Any more bills?"

Patty shuffled through some junk. "Think we got them all. Oh wait." She picked up a thin white envelope. "It's for you."

Cece yawned and stretched. She extended her hand. "Let me see." The block printing on the front made her gasp.

"What is it?" Patty asked.

"It's from Doug." She scrutinized the postmark. *Costa Rica, December 16th, 2011.* Cece swallowed. Her hand shook.

"Aren't you gonna open it?"

"I'm afraid to."

"Why?"

"Because I finally feel like I'm starting to get over him, and I don't want to slip backwards."

"Oh," Patty said, looking at Cece with concern.

Cece put the letter on the table. She pushed it away with one finger, as if it had cooties.

"I brought you girls a pot of tea," Julia said, placing a tray on the table. She looked their faces. "What happened?"

"Cece got a letter from Doug," Patty whispered.

"What's it say?"

"We don't know," Patty said, still whispering.

Julia sat down. "Why don't we know?" Julia started whispering, too.

"Because she's scared to open it."

"I see."

They continued whispering to one another, as if Cece wasn't even there.

"It's from Costa Rica," Patty said. "Mailed two weeks ago."

"Is she going to open it?"

"I'm not sure. Do you think we should open it?"

"Well, not unless Cece wants us to."

"Do you think she wants us to?" Patty asked.

"Would you two quit talking about me like I'm not in the room? Christ! Just give it to me. I'll open it."

Julia put her hand on the envelope and slid it across the table. Cece picked it up and tore the seal. Without hesitation, she pulled out a folded piece of white notebook paper. A small photo fluttered out of the note. Cece picked up the picture. She inhaled, her chest trembling. It was Doug standing in front of a tree in the middle of a cloud-covered forest. Above his head, dangling from the branches, were four monkeys. Cece couldn't take her eyes off the picture. She knew his face so well. He wore a small smile that revealed a dream come true, but a dream that had come with a high price.

One of his companions must have taken the picture. His own camera was slung around his neck, his right hand holding the lens, one finger over the lens cover. Cece had seen him in this exact position a thousand times.

"He made it to the rainforest," she said calmly. She handed the picture to Julia, who looked at it and then handed it to Patty.

Cece picked up the piece of notebook paper. It felt like she had lifted a brick. She read aloud.

Dear Ceece,
I've been in Costa Rica only a few days, and already I love this place. It's beautiful, pristine, like I've gone back in time. I hope it's okay that I'm writing to you. I'm not even sure I'm going to send

this letter, but I need to write it. Every day I see, hear, and smell things I wish I could share with you. A thousand times I've turned and looked for you, thinking I felt you at my side. I dream about you every night. And I think about you every hour. I'm so sorry I hurt you Ceece. I never meant to disappoint you. Seeing you unhappy, and knowing I had made you unhappy, was killing me. I won't even ask you to forgive me. It doesn't matter, because I can't forgive myself. I try to believe that it's for the best, because look where I am. I am a photographer in the rainforest. It's what I always wanted to be. I just wish I could have been everything you wanted me to be, too. I don't know, maybe I will be that man someday. But it'll be too late by then. My timing always did suck.

Cece lost focus. Her tears dropped from her chin onto the paper, smearing the ink.

If I send this letter, and if you're reading it, my guess is you're crying. I know this because I'm crying, too. I haven't cried since I was eight years old. But in the past couple of weeks, I haven't stopped. The guys I'm traveling with just think I have bad allergies, and one of them keeps making me drink this tea that he concocts from leaves and twigs and some root thing. It tastes like shit.

Cece stopped. She smiled through her tears. She almost laughed.

I can hear your laugh in my head. I can see your sad smile.

The letter was like a knife in her heart. Didn't he know how painful this would be for her?

I guess I just want you to know that I'm alive, at least as of, what's the date? December 12th, I think. We're here another week, and then we move on, not sure where. I hope things are going well for you, wherever you are now and whatever you're doing. I know I'm rambling. It's weird, but as long as I'm still writing to you, I feel like part of me is holding on to part of you. They say that time heals all wounds. If that's true, I can't even begin to imagine how much time it will take for me to get over you.

His letter stopped there. She looked at Julia and Patty, their tears flowing as much as hers.

She stood, turned, and slowly climbed the stairs to her room. Cece sat on her bed and read the letter again. He didn't even mention the photo, but she knew him. He would have stuck it in as an afterthought, quickly, before he could change his mind. Half of her felt dragged back to where she was month ago when Doug had left, and the other half was furious. How dare he send this letter? What was the purpose? To assuage his own sadness? To remind her how much they loved each other?

Cece crumpled the paper into a ball and threw it into the wastebasket. She blew her nose and tossed the tissue on top of Doug's letter.

"I'll show him," she said aloud. She went to look at her new dress that was hanging beside her closet. She opened the cover and unwrapped it.

"I am going to look so unbelievably, spectacularly, amazingly sexy in this dress. Brad will lose his mind, and I will have the most incredible holiday fling ever."

Cece turned away from her dress and then, without thinking, she retrieved Doug's note and smoothed the creases. She read it two more times. Sobs racked her body. Cece clutched the letter against her chest, curled up into a ball on her bed, and cried herself to sleep.

CHAPTER 42

The dress enveloped Cece like a smooth glove as Patty pulled the zipper up. The back draped in soft folds over her shoulder blades. Her hair was swept up into a loose bun with thin tendrils of hair around her face and the back of her neck.

"You look like a princess, Ceece. A very hot and sexy princess."

"Exactly what I'm aiming for." Cece faced Patty. "And you, little girl, look downright naughty."

Patty did a turn. She had on a tight, black mini-skirt, high-heel, over-the-knee black boots, and a sparkly silver tank top with plunging neckline. She shimmied her shoulders. "I'm wearing my new push-up. It's like magic—who even knew I had boobs?"

Cece laughed. "Everyone will know now."

Patty spritzed perfume into her top. "Want some?"

Cece turned, and Patty sprayed the back of her neck. She sniffed the air like a dog. "We smell delicious."

"Yes we do," Cece said.

"So, is tonight the night you and Mr. Sticky-buns get . . ."

"Don't say it!" Cece stopped Patty's thought. "My New Year's resolution is to live in the moment." Cece waved her palm through the air as if seeing it in lights. "No more compulsive, controlling, plan-everything-ahead obsession. If it happens, it happens."

Patty smirked. "Oh, it's gonna happen."

Cece raised a shoulder. "I did get that bikini wax yesterday. Can't leave everything to chance."

"That's the Cece I know and love." Patty pursed her lips and made a small frown. "But . . . but you know you don't have to, don't you?"

"What?"

"Sleep with him," Patty said. "I know you Cece. Casual sex isn't your thing."

Patty was right. Ever since reading Doug's letter, Cece felt something pulling her backwards. The tugging on her heart that had begun to subside was worse than ever. But, she thought, with a few glasses of champagne and Brad's irresistible everything, the tugging would vanish. At least for the night.

"Maybe it can be," Cece said. "Maybe I've changed."

Patty shook her head. "I don't think so. You're a hopeless romantic, Ceece." Patty gave her a serious look.

Cece inhaled. "Not anymore I'm not."

"Bullshit," Patty snorted a laugh. "Listen, I'm not telling not to sleep with him. I'm just telling you to be careful. You've already been hurt enough."

Cece twisted some hair around her finger. She took a deep breath. "I have to play it by ear. See how the night goes. Not over-think it."

"You not over-think? That," Patty said with a doubtful smirk, "will be a challenge."

Boomer barked and ran downstairs. The front door opened and slammed shut.

"Hello?" Tom's loud voice echoed throughout the house.

"Sounds like your date has arrived," Cece said.

They walked downstairs together. Cece watched her brother's face light up when he saw Patty, and it made her heart swell. Tom gave Patty a slow kiss on the lips. *This relationship,* Cece thought, *will bloom like a flower in spring. Or crash and burn like a Roman candle on the 4th of July.*

"Nice boots," Tom said, pulling Patty into a hug. "What we could do with those later . . ."

"Christ Tommy, I'm standing right here."

"Oh hey sis," Tom said, giving Cece a kiss on the cheek. "You look totally hot." He gave her an amused look. "Where are Dad and Julia?"

"Left about an hour ago," Cece said. "They're spending the night in the city at some friend's house where they do the happy-new-year at nine, drink 'til ten, be asleep by eleven thing."

"Oh my God," Patty said. "Shoot me if I ever get that boring."

"Are you kidding?" Tom yawned. "I'm ready for that now, and I'm younger than you are."

There it goes, Cece thought, *crash and burn.* She gave Patty a quick hug. "Get out of here you two, Happy New Year!"

Patty grabbed her jacket. "You too! Have a great time, and remember what I said, okay?"

"I will."

"Oh, and I won't be back tonight. I'm sleeping at Tommy's. We're doing it, just so you know."

"Thank you for that." Cece shuddered.

She stood in the doorway and waved. They walked toward Tom's truck, and Cece smiled as she watched two of her favorite people in the world go off into the starry night, full of hope and excitement, and alarmingly poor judgment.

The valet opened the car door, and Cece stepped out in front of a Georgian mansion in Napa Valley. The private estate included the mansion, winery, and vineyards on over two hundred acres of land.

"This is magnificent," Cece said. "Like out of a movie."

"Wait 'til you see the inside." They climbed the steps and entered through cascading lights and giant poinsettias.

Cece felt Brad's hand on the small of her back as he escorted her into the party. In his black tuxedo, he looked like a leading man. His fingers dusted over Cece's shoulders as he removed her coat, giving her goosebumps. He leaned in and whispered in her ear.

"Have I told you how beautifully gorgeous you look tonight?"

Cece gave him a sidelong glance. "You have. Three times."

"I'm glad you're keeping track."

A waiter carrying a tray of champagne glasses stopped beside them. Brad took two flutes from the tray. "Thank you," he said. He handed Cece a glass. "Happy New Year, gorgeous."

Cece touched her glass to his. "That makes four." Cece sipped, her eyes steady on his. "Mmmm, it's the good stuff."

Brad did not leave her side. He introduced her to the people he knew, his hand on her back or around her waist or lightly caressing the skin on her bare shoulder. With every touch, Cece was reminded that she was the date of Brad Redmond, the most desirable, attentive, sexy man in the room. Her regrets and memories melted away with each kiss and sip of champagne. She was in the moment.

The house was spectacular—marble floor, winding staircase, and huge Christmas trees in three different rooms. The two hundred or more guests looked as if a casting agent had selected them. Handsome men in tuxedos, striking women in lavish, designer outfits, and enough diamonds on display to stock a jewelry store.

"This place could be in a magazine," she said.

"It has been," Brad said, eating an olive. "Several times."

"And you know who owns it?"

Brad laughed. "Of course I do. Mitch is one of my oldest clients."

They stood at a tall cocktail table draped with a gold cloth eating appetizers—sushi, shrimp, tiny lamb chops, caviar. A handsome, distinguished-looking man with gray hair and wearing a black tuxedo and bowtie stepped up to join them. He was holding a cut crystal glass filled with amber liquid and ice.

"Finally, our illustrious host appears." Brad shook the man's hand. "Good to see you, Mitch. Great party."

"How are you, Brad?"

"Excellent. I'd like you to meet Cecilia Camden."

Cece held out her hand. "So nice to meet you."

"The pleasure is mine," Mitch said, his eyes admiring.

"Your home is . . . breathtaking."

"Breathtaking," Mitch repeated word, as if it felt good to say it. "As are you."

Cece's heart pounded as Mitch brought her hand to his lips and kissed it with cool lips. "Brad, I must warn you to stay close to this lovely lady. She has caught the attention of a number of gentlemen already."

Cece felt neck and face heat up.

"Believe me, I intend to."

Mitch released her hand and stepped back. He patted Brad's shoulder. "You two have a great night. Cecilia" he said, "I'm delighted you could be here. Finally Brad shows up with a date of whom I approve."

Mitch nodded to Cece with a charming smile and disappeared into the crowd.

"A date he approves of?" Cece eyed Brad.

"That's just Mitch. Has an opinion on everything. Especially women."

"Now I get it, you wanted to impress Mitch," Cece teased. "So that's why you've been pursuing me all these weeks."

Brad picked up his champagne and drank it down. He put a cool hand on the skin between Cece's shoulders and leaned in close to her ear. "I've been pursuing you for many reasons."

Cece lost track of how much champagne she'd consumed. Brad's friends flocked around them, and it became obvious that there was no shortage of women who were interested in Brad Redmond. Blissfully tipsy, she laughed and chatted, charming the women as well as the men. Between the alcohol and the flattery, she felt seductive and adventurous.

After dinner, they went outside for some fresh air. They stood at the edge of the courtyard. A waiter brought them two vodka martinis.

"Oh no," Cece said. "Remember what happened last time?"

"I do. Do you?"

Cece gave him a look. "Did something happen that I should remember?"

"Maybe . . ."

Cece frowned. "Really?"

"No," Brad laughed. "Only that you fell asleep on the way home."

"That's a relief. I hate it when something fabulous happens and I'm too drunk to enjoy it." She looked at him over the edge of her glass.

He looked at her in mock seriousness. "Does that happen often?"

Cece lowered her chin and fluttered her eyes. "Yes, doctor, what should I do?"

Brad cracked up. He put a hand on the back of her neck and kissed her lips, running his hand down her back, over the fabric of her dress. His arm wrapped around her waist and stayed there. They looked out beyond the courtyard to a long, rectangular reflecting pool with fountains at both ends. Colored lights turned underneath, transforming the droplets of water into dancing rainbows. Cece looked further out to the vineyards beyond the pool, illuminated by glass-covered torches. Rolling, grassy hills stretched out behind the mansion for what seemed to be miles.

"I had no idea there was this much money in wine," Cece said.

"Wine, champagne, and believe it or not, olive oil."

"Olive oil, you're kidding!"

"Nope," Brad said. "It's . . ."

"Well," a woman's voice interrupted them. "Brad Redmond, what a surprise."

Brad turned toward the voice. He looked at the woman with his debonair smile. Cece noted she was striking, late thirties, tall and slender. Her dark hair curled around her shoulders, framing an exotic, heart shaped face with emerald eyes. She had smooth, dark skin, accentuated by a strapless, turquoise cocktail dress and nude platform pumps.

"Katrina, how are you?" Brad gave her a polite kiss on the cheek.

"I'm fine Brad. You?"

"Just fine. Thank you."

Cece waited for Brad to introduce her, but he didn't.

Katrina eyed Cece for a moment then turned her attention back to Brad. Cece took a sip of her drink and watched.

"I was hoping I'd run into you. Haven't seen you in a while." She put a hand on his arm and leaned closer. "You still have my number, don't you?"

"I'm sure I do."

Cece was surprised, and intrigued, by Katrina's audacity, coming onto a man who was with another woman. Brad remained impressively composed.

Katrina took a sip of her wine. "Well then, you should use it." She glanced at Cece again. "When you tire of little girls, I'd love to hear from you again."

"Happy New Year, Katrina," Brad said. "Enjoy your evening." He turned away from her just enough to imply that they were finished.

Cece watched Katrina walk across the balcony. A short, balding man put his arm around her and offered her a cigarette, which she accepted smoothly.

"Now that was interesting," Cece licked her lips. "She's stunning."

"Yes, she is." Brad offered nothing more.

"You dated her?"

"Briefly."

Cece drank. She was enjoying needling him. "My goodness, you don't have much to say about her. Let me guess, bad in bed?"

Brad laughed. "Well, you are feisty tonight, aren't you?"

"I'm trying to be." Cece moved closer to him. "You like feisty, don't you?"

He kissed her, and she felt his cool tongue on her lips. "What are you trying to do to me here?"

"Just making sure you have a good time."

"Oh, I'm definitely having a good time. Are you?"

"Absolutely." Cece finished her martini and gave the glass to a passing waiter. "What time is it?

Brad looked at his watch. "Twenty to midnight."

"I'm going to run to the restroom."

"Don't be long," said Brad. "You're my midnight kiss, you know."

"If I'm not back in time, I'm sure Katrina would happily take my place," Cece teased.

"I would probably jump into the fountain before I let that happen."

"Then I'd better hurry," Cece said, running her hands down the lapels of his jacket. "I'd hate to see you ruin your lovely tuxedo."

Cece walked toward the house and stepped inside through the French doors. She found the powder room in an alcove off the foyer. Two attractive women, one blonde and one brunette, stood beside the closed door.

"Hello," Cece said with a friendly nod.

"There's a line," the blonde woman said, smiling apologetically. She wore a simple, red dress, her hair pulled back into a tight, perfect bun.

The other woman said nothing, her face pretty but pinched. She had an unusually small nose, short hair, and puffy lips. In her black, sequined halter-top, black velvet plants and fabulous silver sandals, she reminded Cece of a super-hero. A diamond the size of an almond dangled just above her substantial cleavage.

Cece stepped back and waited.

"Well, from what I heard," the blonde woman said, her voice soft, *"The Nutcracker* was a huge success."

Cece's ears perked up. *They're probably talking about a professional production in the city,* she thought.

"Doesn't matter," the brunette said. "If Ilana Lurensky is as crazy as I've heard she is, that studio will never survive."

Cece felt the blood drain from her face. She leaned against the wall.

The brunette continued talking in a grating, adenoidal voice. "My friend's studio is in the next town over, and she's getting ready to contact some of Lurensky's best dancers."

"She's going to poach them?" the blonde said.

"Poach?" the brunette laughed. "That's an ugly word. She's going to offer them an opportunity."

Cece looked to the side, pretending that she wasn't listening. Her heart pounded as her discomfort gave way to anger.

The brunette toyed with the diamond resting between her obviously fake breasts. "With Ilana gone, her daughter will take over. I hear she's very good, but she has no support. Word is she's shopping for an assistant director."

"My goodness," the blonde shook her head.

Cece clenched her fists. She bit her lower lip.

"And according to my friend, she can't find anyone. Natalie Lurensky is screwed."

"You're wrong." Cece was surprised by the sound of her own voice.

"Excuse me?" the brunette said.

Cece steeled herself, realizing that, for her, anger and alcohol might be a dangerous combination. "She has a very promising candidate."

"How nice," the blonde said.

The brunette raised her penciled eyebrows. "Is that so?"

"It is. Her name is Cecilia Rose." Cece stood taller as she said her own name.

"I've heard of her!" The blonde's eyes opened wide.

Cece focused her attention on the blonde. "I'm sure you have. She's practically famous in Clearwater, danced with Madam Lurensky for years." She leaned in as if she were about to reveal a secret. "And I heard that she was accepted by the San Francisco ballet at the age of sixteen."

"Jesus!" The brunette opened her clutch and pulled out her cell phone. "I wonder if my friend knows about this!" She grabbed the blonde's wrist and dragged her away from the bathroom door.

"But wait, I still have to . . ."

Cece hyperventilated, and the alcove circled around her. The bathroom door opened, and she slipped inside before her knees gave way. She leaned on the sink and looked at herself in the mirror. "Oh my God, what have I done?"

CHAPTER 43

"There you are," Brad said. He was standing in the alcove outside the powder room.

Cece almost fell into him.

"Jesus, are you okay?"

"I . . . I'm fine. I, in the bathroom, I tripped," Cece said, trying to make up an excuse for her odd behavior. "It's my shoes. They're way too high."

Brad looked at her with a worried frown. "Did you hurt yourself?"

Cece smoothed the front of her dress, regaining composure. "No, not at all," she said, smiling up at him as if everything were just fine. "For a dancer, I can be really clumsy sometimes. Let's get some champagne before the countdown."

Across the foyer, guests were beginning to congregate. Cece could not run into those women again. God only knew what would happen once the brunette talked to her friend. The sooner she and Brad had their midnight kiss, the sooner they could leave. She peered out of the alcove into the crowd.

"Cece, are you sure you're okay."

She took Brad's hand. "I am fabulous." Quickly, she led him to a corner of the living room behind by a giant Christmas tree. She pointed. "There goes the champagne! Grab some before they run out."

Brad dashed into the crowd, got two glasses, and returned to their spot behind the tree. "Here you go," he said, handing Cece hers. She gulped half of it down.

"You are really acting strange."

No kidding, she thought. She needed to take control of the situation. And she needed to make sure that Brad would want to leave the party even more than she did. She licked her lips and looked up at him, fluttering her lashes. "It's because I'm a little nervous."

He looked confused. "Why are you nervous?"

She slowly backed him into the wall and leaned against him, tucking them both further behind the tree. "Because . . . because I want you to make love to me."

Brad's Adam's apple bobbed up then down. "Oh."

Cece nodded her head. In her heels, she was almost as tall as he was. She pressed her body against his. With her right hand, she toyed with a button on his vest. She tilted her head. "Would you like to?"

"Absolutely," he said, his voice low and raspy.

Cece kissed him with wet, parted lips. She untucked the back of his shirt and slid a hand up inside it, feeling the muscles in his back tighten at her touch. His skin was smooth and hot. Anxiety from her encounter with that woman and all the champagne mixed with the feel of Brad's strength, and the smell of his cologne. Her adrenaline soared, stirring her passion. Brad pulled her closer, tighter until . . .

TEN . . . NINE . . .

She felt his desire for her . . .

EIGHT . . . SEVEN . . . SIX . . . FIVE . . .

One of his hands reached around and squeezed . . .

FOUR . . . THREE . . . TWO . . ."

Cece looked up at him. "Let's get out of here!"

"ONE! HAPPY NEW YEAR!"

Brad grabbed her wrist and pulled her toward the door.

"Wait, my coat!" Cece reached out. "That one," she said to the coat checker.

They sailed through the foyer amidst the joyful celebration of partiers howling and singing and dancing to the live music. Brad was first in line for the valet. He handed the attendant his ticket, then he pulled Cece behind a tall tree. With his body pinning her against a concrete planter, he kissed her lips, her throat, her neck, his hands everywhere, searching her body through the thin fabric of her dress.

"Your car, sir," an embarrassed voice interrupted them. Cece giggled as they jumped in and sped off.

At the end of the driveway, Brad stopped at a stop sign, and Cece practically crawled into his lap. To hell with what Patty said, casual sex was fantastic! She had never had it before, and she wanted it.

"Where are we going?" Cece asked in between kisses.

"An Inn down the road." Brad took her face into his hands. "I booked a room . . ." his lips were everywhere. " . . . just in case." His tongue entwined with hers, and a moan escaped her throat.

A horn honked at them. They both laughed, and Cece fell back into her seat.

The Inn was only a few minutes away. Cece didn't even pay attention to what it looked like. All she wanted was to get in bed with Brad and leap into what promised to be an incredible night.

A young man stood at the reception desk.

Brad slapped his credit card down. "Checking in," he said. While the man typed into his computer, Brad slipped his hand under the hem of Cece's dress. She felt his fingers on the back of her thigh. She shivered.

"Your name, sir?"

"Brad Redmond. It's right there on the card."

"I . . . I'm terribly sorry, but there's no reservation . . ."

Brad leaned on the counter. "I made it five days ago. Look again." His voice was edgy.

The young man blinked. "I'll get my manager."

He disappeared into the back.

Brad looked over his shoulder at Cece. "They'll figure it out."

Cece moved closer to him. "Okay," she whispered.

The manager appeared. He was only slightly older than the first man.

"Mr. Redmond, I'm afraid we don't have a reservation under your name. Did you call the Inn directly or book it online?"

"Online," Brad said.

The man went to another computer. "Just a minute, I'll check."

Cece grew nervous. The champagne was wearing off. Hopefully there would be a bottle in the room.

"Ah, I see what happened. The reservation was not confirmed. You should have received an email informing you that . . ."

"I never got any damn email," Brad said. "But forget it. Just give me a room. I don't care what the price is."

"Sir, we are booked solid. I'm sorry."

Cece could tell that Brad was getting angry. "Brad, it's . . ."

"Please." He stopped her with his abrupt tone. "Let me take care of this." He turned back to the man with a firm, deliberate tone. "Please make some calls and find me a room."

"Mr. Redmond," the man inhaled, and Cece began to feel sorry for him. "It's New Year's Eve. Every place around here has been booked for weeks or more. I'm terribly sorry."

The man stepped back as if to say: *please leave.*

Brad's jaw clenched. Cece grew more nervous. For a second she feared that Brad would explode. He turned and picked up her hand. "Let's go."

They walked to the car. Brad opened Cece's door and let her in. She bundled herself up in her coat. When Brad got in on his side, she looked at him.

He looked at her. A slight smile formed around the edges of his mouth. She blinked at him. He started to laugh. Cece looked at him with amused puzzlement.

"You're laughing?"

Brad laughed louder. "I'm laughing!"

Cece started to laugh, too. "But what's funny?"

"I've wanted to get you into bed since the day I knocked your coffee over, and here I was so close, and I blew it!"

Cece was delighted that his frustration turned to humor. Her desire, that had started to wane, refueled. She rubbed his leg. "Maybe we need to come up with a Plan B."

"And what would 'Plan B' be?" he asked, grinning at her.

"Where's Dawn?"

"At my house. Having a party."

Cece was shocked. "You let Dawn have a party when you're not home? Are you out . . ."

"Relax. My nephew and his wife are chaperoning."

"Phew! I was about to think you had lost your mind."

Brad leaned over and ran a hand up her leg and underneath the hem of her dress. "Is there such thing as a Plan C?"

Cece cupped his face with both hands. "My parents are away for the night. So is Patty."

"Ooooh, going back to the girl's house," he said, imitating a teenager from another era. "Radical."

"Radical? How old are you anyway?"

Brad started the car. "I am so old that I can't remember the last time I had sex with a girl in her daddy's house." He glanced in Cece's direction. "Makes me nervous just thinking about it!"

"Well," Cece said. "I've never done it in my daddy's house."

Brad smiled and threw the car into reverse. "It's about time you did."

As Brad drove, Cece kept glancing at him. She imagined what it was going to be like to make love to Brad, the first man other than Doug in forever. But as the alcohol worked its way out of her system, reality edged her fantasy aside, and she recalled what she had said to those two women by the bathroom.

How was she ever going to be able to undo that? And what on earth would she say to Natalie? Cece was dying to tell someone what she had done. Maybe she should text Patty. No, that would be a disaster. Patty would think it was hysterical and blab it to everyone.

"What are you thinking about?" Brad asked, interrupting her anxious deliberation.

"Huh?"

He squeezed her hand. "You look preoccupied."

She smiled at Brad. What if she told him? Would he laugh and tell her it was no big deal? Would he be hurt that she was thinking about something other than going to bed with him? Oh shit, she'd almost forgotten. She and Brad were on their way to her house to have sex.

"I've never had, um . . ." A siren blared in the distance as she whispered, ". . . casual sex before."

"You've never had sex before?" Brad nearly drove off the road.

"That's not what I said." Cece laughed. "I said that I've never had casual sex before."

"Well then, gorgeous, you're about to have two 'firsts' tonight, aren't you?" Brad winked at her.

The heat in the car blasted warm air on her feet, and Cece started to get hot. *Two firsts in one night.* She felt herself perspire. What was it that Patty had said? Cece was a planner, a thoughtful, reflective, leave nothing to chance woman, not the kind to run off and have casual sex! She was a hopeless romantic, a relationship kind of girl.

She lifted her hair up to cool off. Brad saw. He reached out and put his hand on the back of her neck. She hoped he couldn't feel her sweat. They stopped at red light, and he pulled her into another deep, long kiss.

On the other hand, she thought, what did that matter? It was a new year. Her resolution was to live in the moment, and that was exactly what she intended to do. Cece could hardly believe what she was becoming—daring, thrill-seeking, adventurous.

"Although," Brad glanced at her. "It doesn't have to be entirely casual."

"What do you mean?" Cece asked.

Brad looked over his left shoulder and merged onto the highway.

"I haven't put all this effort into pursuing you for a one night stand you know."

Cece caught her breath.

Brad touched her cheek with the back of his hand. "LA is only a one hour flight from San Francisco."

"You mean," Cece said. "You mean you want to keep seeing me?"

Brad gave her a look. "Depends if you're good in bed or not."

"What?"

"I'm kidding! Jesus, you do take everything seriously, don't you?"

"So . . ." Cece twisted her mouth, "you want to do the long distance relationship thing?"

Brad's head went back. "Relationship? That's a big word."

Cece began to question herself again. Why would she even say that word? This was her night to be the woman she had never been before. Throw caution to the wind, play it by ear, fly by the seat of her pants, and every other stupid cliché . . .

She looked at Brad's strong, handsome profile. Who cared if he wanted a relationship or not? He was here, now, with her this moment. Not like Doug who was somewhere on the other side of the world in a rainforest taking pictures of toads and toucans and monkeys. Monkeys. The photo of Doug flashed through her mind. She closed her eyes and forced the image of her head. *If you can't be with the one you love, love the one you're with.*

"You know what?" Cece said. "Let's . . . let's not overthink this. Let's just do it."

Brad looked at her out of the corner of his eye. He pressed on the accelerator. "Works for me."

CHAPTER 44

They made out like teenagers at every stoplight. There would be no turning back now.

Cece thought about how everything would play out. Would she offer him a drink first? Would they go straight upstairs, removing articles of clothing along the way? Would he scoop her into his arms and carry her? *Stop!* She chastised herself. No overthinking, no planning, just let it happen. As much as she tried to contain herself, her legs trembled with nervousness.

Brad turned the car into the driveway of the Camden house, still lit up as brightly as it was on Christmas Eve.

"I'm going to park on the street." Brad said.

"On the street? Why?"

"Just to be on the safe side. If your folks come home early, I can sneak away, and they'll never even know I was here."

"Ah, good thinking."

She put her hand on the door and glanced at Brad over her shoulder. She gave him a come-hither smile. "Don't be long. You do not want to keep me waiting."

Brad grabbed her wrist. "Believe me, I won't." His kiss was fast, deep, reckless.

She jumped out of the car and hopped along the driveway in her bare feet, her shoes in one hand, her coat in the other.

"Cece?" A deep voice came out of nowhere. She froze at the foot of the steps. The moon behind him illuminated his silhouette as he rose slowly from a chair.

Doug. Cece gripped the handrail. In the dim porch light, she could see that he'd grown a full beard. He looked thin, but his eyes were large and full of hope.

"What are you doing here?"

"I . . . I had to see you."

"How did you get here?" Cece asked, still immobile.

Doug took a hesitant step toward her. "I took a plane . . . I flew all night from Australia. It was New Year's Eve, and I was at some . . . some party, and it was midnight, and I . . . all I wanted was . . ." He stopped and looked at her. "That's a great dress."

Cece tried to shake the fuzziness from her head. Still slightly intoxicated, she wondered if she was dreaming. "I don't understand."

"I was on the other side of the dateline, so I left the party and went straight to the airport. My second chance at New Year's Eve, and all I could think about was being with you at midnight, but, well . . ."

Cece's heart melted at the sight of him, ragged and worn out and deflated.

"Please tell me I'm not too late, Ceece."

Cece blinked slowly. Maybe he wasn't real but a mere vision. She wanted to move or scream, run to him or run away, but she was paralyzed. Her limbs felt as if they had been disconnected from her body.

A thin beam of light hit Doug in the face. "Hey!" Brad shouted. "Who the hell are you?"

Doug squinted, his hand protecting his eyes. "What?"

"You heard me buddy, who are you?"

"Who are you?" Doug asked.

Cece turned and looked at Brad. He held a little keychain flashlight in front of him. "It's okay Brad, I . . . I know him."

The two men eyed each other, and Cece could read Doug's expression as he put two and two together. His face went rigid. His weary shoulders straightened. His hands clenched. In slow motion, the scene began to unfold. Cece's head swam as if she were sinking into a pool of water. She was an elephant seal lying on the beach, and these two fierce, fiery males were about to fight to the death to win her. *Boy, would Patty love this.*

Brad slowly approached Cece. "Who is he?" His voice was gentle.

Cece looked at Brad, then at Doug, then back at Brad. "He's Doug."

Brad's eyes opened wide. "Doug? Your old boyfriend?"

Cece nodded. Tears threatened. She had trouble breathing.

"I guess I am too late," Doug said. He tightened his jaw. "You've moved on."

Moved on? Cece wanted to tell him no, that she hadn't moved on at all. That she had tried desperately to get him out of her head, but he was stuck there, tormenting her, holding her back. And then, just when she finally felt the tiniest bit of relief, his letter had arrived.

"You left me!" she shouted. "I begged you not to! And now, thirty-two days after you walked away, you show up here? Expecting me to what? Welcome you back like you were on some, some mission to save the world?"

Doug dropped his head. "Just the rainforests . . . "

"Damn right I moved on, Doug. Did you expect me not to?"

Doug blinked at her. "Didn't take you long, did it?"

"No it didn't. Not long at all." Cece looked over at Brad. He was leaning on the railing, poker faced.

"So, while I was slogging through the jungle crying over you, you were out chasing this . . . this stud in a monkey suit?"

Brad took a step. "To be fair, I did most of the chasing."

Doug's eyes bore into him. "Jesus, you're good looking."

"Uh, thanks."

Cece was incredulous. "This is unreal, completely unbelievable!" She threw her hands into the air. "You know what? I'm going inside. You two elephant seals figure it out. You can wrestle in the dirt or man-hug each other to death. I don't care!"

She stomped up the steps and stopped in front of Doug. She poked him hard on the shoulder. "And one more thing. I am a goddamn prize, and you were an idiot to let me go! But since you did, everything's changed. Everything . . . "

Doug grabbed her shoulders with so much force that she stopped breathing. He wrapped his long arms around her like a vice, and kissed her mouth with such desperation and fury that it hurt. Cece felt her body crumble. Her knees buckled, and she started to collapse, but Doug held onto her. Tears streamed down her cheeks, and he kissed them away.

"I've changed, too, Ceece," Doug whispered. "Let me prove it to you, please let . . . "

The sound of Brad clearing his throat interrupted them. "Cece, could you . . . could I have a minute? Um, Doug, do you mind if I just, you know, talk to her for a sec?"

Doug, still holding onto Cece, looked at Brad. "Will you give her back?" He sounded like a little boy who had been asked to share his toy truck.

Brad smiled. "If she wants me to." He held his hand out and motioned for Cece to come down the steps.

Cece sniffed. She looked at Doug. She punched his arm. Hard.

"Ouch."

Cece walked toward Brad. He put his arm over her shoulder and led her away from the porch. They stood facing each other, surrounded by Christmas decorations. Brad looked at her with his dazzling green eyes.

"You want to go back to him, don't you?"

Cece dragged her hand under nose. "I don't know. I'm confused."

"Because of me?"

Cece nodded.

Brad grinned. "I'm glad I had some impact on you, but, well, I can't compete with true love. Even I know that."

"I feel terrible."

"Yeah, well, I get that. I'm in a little pain myself."

Cece laughed, a short, painful laugh. "You . . . you're so nice."

"Please, don't say that." He hugged her. "I really have to work on not being such a nice guy."

Cece toyed with the edges of his lapels. "Then we would've done it in the parking lot outside the hotel."

"Believe me, I wish we had." Brad put his hands on her cheeks. He kissed her forehead. "He'd better be good to you."

Cece felt him let go of her, slowly, regretfully. She watched him take a few steps down the driveway. Then he stopped. He turned. With a slight lift of his head, he flashed his most irresistible smile in her direction. "Happy New Year, gorgeous."

CHAPTER 45

Doug was sitting on the steps waiting for her. His head snapped up as she approached. Seeing him again made her heart pound.

Cece sat beside him, twelve inches away.

"He seems like a nice guy," Doug said.

"He is."

Silence.

"I'm still mad at you," Cece said, looking down at her hands.

"I know it."

"Your timing does suck, just like you said. It always has."

"I know that, too."

Cece turned her head to the side and looked at him. "You grew a beard. And you look skinny."

"That's what men do in the jungle—grow beards and walk a lot."

Cece gave him half a smile. "Did you get me a monkey?"

He reached into his pocket. "I did."

She held out her hand, and Doug placed a tiny, porcelain monkey with a curly tail in it. It was adorable. "Thanks, but I wanted a real one."

"I thought about it, but they'd have thrown me in jail."

Cece closed her hand around the monkey and looked at Doug. "I don't know why you're here."

Doug licked his lips. He took a few breaths. "Remember what I said the very last time we were together? When I left you?"

Cece nodded. But she wouldn't say it. He would have to say the words again.

"I said," Doug's voice cracked. "I said I didn't know how I'd ever live without you."

Tears ran down Cece's cheeks, over her jaw bone and onto her neck.

"As it turns out," he said, "I can't. Nothing I do means a thing if I don't have you."

Doug scooted closer to her, but she couldn't respond. So much pain had hardened her.

"It's only been a month, Cece. You couldn't have stopped loving me already." He grasped her hand. "Please. Say you still love me."

"I do," she whispered. "I still do, but I . . . I hate you, too."

"Okay, well, we can . . . we can work to fix that, can't we?"

"How? Just go back to the way it was before my birthday, before I said what I said that changed everything?"

"No," he said gently. "Words can't be unspoken. I know that."

"Okay, then what? We go home to LA and take up where left off, arguing about everything?" She looked into his eyes. His beautiful, sweet eyes.

"Of course not Ceece. I want to start fresh, to show you that I really have changed. I've grown up." Doug reached into his pocket and pulled out a slip of paper. He handed it to her.

"What's this?" Cece asked as she unfolded it.

"All my passwords."

"What?"

"My passwords, all of them. You know, bank account, credit cards, Netflix . . ." he pointed to the paper. "Even my passport and social security numbers. It was long flight."

Cece started to laugh. "Well, this is a change."

"Try and memorize them, 'cause we're gonna have to shred this." Doug moved a few inches closer to her.

"I suppose you think I should give you my passwords now, too."

"Well, that would only be fair."

She leaned her head on his shoulder, as love, and forgiveness, began to creep into her heart. "Okay. But passwords aren't enough. What else you got?"

"This."

"What?" Cece lifted her head. It was a soft, brown, stuffed kangaroo.

She couldn't help laughing. Did he bring her an entire zoo? "First a fake monkey and now a fake kangaroo?"

"I know, you wanted a real one. But this one is special."

"Oh really? How?"

"She has a baby in her pouch."

Cece rolled her eyes. She put a couple of fingers in the kangaroo's pouch and pulled out a little wrapped bundle. "Very cute." She unwrapped the bundle.

"I hope you like it," Doug whispered.

Cece couldn't breathe. A magnificent single stone in a simple, white gold, Tiffany setting. Doug took the ring. He scooted one step down and crouched in front of her, holding it between two fingers. "I love you more than anything. I want to spend the rest of my life with you. You're the one, Ceece, the one for me."

Tears blinded her. She could barely see the ring. Doug picked up her left hand. He kissed it tenderly. Trembling, he held the ring at the edge of her finger. "Will you . . ."

"Wait." Cece yanked her hand away.

Doug's face drained of color. He looked up. "Wait?"

"I . . . I'm not going back to LA. I mean, I'll go back to get my stuff, but I'm moving. I'm moving home. Back to Clearwater."

"You are? When did that happen?"

"Just now. Just this very second." Cece could barely believe it herself, but it's what she wanted, what she needed to do. "I'm a ballerina, a dancer. I want to teach dance, here, in my hometown, where I started."

"But you hate it here."

Cece shook her head. "Not anymore."

Doug stood. "I guess you've changed, too."

Cece scooted up a few steps on the porch, and the little stuffed kangaroo rolled off her lap and bounced into the driveway. "I'm sorry." She barely got the words out.

Doug put the ring in his pants pocket. He cleared his throat. "Wow. I didn't expect . . ." his voice trailed away.

Cece couldn't move. She had no sensation in her body. Even in her skimpy dress and bare feet, she couldn't feel the cold. She had, quite literally, turned to stone.

She watched as Doug took a few steps down the driveway. He ran his hands through his hair, his curls overgrown and wild. Cece grew frightened. She thought he might do something crazy. And then he did . . .

He turned and faced her. He pointed at the house. "So, do you want to live here with your dad, or should we get our own place?"

Cece caught her breath. "What are you talking about?"

He held his arms out wide. "I'm talking about where we should live."

Cece wasn't sure she understood what he was saying.

"I'm a great photographer, and dance instructors make good money, right? I think we can afford our own little house."

Slowly, the feeling returned to Cece's feet. She stood up.

Doug twisted his back, as if he were stretching. "I think I'd like to live down near the lake. You know how I like to be close to the water. What do you think?"

"Are you serious?"

"Hell yeah I'm serious. I'll go anywhere in the world to be with you. I just want to make you the happy."

"Oh my God! Oh my God!" Cece ran to him. She jumped up into his arms. "Give me the ring!"

Doug spun her around and laughed. "Oh! So now you want the ring?"

"Yes I do! Give it back to me!" Cece laughed and cried. "I love you. I love you so much."

Doug put her down. He took her face into his hands. "Are you sure?"

"Absolutely positive," Cece said.

"So you'll marry me?"

"What do you think? It was my idea in the first place!"

He fell to his knees, reached for her hand, and slipped the ring on her finger.

"It's perfect," she whispered.

Doug stood. He wrapped her in his arms and kissed her. Then he tightened his hold on her as if he'd never let go and buried his face in her neck. Cece felt his warm tears on her skin. They stood there, just like that, glued to each other, while the moon moved through the sky and the new year began.

They never went to sleep. They sat on the porch swing, snuggled under a blanket, and watched the sun come up. Cece twisted the ring around on her finger. She couldn't take her eyes off of it.

"I want to have two babies, maybe three," Cece said.

"Two or three, got it." Doug kissed her hair.

"And they'll all take dance lessons."

"Dance lessons. Okay." Doug kissed her hand.

"Even the boys. But only if they want to."

"Right. Even the boys." Doug kissed her cheek.

"And we'll have dogs. Lots of dogs."

"Uh-huh, lots of dogs." Doug kissed her neck.

"And maybe a cat."

Doug sat up. "A cat?"

Cece cuddled against him. "Just making sure you were listening."

Julie Mayerson Brown

Julie Mayerson Brown lives on the Palos Verdes Peninsula, a rural suburb of Los Angeles, with her husband, two sons, and several rescued boxer dogs. Her work has appeared in the Daily Breeze, Los Angeles Times, Los Angeles Jewish Journal, and Parenting Magazine. An 'at home' mom and community volunteer for over twenty years, she is founding member of Mothers Advocating Prevention, a non-profit organization dedicated to protecting children and teens.

Most days Julie can be found in one of the quiet corners of her local library working on her next novel.

CPSIA information can be obtained at www.ICGtesting.com
Printed in the USA
LVOW081324121212

311330LV00001B/19/P